Mrs. Hudson's Olympic Triumph

by
Barry S Brown

Paperback ISBN 978-1-78705-171-3
ePub ISBN 978-1-78705-172-0
PDF ISBN 978-1-78705-173-7

Published in the UK by MX Publishing
335 Princess Park Manor, Royal Drive,
London, N11 3GX
www.mxpublishing.co.uk

Cover design by Brian Belanger

Praise for earlier work in the *Mrs. Hudson of Baker Street* series:

"Each new book surpasses the others ... Some enterprising TV producer is missing out on a potentially great TV mystery series!"
Over My Dead Body Mystery Magazine

"It is always a pleasure to recommend a Sherlock Holmes novel that retains reader's interest to the very end. This one did."
Sherlockian.net

"... a gloriously complex and improbable scenario ... an entertaining romp ... Mrs. Hudson's a likeable character, and disconcertingly credible."
The District Messenger, Newsletter of the Sherlockian Society of London

"... imaginative plotting ..."
Scuttlebutt, a Sherlockian Newsletter

"... an inherently entertaining and fascinating read from beginning to end ... an enduringly popular addition to community library Mystery/ Suspense collections ..."
Midwest Book Review

"... Brown offers oodles of tasty background ... leads our heroes on a merry chase ... has good insights into character, and he throws out a satisfying cast of possible suspects ..."
Wilmington Star-News

Disclaimer

While many of the actors and events of the 1896 Olympic Games are reported with a proper regard for historical accuracy, the author has not felt himself bound by an unvarying adherence to reality, either in this writing or in the conduct of his life.

Dedication

Remembering the Misfits of Brooklyn, New York, circa 1950—a fairly good softball team, and an outstanding band of brothers.

Chapter 1.
Bound for Athens

"Sherlock, wake up. If I'm to be awake at this ridiculous hour, so by God are you."

The recumbent figure, lost in dreams a moment earlier, opened one eye to confirm the improbable sight the voice suggested. The improbable sight confirmed, opening a second eye did nothing to reduce his confusion. Looming over him, still panting from having ascended the 17 steps to Holmes' bedroom, stood his older brother, Mycroft. Behind Mycroft, half hidden by his bulk, was Mrs. Hudson, her gray hair in unkempt curls reaching to her shoulders and her dark wrapper tight around her.

It was a scene out of place, out of time. Holmes could not imagine the emergency that would bring his brother across the city at any hour, much less at an hour when the sun was barely risen.

"Mycroft, what could possibly require my attention at a time when one's only thought should be of breakfast?" Holmes was sitting upright in bed now, the cover drawn to the midriff of his nightshirt in deference to Mrs. Hudson.

The mention of breakfast had the desired effect on Mycroft. Cocking his head to one side, he considered his brother's observation, then accepted the suggestion contained within it.

"You're quite right. We need to fortify ourselves for the day ahead, and I can describe the situation as well over breakfast as in your bedroom—probably better." Mycroft turned from his brother to the silent presence at his back. "Nothing elaborate, Mrs. Hudson. But if you have some sausages on hand, perhaps a few eggs, and some rashers of bacon. Mycroft had a faraway look in his eyes as he considered what was missing from his impromptu menu. A broad smile welcomed its recall. "Kippers would be nice as well, Mrs. Hudson. And, of course, buttered toast. That should give us a good start."

Holmes grunted agreement, and with only a raised eyebrow as her response, Mrs. Hudson left to explore her larder.

Twenty minutes later, Sherlock and Mycroft Holmes, joined by a still groggy Watson, were reducing the mound of eggs, rings of sausage, rashers of bacon, and stacks of toast that formed the centerpiece of the landlady's table. Without a trace of apology, Mrs. Hudson reported the absence of kippers, for which she was nonetheless grudgingly forgiven by Mycroft.

After paying appropriate tribute to the feast and its provider, he began the explanation of his early morning visit, first issuing a caution that all he was about to relate was to be held in the strictest secrecy — in accord with the express wishes of those at "the highest reaches of government." Pausing to be certain the significance of his statement had been understood, he then made clear his expectation that Watson and Mrs. Hudson would work with Sherlock to carry out the assignment he was about to outline.

"Doctor, you will, of course, be Sherlock's friend and colleague, but not, I fear, his scribe in this undertaking. And you, Mrs. Hudson, will be his housekeeper, being taken on a bit of a holiday — if that's agreeable."

A bemused smile and nod told him it was. Apart from the residents of 221B Baker Street, Mycroft alone knew the role of the diminutive woman who, even as he spoke, was readying a second pot of tea for their refreshment.

"Good. Then let me get on with it. Sherlock, I recognize that you choose to remain oblivious to the world beyond Baker Street, but I must impress on you that issues of war and peace may hang in the balance of the mission you are asked to undertake. May I assume you're aware of the Kruger telegram?" he asked hopefully. He got a blank look from Holmes, but a spirited response from Watson.

"You're referring to the letter sent by the German Government after our unfortunate expedition in South Africa."

Mycroft gave a soft groan. "Yes, it could well be described as unfortunate. It could also be described as an utter debacle. Rhodes used his authority as Governor of the Cape Colony to organize an attack on the neighboring Transvaal Republic without bothering to share his plan with the Foreign Office. He simply sent this fellow Jameson on a quixotic expedition in the hope of creating an insurrection by British laborers working in that Boer territory. As it turned out, Jameson's Raid — as they're now calling it — was such a disaster that Rhodes' own brother was captured and jailed, together with a number of other British subjects. Our government is currently negotiating their release — more's the pity."

Watson frowned his confusion. "But surely then the issue is resolved. The Foreign Office will, I assume, do whatever is necessary to smooth things over just as they always do. How do we come into it?"

Taking note that the plate of sausages had been unexpectedly replenished by Mrs. Hudson, Mycroft paused in responding long enough to make certain he would not be denied access to the fresh bounty. He set one of the plump additions on his plate, but held himself to a single bite before answering Watson.

"That's where the bloody Kruger telegram comes in. Pardon my language, Mrs. Hudson. Kaiser Wilhelm chose to send a telegram to Kruger, the President of the Transvaal, congratulating him on repelling the armed bands that attacked his country. Like it or not — and the Foreign Office doesn't like it — those armed bands were British, and therefore we

8

condemn this insult from the Kaiser. At the same time, no one really knows the significance of the Kruger telegram."

"All of which adds up to what?" Holmes rejoined the conversation, sensing the preliminaries were coming to an end, and his role might soon be made clear.

"All of which adds up to our need to know the meaning of the telegram. It may be an impetuous and therefore meaningless act on the part of the Kaiser, or it may signal his intent to stir up trouble for us in Africa and perhaps elsewhere. We need to know whether it's the Kaiser's chronic inability to think before he speaks, or if it signals something more sinister. And your government has decided that you, Sherlock, are the man to help us find that out."

Mycroft looked intently to his brother, then asked a seemingly frivolous question.

"Sherlock, do you still play at swords?"

Holmes had come forward in his chair, prepared to declare for Queen and country, only to be asked a question he found irrelevant to the heroic mission he envisioned for himself. "If you mean do I still practice with foils, the answer is, yes — occasionally — but what has that to do with anything?"

"Yes, of course, that requires explanation." Mycroft looked longingly to the sausage on his plate before steeling himself to go on. "It's a rather extraordinary situation actually. You're aware the Kaiser's mother, the Dowager Empress Vickie, is our Queen's eldest daughter. Her name is really Victoria, of course, but she's known by everyone as Vickie to avoid the obvious confusion. At any rate, Empress Vickie and her son have a long-standing disagreement about relations with our country. Kaiser Wilhelm feels his mother is too English — as if such a thing were possible. Whatever their differences, Empress Vickie continues to hold her place in Court, and to have use of the royal pouch through which she maintains an active correspondence with her mother. She has her mother's insightfulness, and has routinely provided us a rather keen pair of eyes on events in Germany."

Holmes was aware of his brother's fascination with the intricacies of government, and his very active participation in those intricacies. It was not, however, a fascination he shared, and working his way through them was not the way he wished to spend the morning.

"I'm sure all of that is of great interest to someone, but what has any of it to do with me or my practice with foils?"

"I'm coming to that, Sherlock. I do need to set the stage however." Mycroft took a sip of tea in preparation for outlining the task he had already assured others his brother would carry out.

"As I've said, we need to learn Germany's intentions. Empress Vickie is in a unique position to inform us of them. But we have reason to believe that, in this situation, with the Empress' known affinity for the United Kingdom, we can't rely on the royal pouch. That is where you come in, Sherlock, and where your skill with foils is significant. Empress Vickie will pass a letter to our Queen through one of her ladies in waiting. Or, more accurately, through the brother of one of her ladies in waiting. His name is Count Gerhard Meyerhoff, and he will be attending the Olympic Games in Athens as a member of the German fencing team." Mycroft withdrew a photograph from a coat pocket, and pointed to a balding, square-jawed, stern looking man in a dark tunic and white pants, his helmet under one arm, his free hand stabbing the ground with a saber. He was with two other men dressed and posed the same, each one seemingly determined to outdo the others in fierce solemnity.

"I regret that's the only picture available of the man who is to be your contact. It may help you to know he has a small dueling scar on his left cheek. You can't see it in this picture, but it will be quite noticeable in person. Also, you should know he has excellent command of English, having attended Cambridge. Something the two of you share." Mycroft smiled, thoroughly enjoying the intrigue he was presenting, as his brother knew he would.

"Sherlock, you are to go to Athens as a member of our Olympic fencing team. You will be entered in the foils competition. That will provide an opportunity for two athletes competing in the same arena to meet, and have a letter passed between them. The letter will appear quite ordinary. It will be placed in an unmarked envelope, and will not contain the royal seal. Your contact has been instructed to keep the letter on him at all times to prevent its falling into the wrong hands, and to allow him to effect its transfer at the most opportune moment. Sherlock, you will be serving your Queen and country in a mission that is vital to your country's interest, and you might just win a medal for yourself."

"But why use Holmes in this way? Why not our legation in Athens or Berlin? Surely, our own people are above reproach." Watson set aside the pencil he had been using to draw overlapping squares and circles, having been directed by Mycroft not to take notes on their conversation.

Mycroft did his best to appear to be thoughtfully considering Watson's question while he bit off one then another piece of sausage, but was undone by the contented groan that preceded his response. "I'm afraid no one is above reproach, Dr. Watson. Moreover, the tension between ourselves and the Germans is such that we have to assume our legations are being watched as closely as we are watching theirs."

"I must tell you, Sherlock, I have already taken the liberty of informing the Prime Minister of your willingness to undertake this task, knowing you would not shrink from either the challenge, or your country's need." Mycroft stared pointedly at his brother who stared puckishly back. The exchange of looks amounted to nothing more than pretense; both knew the accuracy of Mycroft's judgment.

"The Olympics will begin in six days, giving you and your colleagues very little time to prepare yourselves. It will take more than three days to reach Athens, going by boat and train. There are reservations in each of your names at the Hotel Grande Bretagné. At some time within your first days in Athens, your German contact will find you. You are to remain at the Games long enough to compete in your event, and return to London immediately afterward with the letter concealed on your person. You will go directly to the Foreign Office where you will meet with the Prime Minister — the Marquis of Salisbury. You are to accept a meeting with Salisbury and no one else. There are people in our government who may well have an interest in seeing the contents of that letter. It is suspected there are some in the Office of the Colonial Secretary who supported Rhodes in his renegade action. Their complicity may be known in the German Court. If so, careers and reputations may be ruined by the information in Empress Vickie's letter." Mycroft took a sip of tea before continuing. "Do you have any questions, Sherlock?"

Holmes stared blankly at his brother, then looked to Watson and Mrs. Hudson, and found he was not alone in being at a loss for words. Mycroft took the moment to devour the remainder of the sausage, then stood to prepare himself for the descent of the staircase whose scaling was still fresh in his mind. At that moment, Mrs. Hudson found her voice and stopped him with a question.

"Does anyone beside yourself and the Prime Minister know these plans?"

"The Queen, of course."

There were no further questions.

It was to be Mrs. Hudson's second trip out of the country, and it had to be shared with Tobias Hudson, her husband of 29 years, the "uncommon common constable" she had laid to rest in Marylebone Cemetery 15 years earlier. She purchased violets, two bunches a penny, from the blind woman at the cemetery gate, and placed them in the small vase set before the headstone describing Tobias as a "devoted husband" and "respected member of the Metropolitan Police Force." It did not reveal that he was the inspiration for the detective agency Mrs. Hudson had founded at 221B Baker Street, or that his instruction was essential to its success — so she made certain to remind him of both at each of her biweekly visits.

Every night the two of them had poured over the crime reports in the *Evening Standard* — murders being their special interest — analyzing what clues presented themselves, what deductions could be made, what information was lacking, and what strategies were needed to obtain the additional information. Once a week or more she had gone to the British Library where she smilingly requested reading materials on poisons, stabbings, shootings, falls and such other mayhem as she could divine. Her requests were filled by unsmiling librarians who would search the next morning's paper for the report of a grisly murder, whose improbable perpetrator they would be honor-bound to report to the authorities. In her travels on horse-cars to and from the library, and her walks to and from the greengrocer and the butcher, she studied people's faces and hands, their postures and gestures; inferring from her analysis their character, vocation and background.

They leased a house with space for lodgers, but did not rent the two empty bedrooms with sitting room between, having decided to wait until Tobias' retirement to become landlords. When Tobias died suddenly from what the doctors called a blood disorder, everything changed. The house at 221B Baker Street would now become the site of the business for which her studies had prepared her. It would become London's first consulting detective agency. As such, it would not only fill her succeeding days and years, it would stand as a lasting tribute to the uncommon common constable who had been her husband.

She was not naïve about the difficulties she would face, nor was she fazed by them. She knew a woman hoping to organize a business in London would be viewed with skepticism. A woman of some years with an uncompromising Cockney accent would be viewed as deranged. She needed a male figurehead for the agency she would run, and the lodging house would provide the bait to find the right man for the job.

She advertised "rooms to let, good location, applicants should possess an inquiring mind and curiosity about human behavior." Of all the applicants, Mr. Holmes looked and sounded the best choice. His considerable height was accentuated by a tendency to look down his long, aquiline nose at his audience. That, and his precise Cambridge diction, lent an authority to his pronouncements that her customers were bound to find reassuring. Moreover, he claimed skills in boxing and with pistols, both of which might prove useful; and he was accompanied by a Dr. John Watson, whose rock-hard steadiness she thought would certainly prove useful. Through the years, Holmes had not always understood his role as figurehead, and Mrs. Hudson had not always appreciated the investigative skills he had acquired. Still, fifteen years after its founding, the consulting detective agency was being called upon for assistance by Her Majesty's Government.

She spread a blanket beside Tobias' grave and told him of the new assignment. "It's a bit outside our usual work, Tobias. Maybe more than a bit, but we couldn't very well turn down a request from the Queen, 'Erself. Mr. Mycroft came to tell us about it. You'll remember Mr. Mycroft is Mr. 'Olmes' older brother, and a very important person in 'is own right. Nobody can say what it is 'e does exactly, but I've 'eard Mr.

'Olmes call 'im 'the most indispensable man in government.' That's the circles we're travelin' in, Tobias, and it's all of it thanks to you," she said, removing a stray leaf from Tobias' grave. "And you know I'd give up every bit of it to be back the way we were. You and me spreadin' the paper across the kitchen table, the two of us together workin' to solve a murder in the East End, or in a fine 'ouse in Kensington."

Her words went from soft to a whisper before becoming a silence that was no less expressive for the absence of words. When she was done, she put two fingers to her lips, transferred the kiss to Tobias' headstone, and promised to be back in two weeks to tell him of Athens and the Olympic Games.

Lord Henry Edwin Sterling, British Envoy Extraordinary and Minister Plenipotentiary to Greece, was not having a good day. His morning began with a request from the Foreign Office that he organize activities "as best he could" to receive the members of Great Britain's Olympic team. His superiors in London regretted they could share only a partial list of names although it was believed most, if not all the athletes would be arriving together the day before the Games. He was to use his ingenuity, and "to avoid any further unnecessary embarrassment for the Foreign Office."

The gratuitous reprimand was a less than oblique reference to purchases made by Lady Pamela that had aroused suspicions in London. The ambassador was certain the allegations were wholly without merit. A self-described amateur archaeologist, who had been a guest at a small dinner party in his home, had, on his return to London, informed the Foreign Office of his certainty that the antiquities in the ambassador's residence were mere copies and not the originals they were purported to be. Since the purchases of the disputed items had been made by Lady Sterling using the household allowance provided by the government, his superiors felt an investigation was warranted. To heap insult atop injury, he had been told that he was to take no part in the investigation, although he was, of course, to give the investigator being dispatched from Scotland Yard his full support.

Lord Sterling was not one to sit idly by waiting for a stranger to clear his wife and himself of any wrongdoing. He decided to do some sleuthing himself before the investigator arrived. He attempted to contact the man who had been his wife's agent in locating the artifacts, but the address his wife had for him did not exist, and the dealer, from whom the purchases had been made, proved equally inaccessible. On the second day of his investigation, a shaken Lady Pamela met him at the door to tell him of a telephone call advising her it would be dangerous for Lord Sterling to continue his inquiries. With that, he decided it might make sense, after all, to rely on the man from Scotland Yard to conduct the investigation.

When the inspector arrived, embassy staff were told he was there to provide additional security needed in association with the Olympic Games. Quizzical looks greeted Lord Sterling's announcement as the need for any security, let alone additional security, had escaped their attention. Lord Sterling met briefly with the new man, and found himself unexpectedly relieved by their brief conversation. The inspector was matter of fact, but understanding of Lord Sterling's situation. He shared the ambassador's concern about the threat he had received, and recommended his continuing vigilance. He reported he would be working with an expert on Greek artifacts dispatched by the Foreign Office, and scheduled to arrive the same day as the British athletes. Lord Sterling was certain the expert would confirm the authenticity of his wife's purchases regardless of Whitehall's suspicions.

But it was neither the demand he provide a reception for the country's athletes, nor even the suspicion of misspent funds that was giving him a bad day, and had, in fact, given him a bad several days. Both of those issues would, he was certain, be resolved in short order. Neither compared to the appalling insult by the Foreign Office in undertaking a major covert operation virtually under his nose, without even informing him about it, let alone inviting his participation.

The belief that he could be kept ignorant of their plans and activities reflected the arrogance of the Foreign Office. There was a special intelligence, they seemed to believe, that was attached to residence in London, and a naïveté that was attached to being stationed anywhere else. He was certain that, in fact, neither the investigation of his wife's purchases, nor the conduct of a major covert operation would remain secret for very long — if indeed, they were secret even now. The Foreign Office was as adept at maintaining confidences as he would have been at swimming the channel between England and France. Already, two telegrams, unsigned and marked to his attention only, had been delivered to him at home by Nikolos, his regular coachman. Both had gone initially to his office in spite of bearing his home address. He had no idea how long they had been at the embassy or whether anyone had seen their contents, but he suspected that one at least had been opened and resealed somewhere in its travels. Each telegram told of a letter written by the Dowager Empress Vickie to her mother, the Queen, that was to be smuggled to Athens by someone operating outside of normal government channels — both telegrams unnecessarily adding the identical phrase, "in case he hadn't gotten the news officially" — both authors knowing full well he hadn't. His informants, he was certain, would share a secret delight in the discomfort their telegrams would be certain to create, all the while contenting themselves they were acting in his best interest.

The plan to distance him from activities taking place on his doorstep had to have been approved at the highest level of government — the very highest. And that was not just infuriating, but hurtful as well. He took it as evidence that, even now, years later, there were some who questioned his reliability, some who would never forget nor forgive his early transgressions.

Not that he hadn't provided them a wealth of material. Throughout university, and for as long thereafter as his father's allowance permitted, he lived from party to party, and fight to fight — and there was always a party and frequently a fight. The parties sometimes led to difficult aftermaths with women who recalled having been promised marriage when he recalled promising far more temporary relationships. The fights created even greater complications, sometimes leading to the need to settle differences across the channel in France where gentlemen could still finalize disagreements with the single shot of a dueling pistol. The parties and the fights increasingly taxed both his allowance and his father's patience. And just about the time the fifth Earl of Middleborough had reluctantly concluded that the long awaited transformation in his eldest son's behavior was never to be realized, Henry Sterling shocked his father and surprised himself with a declaration that the time had come for him to go to work, and to pledge fidelity to one woman. The words were spoken in a weak, but sober moment, and his sense of honor demanded they be acted upon.

He was 38 and lacking marketable skills, but he had a degree with second class honors from Oxford, and he was possessed of an abundance of charm. In short, he had the prerequisites for entry into the family business. Which is to say, he joined his name to the four generations of Sterlings before him who had served Crown and country in the diplomatic service. As he had promised his father and himself, he also acquired a suitable, if somewhat impoverished wife. Lady Pamela, as she became, was the daughter of Baron Zachary Martinson, a trader in commodities, as had been his father and grandfather before him. The success his family had enjoyed lasted until the Great Depression of 1873 when the price of grain and cotton tumbled, and the Baron lost all but the country estate he could no longer fully maintain, and his title which allowed him to introduce his daughter into society. As a precaution, should his insolvency prove an insurmountable obstacle to marriage, he had borrowed sufficient funds to put her through Girton College, guaranteeing she would be able to support herself should it prove necessary.

The family's insolvency was of no consequence to Lord Sterling. He had money enough for them both — or at least his father had — and her family's name, combined with a knowledge of proper etiquette, a reasonable intelligence, and pleasing appearance, was enough to justify a match. In fact, she had proven a worthy partner through their nearly twenty years together, and they had persevered to become finally the British Envoy Extraordinary and Minister Plenipotentiary to Greece, husband and wife.

It had not, however, started well. Their first assignment was a post in New Zealand, arranged by a friend of his father in the Office of the Colonial Secretary. The selection of a post in the distant reaches of the Pacific was seen as providing insurance against the possibility — some saw it as the inevitability — that Lord Sterling would prove himself less than a worthy heir to the family legacy. Indeed, not long after his arrival, their pessimism appeared justified, and distance proved a welcome buffer against a fall from the grace to which he had briefly ascended. The fault was only partly Lord Sterling's, as the previously sedate Lady Pamela did not immediately prove to be the stabilizing force he and his father had anticipated. New Zealand's distant reaches permitted Lady Pamela to be free from the oversight of her benevolently despotic parents. She became suddenly aware that, at 21, she had missed out on a great deal of life, and that New Zealand provided her the opportunity to get quickly caught up. Her husband, almost twice her age, and resigned to adopting the well-ordered life that had long been urged on him, now felt himself obliged to postpone his transformation, and support his wife in her pursuit of a life about which he could, in fact, provide invaluable guidance. For a time, they enjoyed what night life was available in Wellington, and created what night life was lacking. But all that changed with the accident.

They had been driving their carriage back from a dinner party north of Wellington when they were caught in a sudden downpour. The rain, the dark, an unfamiliar winding road, and a rather large quantity of alcohol, helped obscure the girl who had run out to capture the family's dog. The girl would recover, but never again walk properly in spite of the considerable sums Lord Sterling quietly contributed first to her surgeries, then to her rehabilitation and finally to her life. The report, issued by the Colonial Office, emphasized the difficult road conditions and the girl's sudden appearance, but made no mention of the alcohol consumed. The omission fooled no one. Without admitting responsibility, Her Majesty's Government chose to pay the girl's family £500. The incident guaranteed that Lord Sterling's career would proceed at a snail's pace in a climate of continuing distrust, even as it so chastened the Sterlings that they would never again give reason for distrust. Lord Henry Sterling became as focused as he had earlier been frivolous, and Lady Pamela took on the role of dutiful consort with a vigor that other diplomats' wives found excessive and their husbands found charming. Now, just as their adherence to the unerringly straight and suffocatingly narrow had finally been rewarded, the old distrust appeared to have resurfaced as Lord Sterling was assigned to welcome a group of gentlemen athletes, while an unknown stranger was entrusted with securing a message for delivery to the Queen.

The boat, carrying the gentlemen athletes Lord Sterling would be welcoming with less than open arms, left Liverpool with an equivalent absence of fanfare. The truth was that only a handful of British athletes would be participating in the Games, and few of them could be considered top tier performers. A series of missteps by the Games' organizers was largely responsible for Britain's limited representation. Not only had contact with the athletic clubs of Oxford and Cambridge been little and late, the Games' rules and regulations had been sent in French and German, dealing a harsh blow to British pride, quite apart from being unintelligible to all but a few athletes.

Once on board, the athletes who had chosen to make the trip to Athens were counseled by the steward to enjoy what was certain to be only a brief period of decorum. American athletes, he warned, would be joining them in Gibraltar and they were certain to be a raucous lot. He sniffed the last to make clear his sympathies lay with his decorous countrymen.

At the seven o'clock seating, the three passengers from Baker Street chose a corner table seating four, confident the sea of empty tables would discourage anyone from joining them. They had no sooner taken seats and spread their napkins than a tall, narrow-shouldered man in his early 30s positioned himself behind the fourth chair, apparently intent on proving their supposition in error. He pushed back a forelock of jet black hair that had fallen across his forehead, and gave voice to an excitement he appeared powerless to contain.

"You are the redoubtable Sherlock Holmes. Please don't deny it. And this is your colleague, Dr. Watson. Of course it is. I'm Oswald Benton, and I'm on my way to the Olympic Games to do my bit for the Empire. Tennis is my sport, and I should do fine if I can keep the competition away from my backhand." Oswald Benton chuckled about the weakness he readily acknowledged before favoring Mrs. Hudson with a tentative smile.

"But I don't believe I know this lady."

"This is Mrs. Hudson, my housekeeper, who is joining us on holiday to see Athens," Holmes replied on her behalf.

"How delightful for you madam, to see such an exciting part of the world with such extraordinary company." The crinkling around his eyes deepened and the small smile increased a fraction.

He waited as long as he thought it seemly for an invitation to emerge from someone in the group. None did.

"I'll not interrupt you further other than to wish you a very pleasant journey. Might I just ask — I'm afraid curiosity overwhelms me — how do you happen to be going to Athens yourselves? Will you be attending the Games?"

It was, Mrs. Hudson thought, a perfectly reasonable question, and yet it sounded somehow intrusive.

Holmes again answered on everyone's behalf. "Actually, I too will be there representing our country. I will be contending in the fencing competition."

"Splendid, then we're bound to see each other again. It's been a pleasure meeting everyone." With part of a smile still frozen in place, he nodded his compliments to all, and went in search of a table for himself.

As a white-jacketed waiter wordlessly handed them menus, the voice from the newly seated diner at an adjoining table sounded a mix of Scottish brogue and breezy good fellowship. Turning to the voice, the detectives counted as fortunate its owner's amiability. He looked to be two or three inches taller than Holmes, but where the detective was long and thin, the speaker appeared well-muscled in every part of his body exclusive of his eyebrows. His blond hair and moustache, and heroic profile combined with a powerful physique, would shortly lead Athens' residents to regard him as a reincarnation of the gods their forbears had worshiped.

"I couldn't help overhearing your conversation. My name is Launceston Elliot. I'm a participant in the Games myself, and I'm delighted to make everyone's acquaintance." The accompanying smile revealed the expected perfect set of teeth, as well as a genuineness that contrasted sharply with their earlier visitor.

The three detectives nodded their greetings, and Watson asked the obvious question. "Would I be correct in guessing you will be competing in the weight-lifting event?"

The smile broadened to a grin. "Weight-lifting and wrestling although your guess is a good one. Weight-lifting is my preferred sport." The Scotsman's voice rose now to become nearly commensurate with his size. "I believe there's several of us in the room who will be participating in the Games. Might I suggest we all get together in the smoking saloon after dinner?" He looked around to the diners who were now giving him their full attention. "Let us say half eight."

Here and there, throughout the room, diners raised their water glasses to acknowledge Eliot's suggestion before settling back to the green pea soup that had been ladled into their bowls. The meal proceeded for the Baker Street trio without further interruption or announcement.

When, at last, all of the spotted dick had been scraped from their dessert dishes, it was time for Holmes to join the athletes who were rising in stages to make their way to the saloon. A short time later, Mrs. Hudson and Watson left the dining room to stroll the promenade deck, as much because it seemed the thing to do, as to take advantage of the star-filled night and warm breeze. Like those in the smoking saloon, their discussion was about Athens and the Olympics, but while Mrs. Hudson and Watson talked of the future and what they could expect, those in the smoking saloon spoke of their past competitions and shared what little they knew of the

Olympics, and of those who might be their rivals in the Games.

As they neared the stairway leading down to the staterooms, Mrs. Hudson put a hand on Watson's arm to quiet him. It proved unnecessary. Watson, too, saw the figure of Oswald Benton rapidly descending the stairway. They had no wish for a second strained exchange with the tennis player, and so took another turn around the promenade deck before descending the stairway to their staterooms. They congratulated themselves on the success of their escape, and dismissed the matter from any further consideration. It would be reawakened when they met with Holmes for breakfast the next morning.

Overnight, the dining room had undergone a dramatic transformation. As he led the three detectives to a table for six, the steward explained that the tables had been rearranged in larger settings to accommodate the Americans who would be joining them later in the day. The Americans, he explained, traveled in groups corresponding to their university affiliation. Putting the best face on the situation, the steward offered that the arrangement "would give opportunity for people to get to know each other."

Watson grumbled that he already knew a great many people. Unwilling to be discouraged, the steward brightly observed, "One can't have too many friends."

Holmes gave a non-committal grunt, and all three dismissed the man with orders of full English breakfasts. The steward smiled his most deferential, and tried a third epigram before departing. "A boat trip should make for one big happy family."

When the steward was beyond hearing, Holmes carefully smoothed the napkin on his lap and recounted the experience he had been waiting to share.

"Something very curious happened last night. When I got back to my stateroom, I discovered that someone had been there while I was out. Nothing was stolen, and the only disturbance I found was to my jottings on the patterns of bicycle tire treads. In fact, if those notes hadn't been moved from where I left them, I wouldn't have known anyone had been in my room. Still, I find it hard to believe anyone would break into my stateroom simply to learn my ideas about bicycle treads. Mind you, I fully expect such analysis to become a critical addition to investigative procedures in the very near future."

Watson's face had become a dark frown. He told of their seeing Oswald Benton taking the stairs to the staterooms, then raised a more ominous thought. "Could someone suspect the real reason for your trip to Athens, and be looking for evidence to confirm those suspicions?" The question was directed to Holmes, but it was Mrs. Hudson who responded.

"It's possible, of course. Mr. Mycroft 'as said more than once that the Foreign Office leaks like a broken tea kettle."

Further discussion about indiscretions of the diplomatic corps was postponed as the steward again approached their table wearing his ever present smile, and leading the three men who would complete their table.

"Mr. Holmes ... everyone, I've arranged for these gentlemen to join you. Mr. Holmes, you've already met your two Australian teammates, Mr. Flack and Mr. Ramsay, and this gentleman is Mr. Albert Needham from your own city of London. I'll leave you to become further acquainted." The steward left a clutch of menus in the center of the table; then removed himself to smile another guest to a table where he would be given opportunity to expand his circle of friends.

Holmes set himself the task of making welcome the new additions to the table. "Mr. Flack, Mr. Ramsay, and ... Mr. Needham, was it?" The man's somewhat embarrassed nod confirmed it was. "Permit me to introduce my colleague, Dr. Watson, and ... our associate, Mrs. Hudson."

Holmes reported all he could remember about the two Australian athletes from their prior meeting. "Mr. Flack is a distance runner, and I believe an accountant as well, who's been living in London; and Mr. Ramsay is a pistol shot, who's also currently living in London and is also from Australia, although I believe the two of you had never met before last night." The two men nodded agreement. "And I believe none of us have had the pleasure of making Mr. Needham's acquaintance."

Mr. Needham gave the impression that, whatever pleasure others might take in making his acquaintance, he did not share their joy. He was a small man, whose entry into middle age was marked by the acquisition of a considerable paunch and the loss of a considerable amount of hair. He attempted to compensate for the latter by sweeping the lengthy if somewhat sparse remnants from one side across a barren stretch of scalp to meet a fringe of hair on the other side. He gave Holmes a tentative smile; then alternated his gaze between his place setting and his fellow diners.

"I'm glad to meet you, Mr. Holmes. And the rest of you gentlemen and lady as well. I must say I'm a little overwhelmed to be in your company. I'm afraid I'm not engaged in anything nearly as exciting as detective work. Living in London, of course I know all about your accomplishments, Mr. Holmes. And nothing I do is a match for you other gentlemen, what with your running and shooting and such. My own work is in antiquities, and I'll probably be spending more of my time at the Archaeological Museum than at the Olympic Games — although I do hope to get to see some of your exploits while I'm there. But what of the rest of you? Are all of you participating in the Games? I know at least one of you is not." He gave a half smile to Mrs. Hudson which she returned in kind.

Before anyone could answer, a waiter arrived with the breakfast orders for the Baker Street trio, and ready to take the orders of those who had joined them. Seeing the servings he had set down, only Needham opted for the full English breakfast, Flack reporting that runners followed different training regimens than other athletes, Ramsay saying the voyage had him feeling the least bit queasy by way of explaining his order of tea and toast.

"I do envy you blokes who can eat what you choose and still be in condition for your events," Flack said. "If I were to eat one of your English breakfasts, I'd leave half of it behind before I made it to the finish line." He gave a quick glance to Mrs. Hudson, and she noted his face retained its cheerful expression even as he asked her forgiveness. "Begging your pardon, ma'am." She nodded acceptance of his apology, and he continued, looking to the three non-athletes at the table.

"As I was saying last night, I'm a distance runner — although the truth is I haven't been doing the running I should have to prepare for my events. You see, I came to London to do an accounting job, like Mr. Holmes said, and to see for myself the most exciting city on the planet, and I'm glad I did, but all that sitting has got me at a bit of a disadvantage for my races. Not that I won't do all I can for Victoria at the Games. By the way, the name is Edwin, but my friends call me Teddy, and since we're now all gonna be friends, I hope that's what you'll call me."

The hush that came over the table had nothing to do with Flack's offer of friendship, and everything to do with his indiscreet language in what had been up to then a pleasantly light-hearted exchange.

Watson voiced the concern that was felt around the table. "Mr. Flack, I understand that your home is a great distance away — virtually the other side of the world—so you may perhaps be forgiven your intemperate reference to the

Queen, but you should be aware that one never refers to Her Majesty by her given name alone. Frankly, I don't see how you could have lived in London for any length of time and not be aware of that."

Watson waited for the man's abject apology, which he was prepared to accept with a display of magnanimity that would form a striking contrast to the Australian's graceless behavior.

Instead of apology, however, his words were greeted with a roar of laughter from the man whose coarse behavior seemed to have no limit. Only Flack's frantic hand waving while he labored to gain control of himself kept Watson from expressing the disgust he felt for the young man's behavior. Flack finally gained control in brief spurts of speech punctuated by lingering small bursts of laughter.

"I'm sorry, you thought I meant the Queen when I said I'd do my best for Victoria." The same unwelcome volley of laughter. "I assure you I meant no such thing. Victoria is where I'm from. It's the colony in Australia where I live — at least when I'm not living in London. It's just the same with Ramsay over there. He's from the city of Palmerston and he's representing South Australia in the Games. And if you want to know about the size of Australia, just pay attention to how Ramsay talks. If he hadn't told me where he's from, I'd of thought he was from another bloomin' planet."

The man, whose language skills had been called into question, smiled sheepishly before speaking. "I feel I should speak slowly so as to be understood. I'm Durand — Dewey, if you like — Ramsay, from Palmerston, as Teddy says, and I'll be taking part in the pistol competition. I do represent South Australia, although I recognize that all of us represent the Queen and the Empire as well."

Watson frowned acceptance of Flack's explanation of his behavior, and turned his attention to the second Australian,

"What sort of work do you do in South Australia, Mr. Ramsay?"

"Nothing very exciting, I'm afraid. I've got a building supply business, and I do some home building and home repair."

"You see, didn't I tell you," Flack said triumphantly to an audience that was struggling to find the nuance in speech that distinguished one man from the other. "Well, we won't be far apart for long. The Great Northern will see to that. Right, Dewey?"

"The Great Northern." Ramsay paused a long moment, appearing to consider his response. The delay had the effect of causing those at the table to have a sudden interest in learning the opinion of someone they barely knew on a subject about which they knew nothing. There was palpable relief when he finally spoke. "Yes, I suspect you're right. It will very likely bring us closer together."

Flack held off his assault on the cinnamon and oatmeal set before him to share an additional thought about the Great Northern. "Of course, there's no question it will take a while to make it to Palmerston."

Watson was again the first to give voice to a question he shared with others. "What exactly is the Great Northern?"

Flack and Ramsay looked to each other to determine who should respond to Watson's question. Finally, Ramsay pursed his lips and extended an open hand to Flack, giving him license to speak on behalf of the two of them.

"The Great Northern is our newest railway. It follows a north-south route that will have it starting in Port Augusta not awfully far from me, and ending in Dewey's Palmerston. Of course, up to now it's only got as far as Oodnadatta."

Watson chose not to learn where or what Oodnadatta was, fearing it could lead them deeper into Australian trivia. But Flack's explanation triggered another person's curiosity. Albert Needham led slowly and apologetically to his question.

"I have to admit I don't know a great deal about these things. I mean it's all so far removed from our experience in England. But I have read about the railroads in America. America is sort of a hobby of mine. They've got the Indians over there as you probably know. Anyway, from what I've read, the Indians caused a lot of problems for the building of their railroads. I know you don't have Indians, but I believe you have people who are a good deal like America's Indians. Wouldn't they create some of the same kind of problems for your railroad?"

He looked to both men for response. This time Flack extended an open hand to Ramsay, and waited his response.

"You're undoubtedly right, of course," Ramsay said. "The natives are capable of creating significant difficulty."

The short response, delivered in Ramsay's low-key fashion, clearly did not satisfy Flack. He seemed barely able to contain the feeling behind his words.

"You can call them natives if you like, Dewey. That's certainly a nice civilized name for them, and maybe there's some where you live that deserve it. But I'd call them by their right name — aborigines — or better still, aborigine devils. I don't mean to sound cruel," Flack turned to the others at the table, "but there's been too many of my countrymen killed or burnt out of their homes for me to gentle my talk about them." Flack shook his head in vigorous support of his own observations before turning to another subject.

"But enough of that, we haven't heard anything from Dr. Watson and Mrs. Hudson. What do you people do back in England, and what brings you to Athens?"

With a nod to Mrs. Hudson, Watson spoke first. He described himself as a physician, retired from the military, who now lived in the same lodging house as Holmes and sometimes worked with him on his cases. Mrs. Hudson reported herself as "just a 'ousekeeper for the two gentlemen, who were good enough to take me along for a 'oliday on their

30

trip to Athens." She planned, she reported, to be at the Games to cheer for Mr. Holmes, but now she'd be cheering for Mr. Flack and Mr. Ramsay as well. Nobody found it necessary to have Holmes explain who he was.

When their meals were done, and all but Flack and Mrs. Hudson had lit the cigarettes offered by Holmes and Needham, they pushed back from the table, sharing compliments of the day, and the hope they'd all see each other again very soon. They exited slowly, Holmes, Flack and Ramsay stopping at several tables to pay their respects to the athletes they had met the night before. By the time they had exited the room, each was prepared to spend a relaxing few hours reading, writing letters, strolling around the deck, or simply staring out to sea in advance of the scheduled invasion by the Americans.

At mid-day, the event dreaded by the steward, and awaited with curiosity by everyone else, came to pass. Fourteen American athletes boarded the ship in Gibraltar as well as some friends, family, and a handful of reporters. Most of the American Olympians were either on temporary leave from their studies at Princeton, or had been recruited through the Boston Athletic Association, with the majority of those proud Harvard men. As the steward predicted, the American presence transformed the remainder of the voyage. When present, they dominated everyone's attention; when absent, they became the sole topic of conversation. During the day, they were, in the words of one of the reporters, "slaves to conditioning." Using deck chairs they cordoned off a section of the promenade deck where they gathered for two hours every morning and two more in the afternoon. In twos, or threes, sometimes individually, they repeatedly flexed arms and legs in prelude to skipping rope and lifting dumb-bells, after which some practiced race starts, one hurdled the deck-chairs barrier, and another lay on his back with his legs in the air pedaling an imagined bicycle.

The nighttime regimen provided an equally dramatic departure from earlier routine. After dinner, the Americans commandeered the saloon where they proceeded to demonstrate their knowledge of lyrics for as many popular songs as they could crowd into the space between dessert, and taking to their beds for the full night's sleep their training demanded.

Accompaniment was provided by a succession of piano players, and a single virtuoso on the five-string banjo. The room first rang with a spirited, if not entirely harmonious rendition of *Daisy Bell* led by the young man from the Boston Athletic Association who had earlier been hurdling deck chairs. Cajoled by the hurdler's insistent waves, the passengers, who had formed an appreciative, if somewhat mystified audience to that point, now joined in the song's choruses, paying somewhat greater attention to the niceties of beat and harmony than the Americans, but lacking their fervor.

The same pattern of Americans leading with all others close behind, was next on display for *There'll Be a Hot Time in the Old Town Tonight*, then for *The Band Played On*. There followed a succession of songs drawn from America's vaudeville stage, some of them known to the British audience and some not, all of them following the pattern of greater enthusiasm than harmony from the American side. Finally, a sweet tenor from Boston stepped forward to sing *Little Lost Child*, and by the time the song's policeman had reunited the baby girl with the woman revealed to be his own estranged wife, there was barely a dry eye in the room. A Princeton man followed with a stirring rendition of *When the Roll is Called up Yonder*, which seemed a fitting way to end the evening. Amidst applause for and by themselves, nearly all trundled off to their staterooms, a few remaining behind for one last cigarette. Mrs. Hudson smiled her leave taking to the men she sat between, Albert Needham, who had added an unexpectedly lusty baritone to the group effort, and Oswald Benton, who had grimaced his way through the evening's entertainment. Durand Ramsay waited to hold the door for her, and she noted he was turning an unbecoming shade of olive green. Thereafter, he spent a good deal of time in his stateroom or at the ship's rail.

The Americans' relentless preparation for the Games served as a cautionary tale for the Empire's athletes, none more so than Holmes. In the narrow confines of his stateroom, he copied the bending and stretching he had witnessed, and practiced thrusts, parries, and strategic retreats in repeated battle against an imaginary opponent. By the time the ship put in at Naples, Holmes was feeling more confident in his skills, to the extent that winning a medal for Queen and country no longer seemed quite as distant a dream as it had at Mrs. Hudson's breakfast table.

The Americans and the Empire's athletes disembarked in Naples, and filed into separate cars of the train taking them to Brundisi. The boisterous Americans became an instant object of curiosity for the car's other passengers — a situation that seemed to cause them no concern. The Empire's athletes made an effort to appear indistinguishable from their neighbors, an impossibility as long as the blond giant, Launceston Elliot, was with them.

The ferry to Piraeus from Brindisi brought the American and Empire athletes back together, renewing the warm Anglo-American relations forged earlier. The good fellowship continued in evidence during the fourth and final leg, a train ride from the Piraeus harbor to Athens.

Once arrived at the Athens station in mid-afternoon, the athletes from Great Britain and its Australian colonies were met by a young man whose effort to communicate authority was largely undone by his age—or, more precisely, its lack—and the uncertainty with which he welcomed the people he described as "his countrymen." He introduced himself as Thomas Fitzhugh, assistant to the deputy ambassador of the British embassy. The ambassador and the deputy, he declared, were detained by urgent business and unable to be at the train station to welcome them, but wished to invite everyone to the embassy for a small reception. His unenthusiastically proffered invitation was unenthusiastically received by his audience. Nearly four days of travel had led to a longing for the comforts of the hotels that awaited them. Nonetheless, only three people begged off. Oswald Benton, the tennis player, gave the somewhat dubious excuse of having promised to join an old school friend on his arrival. Durand Ramsay gave the more plausible rationale of still suffering from the motion sickness that had kept him close to the rail when at sea, and within easy reach of a lavatory when on land; and Albert Needham acknowledged the exhaustion all the rest felt, but were loathe to claim, and with profuse apology excused himself from the festivities.

The assistant to the deputy ambassador handed each person a card restating the ambassador's welcome to Athens, as well as giving the telephone number and address of the embassy, and of the ambassador's residence should an emergency arise after business hours. After all cards had been distributed, pocketed, and forgotten, and everyone's bags collected, there was a pairing off as athletes entered the brigade of waiting carriages.

The carriage ride to the embassy revealed a city primed for two celebrations. Floral arches greeted the carriages as they entered downtown Athens. At the center of each arch, flowers were arranged in the shape of shields within which were the letters, "O A" which they were later told stood for Olympiakoi Agones — Olympic Games — and the dates 776 BC – 1896 AD. Multi-colored bunting decorated the buildings they passed and the balconies of many homes, while green wreaths hung on their doors. Other banners depicted a lamb and cross, heralds of the Easter week that would begin the next day, coinciding with the opening of the Olympic Games. The holiday would permit greater attendance at the Games, even as the Games would hold down Easter week's church attendance.

The British Embassy was located in what had once been a private home in Klafthomonos Square. Its architect seemed to have used a wedding cake for inspiration, albeit a somewhat squat wedding cake. On top of two broad stories he had placed a narrower third, distinctive from the others in having a balcony across its front. The Union Jack flew from a pole in the small patch of green fronting the building, the single, and essential, indication of the building's purpose.

The center hall that daily served as a waiting area for visitors now struggled with little success to achieve a party atmosphere. Chairs had been moved to a side wall and a white sheet thrown over the receptionist's long desk, transforming the room from its usual role of providing guests an austere welcome to a new role of providing guests an austere celebration. Two young men in kitchen whites carried trays of wine glasses. When those were distributed, the young men disappeared, not to return until sometime later, and then only to collect the empty glasses. The embassy staff circulated through the clusters of athletes, asking the obligatory questions about their sport, where they were from, their families, what they did at home; then offering advice about Athens, what to see and places to go if they had the time. Both the embassy staff and their guests were relieved when Lord Sterling arrived to bring the affair to its climax, and start it towards its conclusion.

The ambassador entered from the corridor beyond the reception hall, wearing a smile so lacking in warmth it might have wilted the room's flowers—if anyone had thought to provide flowers. A great bear of a man he stroked a full beard more gray than black as he strode to the room's center. Members of his staff parted to allow him a path, mumbling acknowledgement of his presence more than giving him greetings. For his part, the ambassador, as Mrs. Hudson observed, appeared to take no notice of his staff's reaction. But there was more to his behavior than simple autocracy. For one thing, staff seemed surprised or put off by his lack of response to them, suggesting they were not accustomed to being ignored. The uncharacteristic behavior toward his staff, the frequent stroking of his beard, and the forced smile indicated to Mrs. Hudson that something other than welcoming visitors to Athens was preying on his mind.

Her musings were interrupted by a Scottish brogue that could only belong to Launceston Elliot. "A' last, the great mon has come to greet us. Now perhaps we can get on with the day. I imagine you can do with a bit o' rest, Mrs. Hudson, as can we all."

Mrs. Hudson was relieved of the need to devise a diplomatic response to Elliot by the ambassador's call to order. "Ladies and gentlemen, please give me your attention." He gave the group a few seconds to quiet before continuing. "It is my great pleasure to welcome our outstanding athletes, and their families and friends to Athens and the Olympic Games. I want all of you to regard the embassy as your constant resource while you are here. Please don't hesitate to call on any of us for whatever need arises. Now, join me in raising a glass to the success I know we will enjoy in these Games." He waited until he deemed the number of glasses raised to be sufficient, then took a sip of his own, and began strolling from one cluster to another sharing with each the same frozen smile. After he had circulated through the room, he called a "thank you for coming" to the crowd, set his glass on the tray a newly arrived waiter held out to him, and began a slow, but deliberate exit from the reception area. In the unlikely event the message was lost on anyone, an announcement was made that carriages had been called to take people to their hotels. The festivities had consumed slightly less than half an hour.

The unadorned colonnaded front, and the massive bare urns on either side of the Hotel Grand Bretagné's entrance were a stark contrast to the richly decorated buildings they had passed on their carriage ride. It appeared the conviction of the hotel's management that no special adornments were needed; the Grand Bretagné was, of itself, adornment enough for anyone.

The hotel's reception area continued the theme of elegance without ceremony. Great frames of knotted gold molding held within them either silvered mirrors, or paintings depicting the ruins of ancient Greece. Statues, set discreetly about the room, depicted mortals, male and female, of heroic proportions, as well as figures from the panoply of gods seen as controlling all human destiny in the days when Greece stood at the center of world civilization. And even as the glories of an earlier age were everywhere in evidence, above them a multi-tiered electric chandelier bathed the reception area with light, promising that all the conveniences of 1896 would be available to them as well. As they stepped across the room's threshold, the three detectives were instantly joined by three uniformed porters, all of whom shared an expression of bored disinterest that belied the energy they exhibited in snatching the detectives' bags and preceding them to reception. After registering, they were shown to rooms that were in themselves unremarkable, but afforded views from private balconies of the Olympic stadium and the King's palace in the near distance, and the Acropolis and Parthenon not far beyond.

When they'd unpacked, changed, and had their fill of the view, they came together for an early dinner. They had in mind to eat quickly in hopes of capturing what daylight they could to explore the city. Watson and Mrs. Hudson planned to walk in the direction of the palace, while Holmes was anxious to see the Zappeion, the arena in which he would be competing in just two days, and where he was scheduled to meet the German courier at some unspecified time. As the waiter approached, they steeled themselves for what they saw as the inevitable consequence of dining in a country whose language, and whose very alphabet was unknown to them. They were relieved to find themselves handed menus written in English as well as Greek, negating a need to rely on the halting English with which their waiter greeted them.

They opted for modest experimentation with the new cuisine, excusing their caution as a desire to avoid the risk of indigestion interfering with their duties. Mrs. Hudson ordered chicken with rice and Watson roast lamb. Holmes ventured a little farther afield, ordering stifado which appeared to him to be a sort of stew, and therefore reasonably safe. The restaurant was located directly below their balconies, and from their outdoor table gave them the same view of Greek landmarks.

As they ate, the room began to fill with several of the people with whom they had shared their travels the past several days, all of whom seemed equally intent on an early dinner and the potential for some sightseeing before getting to bed. They exchanged waves with the weightlifter, Launceston Elliot, whose blond good looks instantly outshone the attractions of ancient civilization for several young ladies, while becoming a source of undisguised displeasure for their male escorts. He was joined by Grantley Goulding, a British hurdler, who drew a friendly wave from Holmes, but whose swarthy, richly mustachioed features excited none of the admiring attention shown his companion. Oswald Benton entered the room a short time later, nodded his respects to their table, before directing the maitre d' hotel to seat him at an unoccupied table against a far wall. He was followed by

Flack and Ramsay, the one loud and passionate, the other reserved and cautiously optimistic that his appetite might be returning. The Americans, who been such a vibrant presence the past several days, were nowhere to be seen.

When they had finished eating, the three detectives made good their plans for sightseeing. Mrs. Hudson and Watson started for the gardens beyond Syntagma Square and a view of the palace. Holmes walked to the Zappeion, where he hoped to accomplish his assigned task of receiving the Dowager Empress' letter from the German courier, and his chosen task of winning a medal for his prowess with foils. The arena, where those glories were to occur, was something of a letdown to Holmes. Its eight-columned center section suggested a grandeur that was quickly undone by the line of low nondescript buildings extending from its either side. He turned his attention to the matter at hand, climbed the seven steps at the building's center, and entered the arena.

Striding to the stadium's platform, he assumed an on-guard stance, and with his body erect, pushed off his back foot, keeping his right arm holding the imaginary foil parallel to the ground, his left arm in the air, and his left leg now extended behind him as he lunged forward. He pursed his lips, his movements did not quite flow together as they should have. He repeated the advance and lunge, a second, third and fourth time. Satisfied with the last, he followed it with a strategic retreat, becoming aware as he did so of a solitary figure emerging from the shadows of the spectator area below the arena's balcony, where he had doubtless been watching Holmes the whole time. He launched into a feint, and held his position long enough to consider the man without seeming to, employing the observational skills acquired from his years with Mrs. Hudson. His silent onlooker was fiftyish, wore a frock coat and striped trousers, and had hair, beard and moustache the color of newly plucked carrots, all of it neatly trimmed and of moderate length. Indeed, everything about him appeared neatly trimmed and moderate. Holmes judged him to be an official, perhaps with the Olympic Games, perhaps with one of the several governments whose athletes would be represented.

"Hello, do you speak English?" Holmes spoke slowly, and with labored enunciation as if his doing so would allow him to be understood regardless of the language the man in the shadows spoke.

"I do, indeed," came the response in diction revealing English to be not only his first language, but to have been carefully cultivated, likely at Eton or Harrow, before being finely polished at Oxford or Cambridge. "May I take it you are a member of our fencing team?" the voice continued.

"I am. I will be participating in the foils competition. I am Sherlock Holmes. And are you here at the Games in some official capacity?"

"No, not official. I'm here solely as a spectator, delighted to cheer on my countrymen." The man stopped to look around as if becoming suddenly aware some explanation for his presence was in order. "I was curious to see a sports arena and wandered to the one that seemed nearest my hotel. But please go right on with what you're doing, Mr. Holmes. Pretend I'm not here." With that, the man acted to fulfill the pretense he suggested. He flicked on a smile, flicking it off when it seemed to have accomplished its purpose, and crossed the hall to an exit. He paused, holding the door part way open. "I do wish you well ... with your swords. Good evening." He left without giving his name; Holmes was aware he was far too well-mannered for that to have been an oversight.

At the hotel Holmes described the encounter to Watson and Mrs. Hudson, who had returned from their walk. Mrs. Hudson scowled her concern about the neatly turned out stranger. "We 'ave to suppose that, as we talked about, there may be some who know of Mr. 'Olmes' mission and the letter. And if one of them knows that much, 'e may even know about this Zappie place. So 'e goes over there to get the lay of the land—so to speak—only 'e runs into Mr. 'Olmes, and decides to make a quick getaway without stoppin' for introductions."

"What do you suggest we do about it, Mrs. Hudson?" Watson asked.

"There's not much we can do except stay alert, and wait for our mystery man to make 'is move. It shouldn't be long in comin', what with our German friend due 'ere shortly."

"Well then," Holmes said, "let the games begin."

Chapter 2.
Two Murders

At breakfast the next day, talk turned to the opening of the Olympic Games. Attention had been so focused on the responsibility Mycroft had set upon their shoulders that, apart from Holmes' brief effort to recapture bygone fencing skills, scant attention had been paid to the great spectacle about to unfold. Now, all three detectives found themselves looking forward to the prospect of witnessing a pageant whose like hadn't been seen for more than 2000 years. For two drachmas each, Watson and Mrs. Hudson had purchased tickets for the afternoon's opening ceremony. Holmes wouldn't need a ticket. He would be on the track of the Panathenaic Stadium where he would join with athletes from all the participating countries to be welcomed by Greece's King George.

They finished their meals, and had in mind a stroll around the hotel, when a familiar figure appeared in the dining room's doorway. He was a small, well nourished, clean shaven man of about 50 with a great shock of dark hair that seemed to have sprouted without warning or rationale from a place beyond his high forehead. The detectives recognized him from the reception the day before where he had been so constantly at the ambassador's elbow, he seemed very nearly an appendage of the man. Now, he was clearly on a mission. His eyes were a fierce squint as his head slowly swiveled to capture every corner of the room until, spotting the three of them, his eyes returned to nearly normal size, and he proceeded to maneuver his way around tables with a grace and speed that belied his well-rounded figure. On arriving at their table, he struggled with limited success to observe the decorum expected of visitors to the dining room of the Grand Bretagné Hotel.

"Thank goodness I found you. You *are* Mr. Holmes?" He looked accusingly to Holmes who reluctantly granted the point. "And this is Dr. Watson of course." The small man's discovery was rewarded with a cautious nod. "And ... madam." He directed a quizzical stare to Mrs. Hudson, and proceeded to ignore her thereafter.

Confirmed in his judgment about the principals, he took the single empty seat at their table without waiting to be invited. Leaning into his audience, his eyes again narrowed as he spoke as confidentially as his excitement would allow, entirely oblivious to the attention his effort at secrecy was garnering from all parts of the room.

"My name is Coopersmith, Spencer Coopersmith. I'm the deputy chief of the British embassy. We have a situation, Mr. Holmes — a very serious situation. I need to have you and your colleagues accompany me to the ambassador's home." With that, he pushed back his chair, and rose to pursue the same circuitous path out of the room he had employed on entering it. He found himself, however, a leader without followers. The three people who should have fallen in line behind him remained seated, their faces a mix of confusion and astonishment. He returned to his seat and leaned still closer, his voice now a hoarse whisper.

"Please, you must come. There has been a murder. Two murders. Lady Sterling is dead. So is a gentleman we haven't yet been unable to identify. Both of them shot. And Lord Sterling has disappeared."

On this second try, the three detectives rose as one to follow Coopersmith to the coach he had waiting. "The ambassador's house isn't far," he informed them, "we could comfortably walk there, but it will be easier to talk in the carriage."

He directed them to a coach, whose driver was a burly man in his early fifties wearing a somewhat battered top hat that appeared designed to match his tattered frock coat. He studied his passengers without greeting or change in expression, urging his little horse on after the last of them entered his coach.

Throughout the short ride to the ambassador's residence, Holmes and Watson took turns peppering Coopersmith with questions, routinely interrupting his answers with additional queries to gather what information they could in the limited time available.

"When were the bodies discovered and who found them?" Holmes asked.

"The housekeeper found them. A Mrs. Kasiris. It must have been a dreadful sight. I can't even imagine it."

"What time was that?"

"Half six. Half six is when she gets to the ambassador's home. She's very prompt. A fine woman, somewhat stand-offish, I suppose ..."

"Who determined the two people were, in fact, dead?" Watson asked.

Coopersmith was taken aback by the question. It hadn't occurred to him that the two people could have been anything other than quite dead at the time they were discovered. "I suppose that would have been Nikolos—the man who is our carriage driver. He's sort of the ambassador's own coachman. You see, Nikolos speaks English, which is very unusual for a coachman. He was actually raised in Australia, but his family got homesick and returned to Greece. He ..."

"When did this Nikolos view the bodies?" Watson asked.

"That would have been right away. As I say, Nikolos is the ambassador's own coachman — not in the sense of being in his employ, but being always on call to the ambassador. Personally, I think the ambassador is far too trusting of the man. If it were up to me, I wouldn't allow him anywhere near the embassy. As far as I'm concerned, Nikolos needs to be watched constantly or he'll steal anything that isn't nailed down."

Sensing the unease he was creating for his audience, Coopersmith returned to the question put to him. "He would have been sitting outside the residence waiting on the ambassador who liked to get an early start to his day. Anyway, it was Nikolos who inspected the bodies. After that, Mrs. Kasiris sent him to give me the terrible news. I cabled the Foreign Office, although it's a little early for them, and knowing that you were attending the Olympic Games, Mr. Holmes, I decided to contact you at your hotel."

Coopersmith revealed he had said nothing to the Greek police, although he planned to inform them after Holmes had an opportunity to investigate. Since it was the home of the British ambassador, he felt justified keeping things to himself. Coopersmith allowed himself a small smile commensurate with his small deception. He did not report his second deception, that of also keeping the deaths from the Scotland Yard inspector who had arrived the day before. No one had suggested he inform the man, and besides he wasn't supposed to know the new arrival was a Scotland Yard inspector. Of course, he had known it before the detective even boarded the boat in Liverpool. Secrets were the major currency of the diplomatic corps. They were to be surreptitiously, but assiduously gathered, and once acquired, to be hoarded until time and circumstances would allow their revelation the greatest impact. Coopersmith had come into a windfall regarding Lady Sterling's purchases and the detective dispatched from London to investigate those purchases, and he planned to hoard his wealth for a while.

"What do you know of the ambassador's movements last night?" Holmes asked.

Coopersmith's face creased into a severe grimace and his lips became so tightly clamped, the three detectives feared for a moment they'd learn nothing more before their arrival at the ambassador's home. But the moment passed. Coopersmith's face unclouded and his words gushed forth.

"I don't want to raise question about the ambassador, but there was this one thing that was a bit of a curiosity. Lord Sterling called his wife after the reception for the athletes to tell her he'd be delayed getting home until nine or ten because of preparations for the Olympics, and she shouldn't wait dinner on his account. Of course, when we heard that, we were all prepared for a late night ourselves. But then, around six or maybe a little later, he tells us we can all go home, he's changed his mind, that there's nothing that can't wait until morning. Well, of course everyone was out of there like a shot. I had a report I had to get out, so I stayed behind for a while. My door was closed, but I thought I heard Lord Sterling leave together with Miss Pershing, our receptionist. You might speak to Miss Pershing about it. It's common knowledge they sometimes left together." Coopersmith looked to the three members of his audience to make certain his comment was understood. He found his audience staring back impassively.

Holmes asked the question he knew Coopersmith was dying to answer. "Is there something we should know about Lord Sterling and Miss Pershing?"

"I don't want to appear to be telling tales, Mr. Holmes, and normally I wouldn't say anything — I mean it's really nobody's business — but with two murders ... Anyway, it's likely nothing more than talk, but the two of them have been seen having dinner together — Athens is not a big enough town to hide that sort of thing. Of course, Miss Pershing is more than 30 years his junior, but then Lady Sterling is ... was nearly 20 years Lord Sterling's junior."

There was a brief pause while Holmes considered how to phrase a follow-up question regarding Lord Sterling's possible infidelity. Watson seized the moment to follow another line of inquiry about the ambassador. "Mr. Coopersmith, do you know if Lord Sterling owns a revolver?"

"I don't know what he has at home; there is a revolver in his desk drawer in the office, although it's not strictly speaking his. It's the embassy revolver, but it's kept in the ambassador's office in the interest of safety. The ambassador's door is the only one with a lock." Coopersmith pretended a sudden awareness of the implication of Watson's question and his own answer. "But you can't think ... It's just not possible." For a second time, Coopersmith found himself facing blank stares.

"What can you tell us of 'ow Lord and Lady Sterling got along with each other? And did they 'ave any enemies?"

Coopersmith was taken aback, not by the questions, but by the questioner. He would have ignored her except for the intense stares of Holmes and Watson who appeared to see nothing amiss and were waiting for his response. He looked solely to them as he responded to Mrs. Hudson.

"You have to understand that simply being the ambassador, or the deputy ambassador for that matter, puts you in a position where you're going to have enemies. It can't be helped. Like right now, it's no secret we're having disagreements with the Germans, and it's the ambassador who has to voice those disagreements. That's bound to ruffle some feathers."

"When it comes to people who work at the embassy, of course a man in his position has to do things that please some people and upset others. And I suppose there'd be general agreement that he can be quite demanding — but every bit as much of himself as of anybody else. Everybody understands that comes from a sort of image he has to overcome. It's well known he came to the diplomatic service late, and that he was rather a madcap before settling down, getting himself in some scrapes, and even an occasional duel."

Raised eyebrows and a small tilt of his head underscored his point.

"How did Lord Sterling come to enter the Foreign Office?" Watson's curiosity led him to stray for the moment from the murder investigation. In truth, he voiced a curiosity he shared with his colleagues.

"As I say, there's no great secret about it. His father worked out an initial appointment in the Colonial Office which put him in New Zealand for his first posting. He had a little bit of a problem there, an unfortunate accident he had to put behind him — which he obviously did. I see no reason to get into the sordid details."

Before Coopersmith could be cajoled into providing the sordid details the Baker Street trio was anxious to learn, the coachman pulled their carriage to a halt in front of an imposing two story red brick home topped by a Spanish tile roof with tall chimneys at either end. On its first level, pairs of bay windows with pale white shutters stood on either side of an oversized double door entrance. The windows on the second level continued a pattern of white against the red brick through the thick frames surrounding them. All of the owner's imagination or resources appeared to have been depleted in the design and building of the home with nothing left for landscaping. As a result, the house was surrounded by a great expanse of well-manicured, but totally bare lawn.

Coopersmith directed Nikolos to wait, and the detectives fell in behind him as he hurried up the gravel walkway. His knock triggered a woman's shout from somewhere deep inside the house, assuring them the door was unlocked. The reason for the woman's inhospitality was immediately apparent. In the hall, a few yards from the door, a man lay in a pool of blood that looked to have oozed from several channels. The bald head, and the small scar on his left cheek identified him as the man whose photograph was tucked into Holmes' coat pocket. In response to shouted directions from their unseen guide, they continued along the hall, past the parlor on one side and Lord Sterling's study on the other, and through a door to the dining room where the body of Lady Sterling lay a few feet from the sideboard partly covered by a blanket. On the sideboard was a tray holding two cups, one filled with tea, the other turned on its side. The several pieces of a teapot lay next to Lady Sterling, its brownish contents no match for the torrent of blood that engulfed it. As with the man they knew to be the German courier, Lady Sterling's body suggested she had suffered a number of wounds leading ultimately to her death.

Watson's preliminary study of the bodies suggested the shots had come from fairly close range, ten feet was his estimate. He counted three bullets in each, none of them striking their victims' vital organs, but the combination sufficient to immobilize them while they slowly bled to death. In the course of his study of the man's body, Watson took the opportunity to look for the letter he should have been carrying; then loudly announced his findings from both his examinations.

"Judging from the stiffness of their muscles, the two people appear to have been killed about 12 to14 hours ago. I'm afraid there's nothing on the man to tell who he is or what he was doing here."

While Holmes joined Watson in examining the bodies, Mrs. Hudson mumbled something about "givin' comfort to the 'ousekeeper," and ascended the stairs to where Mrs. Kasiris had sequestered herself.

Holmes stepped back from his examination of Lady Sterling to take stock. "Shot by someone who appears not very expert with firearms. As you said, Watson, whoever it was managed to miss the heart and the brain in spite of firing several shots at each of the victims from a relatively short distance. Lady Sterling and her visitor would seem to have been about to have tea when they were surprised by someone.

Nothing in the house appears to have been disturbed, and there's no suggestion of anything being taken ...." Holmes paused to search for Coopersmith, but the deputy ambassador had stationed himself in the parlor, out of sight of the bodies and beyond the earshot of Holmes and Watson.

"Except for the letter, of course, which Mycroft assured us he was to have on his person at all times. And what do we make of the absent Lord Sterling? Did he have reason for jealousy? Is that one of the 'sordid details' Coopersmith was loathe to share? Did Lord Sterling leave work earlier than he told his wife he would in an effort to catch her with her lover? It appears the killer did not have to force his way into the house. That supports the theory of a jealous husband, but where then is the letter? There would seem no reason to rummage through the pockets of a man killed out of jealousy. I suggest we join Coopersmith to question him about the state of the Sterlings' marriage and get into those sordid details."

At the entry of Holmes and Watson, Coopersmith stopped pacing the length of the parlor, and took to firing a stream of his concerns at them, and the ceiling and the wall behind them. "It's horrible. I just wasn't prepared. It's horrible. Are we done? I need to call in the Greek police, and I really should update the Foreign Office, although I have no idea what I can tell them. I can't understand who would do this terrible thing." Then it all came together for the deputy ambassador in a moment of sudden enlightenment. "The Germans. Of course, the Germans. They could have committed the murders, and then taken Lord Sterling hostage."

Holmes attempted to reduce the risk of the deputy ambassador launching a preemptive strike against Germany on behalf of the United Kingdom. "We've only just begun the investigation, Mr. Coopersmith, and we need to gather a great deal more information before reaching any conclusions."

It was to no avail. Coopersmith was already lost in the vagaries of the international intrigue he had concocted, and took no notice of Holmes until a question forced the deputy ambassador's return to reality.

"I have to ask you about the relationship between the Sterlings. It appears that last night Lady Sterling was entertaining a male visitor by herself. Would she have been in the habit of doing so?"

"Not in the habit, Mr. Holmes, certainly not in the habit. You do understand Lady Sterling is — was — the ambassador's wife. She'd be called upon to entertain — as you put it — all sorts of people from time to time. I admit the hour is unusual, but I feel certain nothing unseemly would have been going on. I do hope you won't mention any of that to Whitehall ... or the press."

"I'm not in the custom of spreading tittle-tattle, Mr. Coopersmith, but this *is* a murder investigation. I will need to explore aspects of the couple's relationship that may be relevant to the murders. Am I correct that Lady Sterling was a good deal younger than the ambassador?"

Visions of the Teutonic menace temporarily receded to the background. Murder was unfortunate, but was an event the Foreign Office could not have expected him to foresee. Therefore, it constituted no threat to his career. Adultery, on the other hand, was an event he would have been expected to recognize, and about which he should have informed his superiors. He now regretted his earlier comments about Miss Pershing, and reverted to his earlier strategy of hoarding information.

"I can't say I appreciate the tenor of this conversation, Mr. Holmes. There is a disparity in their ages, but the gossip about their marriage is almost certainly just that — gossip — and I'd remind you the ambassador and Lady Sterling have been married for more than 15 years."

Holmes shrugged, "Nonetheless, I need to know something about this Miss Pershing."

"There's nothing, I'm sure. I'm sorry I mentioned it. She's a young receptionist who joined us a few months ago. Her father is with the Colonial Office, and her mother is from Greece so the girl is fluent in the language. The ambassador is almost certainly just being supportive of the young woman. More than likely it's something paternal. You know Lord and Lady Sterling have no children." Coopersmith arched his back, increasing his stature too minutely to achieve the effect desired. "Now, I really must inform the Greek police. I'm afraid they'll be quite upset if I delay any longer, and one must maintain some semblance of good relations with the local authorities. Also, I need to communicate with my superiors and with embassy staff who know nothing of these events. This will be a terrible day. A terrible day." Coopersmith gave a small shudder in anticipation of his terrible day before starting for the hall and the front door.

"I take it you will join me at the embassy when you're through here and let me know your findings." Coopersmith didn't wait for an answer; he was focused on avoiding any glimpse of the body in the hall, and removing himself from the scene of the murders he would spend the rest of his day describing to one group or another. Holmes was left to wonder about Lady Sterling's liaisons, if, indeed, there had been any.

Mrs. Hudson found herself in the unexpected position of playing hostess in a house that was not her own. She shepherded Mrs. Kasiris into Lady Sterling's upstairs study, and invited the woman to choose one of the three chairs available. The tall, slender woman screwed her well-chiseled features into a tight grimace as she assessed her options. She rejected the chaise lounge with a quick glance, frowned dismissal of an easy chair, and finally selected the secretary's chair, turning it away from the roll-top desk before setting herself on its edge.

Mrs. Hudson seated herself in the easy chair the housekeeper had rejected, and made a quick study of the woman before speaking. The absence of a ring made clear she was neither married nor a widow despite her title. They would have had to amputate to remove Mrs. Hudson's ring or that of any widow she'd ever known. Her decision to perch uncomfortably on the least comfortable chair in her mistress' study signaled her hesitancy to step, however briefly, out of the role of service. Mrs. Hudson had known such women. Lacking families of their own, their lives became bounded by the lives of the families for which they worked. The family's successes and failures, joys and sorrows were theirs to share, although in decidedly muted fashion. For some, it would continue like that until the grave; for others, that attachment would end with their finding someone with whom to start their own families. For Mrs. Kasiris, there appeared the distinct possibility that that someone had entered her life, but not yet become part of it.

The housekeeper showed the expected alarm at finding the bodies of her mistress and a strange man on her arrival, but not the grief that would have been seen if the relationship to the family were all. Her loyalty was professional, not personal. It suggested not only the possibility of there being someone else in her life, it suggested as well the possibility of finding a breach in the wall of resistance her tight-lipped stare implied.

"I take it you speak English, Mrs. Kasiris?"

"I have some English, ma'am. I work for a family where the master was in shipping. He was sent to Liverpool in your country, and the family with him. We was there 11 years. I only come back a year ago when the master died and my mistress went to live with her family. That's when I hear

Lord Sterling is looking for someone who has English. It was the Good Lord looking out for me."

Mrs. Hudson smiled in recognition of God's magnanimity. "Tell me, Mrs. Kasiris, is everything downstairs exactly the way you found it?"

"Yes ma'am, I don't go near the bodies. Nikolos was waiting outside for the master like every morning, and I ask him to come inside and look at the bodies. When he tells me everyone is dead, I send him to Mr. Coopersmith, and I go upstairs to find something to put over my mistress' body. It wasn't right, her lying there like that. I took blanket and covered her best I could. That's the only time I go near the dead body." The woman gave a small shudder of remembrance before turning back to the present. "Has somebody been called to take away the bodies? Have they found Lord Sterling? The master should know what's happened."

Mrs. Hudson ignored the housekeeper's statement, not revealing her certainty that Lord Sterling was already well aware of what had happened. "I'm sure the bodies will be removed before long, but we'll 'ave to wait for the police to get a look at them." She paused to try a smile of reassurance, and spoke softly.

"What can you tell me about the man downstairs?"

"I never see him before last night. He had German name, Meyer something, and she called him Count. Lady Sterling said he was friend she knew from college. She went to a lady's college, you know. She said this Count Meyer something was close by at the men's college in Cambridge." Mrs. Kasiris sniffed her disapproval of either the evening visit, women's colleges in close proximity to men's colleges, or the Count, perhaps all three.

"He come here sometime after five, saying he had come direct from the train to see Lady Sterling. I heard him say he hadn't even stopped to get his bags, but had them sent to the hotel. I suppose he wanted to impress my lady. I told her I stay if she liked even though I leave at six after I set out dinner. But she said she'd be fine. Of course, if I had known ...." The housekeeper's voice trailed off and her jaw reset as she stiffened still more in the chair she only partly occupied.

Mrs. Hudson spoke firmly to the suggestion of dereliction of duty on her part. "There could be no way for anyone to know what was goin' to 'appen. The only one to blame is the person who did this terrible thing." With any thought of the housekeeper's misfeasance dismissed, Mrs. Hudson turned the conversation back to her investigation. "I'm just wonderin', Mrs. Kasiris, about keys to the 'ouse, and whether there's any keys gone missin'?"

A small blush showed before the housekeeper spoke. "There was this one, ma'am. A key went missing two or three months ago. It was an extra key kept in the master's study. Lord Sterling was very upset about it and would not make another one."

Mrs. Hudson greeted the news with a small series of nods. She adopted a studious look as if the information was fraught with significance, although the timing of the key's disappearance, combined with the woman's blushing as she described it, suggested it had more to do with the housekeeper's "someone" — of whose existence she now felt certain — than it did with the murders. In any event, the revelation of the small lapse in the household's functioning might pave the way for discussion of more serious indiscretions. It was time to try to ease into such a discussion.

"Mrs. Kasiris, it's critical we know everythin' that might lead us to find your lady's murderer. Because of that I need to ask you some questions that will be gettin' into the Sterlings' private life. I'll only be askin' you these things so we can find Lady Sterling's murderer. And I'll only be tellin' what you tell me to Mr. 'Olmes, the world-famous detective who'll be the one to find out who that person is and turn the murderer over to the police." Mrs. Hudson waited for the housekeeper to think it through. When the lines in her forehead began to slowly disappear, she began the questioning she'd promised.

"Mrs. Kasiris, we know that all married couples 'ave their little arguments. Me and my own Tobias 'ad a wonderful marriage, but it wasn't like we never 'ad our little spats. I'm thinkin' there must 'ave been things that set off spats for Lord and Lady Sterling, like things can for any married couple."

Mrs. Kasiris rocked from side to side at the edge of her chair, and twice cleared her throat before answering Mrs. Hudson. "They was a devoted couple, Mrs. Hudson. They're not the first family I work for, and I saw arguing in some that got pretty loud. There was none of that with the master and my lady. Of course, like you say, they sometimes disagreed about things. They wouldn't be human if they didn't. For one, Lord Sterling had to have his cigars, but their smell bothered my lady. She asked him to smoke in his study, but he would forget now and then, and my lady would get upset with him, but right after, everything went back to the way it always was between them."

Mrs. Kasiris looked to Mrs. Hudson with the beginnings of a smile. She had given the strange talking woman what she asked for without saying anything against her mistress. It occurred to her that now she needed to even up the score, and talk about a time when Lord Sterling became upset with her lady.

"There was, too, this one time the master complained about the money my lady wanted to spend on her parents. The master brought Lady Sterling's parents, Baron Martinson and the Baroness, to Greece. He got them a house in Acharnes, little way north of here, so my lady could be close to them on account of her father not being well, and her mother needing help sometimes. The master was very good about that. Except he thought my lady was spending too much money on furnishing the house. She promised to be careful about the expenses and that was all. It never came up again."

With two trivial conflicts revealed, the housekeeper hoped she was done, while Mrs. Hudson hoped the housekeeper would now be open to discussing more significant issues. Mrs. Hudson pressed for the realization of her hopes.

"I need you to tell me about the male guests Lady Sterling 'ad to the residence."

Mrs. Kasiris again explored the sides of her chair before settling back in its center to face the inevitable.

"It wasn't like there were a lot, Mrs. Hudson, and they were — most of them — friends of the master. They would come for lunch or sometimes for tea in the afternoon. It was only yesterday that someone was here at night."

Mrs. Hudson had no interest in learning anything more about Count Meyerhoff, and a great deal of interest in learning about Lady Sterling's other men friends. "Was there anyone she saw more often than 'er other guests?"

"I'll say nothing against my lady, Mrs. Hudson. She and the master were always good to me, and I can tell you I'll be lighting a candle for my lady before the day is out." Her preamble complete, Mrs. Kasiris lowered her voice, and looked from Mrs. Hudson to the door behind her as she began to reveal what she'd held in confidence until now.

"If you think it could help find the terrible person who did this thing, Mrs. Hudson, your Mr. Holmes should know there was one man who visited her a great many times. A young man, younger than my lady, and I suppose some might say nice looking." She shrugged her own indifference to such superficialities. "He was here regularly to help her with buying Greek bowls and statues and things for the house. One time she had Nikolos take her to where he worked — maybe more than one time. Anyway, whenever he come, the two of them sat with each other in the front parlor with the door closed, and Lady Sterling tell me not to come in unless she rang. Once I thought she wanted tea, and when I go in, the two of them are close together, looking at a book he brought with him. Lady Sterling was very upset, and told me to set the tray down and leave." Mrs. Kasiris pursed her lips before sharing her last and most crucial piece of information. "The man's name is Theodore Bikelas. I could write it in English if you want."

Mrs. Hudson had her do so. "Did Lord Sterling ever say anythin' about Mr. Bikelas, or any of the men who visited Lady Sterling?"

With the secret she had been holding now revealed, the housekeeper had only to restate the justification given her by Mrs. Hudson before sharing all that remained. "There was this one time — I'm only telling because you say it could be important. I was in the hall upstairs. They didn't know I was there and they didn't make their voices soft." Mrs. Kasiris looked to Mrs. Hudson to make certain her innocence was understood, and was rewarded with a small sober nod.

"Lord Sterling tell her she shouldn't be seeing men alone at home. He said there was starting to be talk at the embassy. She tell him I was always there — except she said my name of course — and that he knew all the men except Mr. Bikelas, and that he was only there to help her buy nice things for their house. And she asked him, didn't he want her to make the house look nice? Then, she told him she could just as well ask what went on in his office. Lord Sterling said something I couldn't hear, and Lady Sterling said something about using her own judgment. After that, Lord Sterling came out of the room saying he didn't want to discuss it further." With her report complete, the housekeeper's body became a little less stiff, and she allowed herself to drift a little closer to the back of her chair.

"Thank you, Mrs. Kasiris. I'm sure what you've told me will be very 'elpful in bringin' to justice whoever 'as done this terrible thing. I'll not bother you any more for now, although there may be other questions later."

"I'll be here, ma'am. I know the master will be back, and I mean to be here for him. There's things to be done in the meantime, silver to be polished, and furniture waxed, crystal to be cleaned, lots of things. I must have everything ready when he comes, and it must look the way my lady would want."

Mrs. Hudson asked if she could bring the housekeeper some water or some tea, but Mrs. Kasiris said she was fine. As Mrs. Hudson left, Mrs. Kasiris followed her out of the room, but not down the stairs. She stood at the railing that ran along the corridor on the second landing overlooking the ground floor. She would stay upstairs until it was cleared of the bodies of her mistress and her visitor.

The three detectives delayed leaving until five uniformed officers of the Greek police arrived in response to Coopersmith's call. Scowling and groans made clear what language differences could not at their finding themselves an apparent afterthought in the investigation. Mrs. Hudson concluded that the deputy ambassador's wish for a semblance of good relations with local authorities was not to be fulfilled. Holmes and Watson employed hands and facial expressions in an effort to achieve a more cordial exchange, but succeeded only in learning that the man in charge of the Greek police was Theophilus Paparrigopoulos, a name that was not so much dismissed from memory as never incorporated into it. The brief effort at civility ended with a round of formal handshakes among the men and respectful nods to Mrs. Hudson — whose presence was as much a mystery to the police as the bodies they had yet to explore — after which the three detectives went in search of a place to share their findings and suspicions. A small café, a street north of the ambassador's home, was found inviting. They ordered Greek

59

coffees and Lazarăkia, a spice bread which, they gathered from their waiter's broken English, was only available during Easter week. After first agreeing that the spice bread was a most happy choice, and communicating their judgment to the waiter through a series of smiles and nods, the three detectives began to share their thinking.

Holmes detailed the difficulties he saw in the conflicting evidence. "As I said to Watson, at first blush it is tempting to view Lord Sterling as our prime suspect. He leaves the office early after telling Lady Sterling he'd be home late. He surprises her with a strange man, thinks he's her lover, and shoots them both in a fit of jealous rage. I would wager, by the way, the revolver kept at the embassy is no longer in his desk drawer." Holmes looked to his two colleagues to see if either would take up his challenge. When neither did, he continued. "But then one comes to the missing letter. If Lord Sterling killed the two of them in a fit of rage, why would he stop to steal a letter directed to the Queen — indeed, how would he even know this man was carrying such a letter? The disappearance of the letter throws everything into confusion."

Watson nodded his concurrence before adding his own comment about the confusing evidence. "We also know from Coopersmith that Lord Sterling was a good enough shot to survive some number of duels. Is it likely that he would require three shots to dispatch each of his victims at close range?"

"There's somethin' more to think about," Mrs. Hudson began. "If it doesn't make sense to think of a jealous 'usband stoppin' to take a letter, does it make sense to think someone who's come to steal a letter would go through the 'ouse lookin' for Lady Sterling so 'e can shoot 'er too, when 'e could just duck back out the door without being seen? No, there's only one way it all makes sense."

Mrs. Hudson paused to pull off another piece of the spice bread, and appeared to savor it while Holmes and Watson waited to learn how it all made sense. A swallow later their patience was rewarded.

"I'm thinkin' the murders and the stealin' of the letter were done by two different people."

Watson's face creased its way to a consideration of Mrs. Hudson's reasoning, then cleared with his acceptance of that reasoning. Holmes began a steady drumming of his lower lip with his index finger, searching for another conclusion to fit the findings they had described. Mrs. Hudson ignored the two of them and continued to munch on spice bread.

Holmes finally abandoned his search, and raised another concern. "That is certainly something to consider, Mrs. Hudson, but we still have the problem of understanding why, if he's not the murderer, the ambassador has disappeared and where he's gone."

"That's true, Mr. 'Olmes." For a moment she looked longingly at her plate which now contained only the few crumbs remaining from her portion of the spice bread; then turned her attention again to the task at hand. "The Olympic ceremony is still a good three 'ours off. That gives us time to see what we can learn at the embassy. There may be some there who can shed light on our problems. In particular, I'd like a talk with this Miss Pershing to see whether there's anythin' more to 'er and the ambassador than a lot of nosy people with not enough to do. First though, Dr. Watson, are you plannin' on finishin' the rest of your spice bread?"

Atop a coach parked a little way beyond the embassy's entrance, Nikolos smoked a cigarette and leisurely leafed through a newspaper. He looked up at the approach of his earlier passengers, gave them a curt nod of recognition, tipped his hat to Mrs. Hudson, and turned back to his paper. Inside the center hall, now restored to its proper role of providing visitors a formal welcome, an attractive young woman sat behind a desk whose only adornment was a placard that held the word "Reception" in English and Greek. Mrs. Hudson guessed they were meeting Miss Pershing. The young woman tried for the smile that likely came automatically at other times, but had to settle for a wide-eyed stare. Mrs. Hudson concluded Coopersmith had shared news of the morning's events with staff.

"Welcome to the British Embassy. How can I be of service?"

"We're here to see Mr. Coopersmith," Holmes announced.

"Do you have an appointment with the deputy ambassador?" Again, the effort to manufacture a smile fell short.

Holmes ignored the question. "You may tell Mr. Coopersmith that Sherlock Holmes and his colleagues are here to provide the assistance he requires."

Moments later, they were joined by the solemn young man who had greeted them at the Athens train station the day before. He nodded importantly to Miss Pershing, who introduced him as Mr. Fitzhugh, Mr. Coopersmith's assistant, a sudden but very becoming blush overtaking her cheeks as she did so. For his part, the young man glanced to her once, then again, longer this time as she turned her attention to the papers on her desk. It was apparent to Mrs. Hudson that the two young people shared a relationship, or more likely, judging by their deliberate inattention to each other, would like to share a relationship. With a last look to Miss Pershing, this one resulting in a demure glance from the receptionist, Mr. Fitzhugh recaptured the air of authority appropriate to his position as assistant to the deputy ambassador, and led the three detectives to a small conference room where Coopersmith joined them, wearing an expression that made their somber guide appear jolly. After summarily dismissing

Fitzhugh, he shared with them the several reasons for his discomfort.

"Have you learned anything I can share with London? Whitehall is all over me, as I'm sure will come as no surprise to you. I have telegrams to answer from the Prime Minister and the Foreign Office, and I'm expected to be in touch with them every two hours. I have to deal with a distraught and anxious staff, and I need to prepare a statement for the press before they go off on their own and report every rumor they hear — and there are many — and, with all that, I'm still expected to represent our country at the opening of the Olympic Games." Becoming suddenly aware of the presence of Mrs. Hudson, Coopersmith blinked himself to a stop.

"What I have to say is confidential. The fewer people involved the better. I mean no disrespect, madam, but was it necessary to bring this woman to these briefings?"

The comment was directed to Holmes, but was answered by the woman in question.

"Goodness, Mr. Coopersmith. I wasn't about to stay by myself with a lot of people who don't even speak my language. Not after seein' all those bodies and all that blood, and knowin' there's a murderer on the loose. But I'll wait outside if it'll make you feel better. I'm sure I'm safe 'ere in my own country's embassy."

"No, no, that won't be necessary. You already know most of it anyway. Besides, you're not the first surprise I've had since getting back to the embassy. As if two murders and Lord Sterling's disappearance weren't enough, I have two members of the service staff who have got it into their heads that because they can ride a bicycle, they should participate in the Games as members of the British team. I'll deal with them later." Coopersmith waved away any further discussion of murders, a missing ambassador, or kitchen staff masquerading as bicyclists, and taking a deep breath, he spoke to the latest dilemma placed in his lap.

"There is something additional I need to share with you. I don't know that it has any bearing on the murders, but I suppose it might. I was only informed of it officially this morning." He looked to Holmes and Watson with what he hoped was a meaningful stare before continuing with the information he had been informed of unofficially days before.

"It has to do with an investigation whose findings could prove embarrassing to the embassy, and indeed, to our country. In fact, even the knowledge that an investigation is being conducted could prove embarrassing. For that reason I must ask you to keep what I'm about to tell you in the strictest confidence." He gave an uncertain nod to Mrs. Hudson, whom he suspected suffered the liabilities of her sex when it came to secrets, but whom he hoped would be controlled by the two men.

"There's nothing certain, but it appears Lady Sterling was hoodwinked by an unscrupulous dealer in Greek antiquities — or rather in faked Greek antiquities. She made purchases of a number of items for the ambassador's home in good faith relying on his recommendations. In any event, it now appears the embassy and the government spent a significant amount of money on worthless copies instead of the valuable originals Lady Sterling thought she was purchasing. The situation has resulted in the Foreign Office requesting the assistance of Scotland Yard to disentangle this very delicate situation. An inspector from the Yard has already been detailed to the embassy. He arrived in Athens two days ago. Ambassador Sterling met with him at that time, and listed him as a security officer assigned to handle safety concerns associated with the Olympic Games. No one except the ambassador and myself — and now the three of you — have been told the true nature of his mission. However, as of this morning, he has been given another assignment. He is to involve himself in this latest dreadful turn of events, but he cannot reveal his association with Scotland Yard lest he compromise his ability to look into the purchase of antiquities. Since you will be exploring the murders, it is obvious that you should know of each other and begin to work together on both issues. It's my understanding, Mr. Holmes, you have frequently joined forces with Scotland Yard in the past. You may even know the inspector who's been sent. His name is Lestrade."

Watson was the first to find his voice after a long moment of silence accompanied by open mouths and widened eyes. "We would be pleased to speak to this Lestrade, and perhaps others on your staff who may be able to shed light on these terrible events."

Coopersmith shrugged acceptance of Watson's request. "I would only ask you to observe the propriety appropriate to the situation. I have apprised staff of the deaths at the ambassador's home, and as I'm sure you can appreciate, everyone is quite upset. Now, I really must get back. I will ask Mr. Lestrade to join you."

As he rose to leave, Coopersmith found his exit suddenly blocked by two strapping young men in the whites of kitchen staff. Having thrown open the door, they now stood at the room's threshold, seemingly defying the deputy ambassador to work his way past them. Barely visible behind them, a young woman was intent on explaining her obvious inability to contain the intrusion of the two men.

Coopersmith turned first to the hapless woman. "It's alright, Miss Patras, you may go back to your desk." He then attempted to assert an authority over the two men he was not certain he possessed, and they appeared certain he did not.

"What is the meaning of this, Mr. Battel, Mr. Keeping. You can see I'm in a meeting."

"I beg your pardon for that, Mr. Coopersmith, gentlemen, lady, but time is near out, and we haven't had a decision about the Games. We've got to change if we're to get to the ceremony, and we still need to get our bicycles ready for the races." The man Coopersmith addressed as Mr. Battel had relaxed his posture in the course of his short speech. Now, he again stiffened to attention. "This is about making a showing for our Queen and country. Which me and Mr. Keeping are wanting to do. We're bicyclists, and we're good ones."

Coopersmith, too, stiffened after recovering from his initial surprise. "Yes, well, be that as it may, you're also paid servants, and the Games are for amateur gentlemen only." Coopersmith took a step toward the door, considered the risk associated with taking additional steps, and decided instead to appear adamant from a safe distance. "There's more than enough to keep you busy with work here at the embassy. I'll thank you to return to it now."

"One moment if I might, Coopersmith." The voice belonged to Holmes; the tone to God. "Surely, the rules about who may and may not participate are subject to interpretation. One of the Olympic athletes on board our ship, a Mr. Flack, works in London where he keeps accounts. That man must surely be in another's employ. Just as these young men are."

"It's not the same at all. Your Mr. Flack is not a servant. He has the standing of a gentleman."

Watson gave voice to the distaste his face reflected. "I fear, Mr. Coopersmith, your argument suggests there is something improper or unworthy in the work of your own staff. I find it hard to believe you truly believe that. I certainly hope you don't."

"These men are not part of my staff; they are part of the kitchen staff. Would you describe your housekeeper as part of your investigative staff? Of course not — no offense, ma'am. There are standards all of us have to maintain, Doctor."

"And there is snobbery none of us have to tolerate, Mr. Coopersmith," Holmes observed drily, "I'm not certain that your colleagues in London would hold the same view, or be as willing to deny opportunity to their employees."

Holmes' words hung in the air for just moments before Coopersmith threw up his hands and blurted out his response. "I simply have too many things to do to waste time on this. Mr. Battel, Mr. Keeping, you may take part in these Games, but I will expect you to make up the hours you miss riding your bicycles, and to be here to get your work done at all other times this week. Mr. Holmes, I will summon our security officer, Mr. Lestrade, and he can arrange for you to meet with whatever staff you wish. Right now, I must see about responding to the concerns of the Prime Minister." A solemn Coopersmith followed his jubilant servants out of the meeting room.

Lestrade's eyebrows threatened his forehead as he nodded greetings to the familiar trio he now found in unfamiliar circumstances. "Mr. Holmes, I suppose I should never be surprised to find you wherever there's been a murder. Still, you seem to have come a long way to involve yourself with this one."

"You are aware, Lestrade, that I'm competing in the Olympic Games"

"I had heard that, and I was looking forward to taking in your performance. But I didn't know you'd be bringing along a cheering section," Lestrade nodded his compliments to Watson and Mrs. Hudson. "Still, I'm finding it hard to believe, Mr. Holmes, that you've come all this way solely to enter a fencing contest. In fact, there's a good deal of gossip about a secret letter making its way to Athens for transmittal to Whitehall, although no one seems to know very much beyond that. Of course, no one is aware that Sherlock Holmes has a brother importantly placed at the top reaches of the government. Rest assured no one will learn of that, at least not from me."

Looking to his audience's raised eyebrows, Lestrade grinned before continuing. "You'll find, Mr. Holmes, that learning other people's secrets is a full-time activity here. I'm quite certain several people are aware that I am here to investigate Lady Sterling's apparently fraudulent purchases although no one will say so. Anyway, when I learn that Mycroft Holmes' brother is coming to Athens at the same time a secret letter is scheduled to arrive, I can't help wondering about the coincidence. But before we get into that, I have to ask how you happen to be here, Mrs. Hudson? Please don't tell me you've quit your kitchen to assist Mr. Holmes' in his investigations."

Mrs. Hudson chuckled at Lestrade's outlandish suggestion, before recounting again her unwillingness to stay alone in light of the murderer in their midst.

Lestrade nodded thoughtfully, but said nothing before turning again to Holmes. "Mr. Holmes, Coopersmith tells me he has informed you that I've been asked to expand my investigation and look into these murders as well as Lady Sterling's purchases, and that you and I are to work together to bring the murderer to justice. Indeed, it seems to me quite possible that the fraudulent purchases are tied to these killings."

"Why do you think that, Lestrade?" Holmes asked.

"I was told by Lord Sterling that his wife received a telephone call threatening the ambassador if he continued to make inquiry about her purchases. He quit his investigation immediately, but it could be that our murderer didn't know that and chose to eliminate any danger of being found out. He goes looking for the Sterlings at a time the two of them could be expected to be home and alone. He finds instead a visitor and has to kill him before getting to Lady Sterling. He flees the scene without finding Lord Sterling. The ambassador comes home to find his wife dead, knows he's next, so he goes into hiding."

"Of course, there's a competing theory believed by most of the embassy staff. They will tell you the murders are most likely the result of the ambassador's jealous rage. He comes home, finds his wife with another man and kills them both, then disappears. It's certainly not unreasonable, although it may be nothing more than guesswork based on gossip."

"Then, of course, we have Coopersmith's theory of a German plot, but I think we can forget that," Lestrade added.

"How far have you gotten in your investigation, Inspector?" Watson asked.

"I've only just started of course. I've been trying to collect information about the cost of the items purchased by Lady Sterling. I haven't come across the receipts yet, but according to her rather meticulous records, it comes to quite a sum. I've also learned that Lady Sterling's agent in the purchases was a man named Bikelas. I have yet to locate him. To tell you the truth, Mr. Holmes, my investigation promises to be considerably more difficult than it need be. For the moment, the Foreign Office has directed me to hold off on any activity until the archaeological expert they're sending has opportunity to review the items and verify they're fakes. You may have met him, he was supposed to be leaving on the same boat as you. Man named Needham, Albert Needham." Lestrade looked to Holmes and acknowledged the nod he got from the detective with one of his own.

"I haven't seen him yet. I guess he's still resting up from the trip. Anyway, as best as I can tell, everyone believes the items at the ambassador's residence are fakes, but the Foreign Office doesn't want to be caught short on the chance they turn out to be genuine. And that's not the whole of it, Mr. Holmes. I can't contact the Greek police for fear of embarrassing our government — not that I could talk their language if I could contact them — and I have to tread lightly at the embassy since I'm supposed to act as if no one knows the real reason I'm here." Lestrade crushed a half-smoked cigarette in the ash tray, making clear his frustration if his words proved insufficient.

"And what of yourself, Mr. Holmes, what about your assignment? As I say, I know about a letter. I think you'll find the embassy's cleaning lady knows about a letter. What can you tell me about it, and do you believe that it might provide another way to explain these murders?"

Holmes avoided eye contact with Mrs. Hudson. He was determined to tell all — or nearly all — to Lestrade and chose not to risk finding Mrs. Hudson in disagreement. His concern was unnecessary. There was no disagreement.

"What I share with you must, of course, go no further." With occasional additions and clarifications from Watson, Holmes told Lestrade of Jameson's Raid in South Africa, the German telegram expressing support for the victory against the British forces, and the letter being sent to Queen Victoria by her daughter that might or might not clarify German intentions, and might or might not reveal details of British involvement in supporting or frustrating the Raid. "The letter in question has gone missing, and its courier is the man who was killed with Lady Sterling."

For a moment, a low whistle was Lestrade's only response to Holmes' tale. Finding his voice, he asked the status of Holmes' investigation.

"We're still gathering information. You know we only arrived yesterday, and like you, we found out about the murders a few hours ago." Holmes went on to describe the results of their investigation at the ambassador's residence, including the deduction that the robbery of the letter and the murders could be unrelated.

Lestrade grunted at the last, opened his mouth to speak, but closed it again as there came a knock on the conference door followed by the return of Coopersmith. As before, he dispensed with pleasantries and got immediately to the issues of concern to him.

"I've been in communication with London, and there's a great urgency felt about your getting these things resolved as quickly as possible. As we speak, Parliament is being informed of the murders and the ambassador's disappearance. That means the papers will have the story and the pressure will just keep building. It will be a miracle if we don't all lose our positions. Not the two of you of course. I mean the rest of us."

The deputy ambassador fell into a chair overwhelmed by the problems he faced and the catastrophe he predicted. "I'm to give you all the help I can, and you're to have anything you need." Coopersmith came suddenly forward in his chair, anxious to share a new thought. "Of course, you will now be giving up your plans to compete in the Games, Mr. Holmes. I'm sure you'll agree you need to devote your full attention to these crises."

Coopersmith's words carried the spirit of command, but his tone made clear they reflected nothing more than his wish. Holmes had no intention of allowing murders, disappearances, or fraudulent purchases to interfere with the demonstration of the fencing skills he had been taking pains to hone.

"I think there is still value in retaining this disguise. I may yet learn things I could not if I became known to everyone as a consulting detective." Holmes sounded as authoritative as Coopersmith had sounded uncertain, although in fact he had no idea what things he might learn in the guise of an Olympic athlete.

It was barely noon. Coopersmith had a full day ahead of him, and there were still things to be readied for the Games — which were proving to be an increasingly pointless diversion. The deputy ambassador was somewhere well beyond the end of his rope. "Well then, do as you wish. I only hope you know your business. In any event, I'll ask you to keep me informed every step of the way so I can keep Whitehall informed."

With Coopersmith's frustration apparent, Watson chose for himself the task of calming roiled waters.

"This has been a difficult day, and I fear nerves are somewhat frayed. It's not going to be easy on any of us, but we — all of us — will need to work together if we are to get through this — as I'm sure we can."

"I agree with Dr. Watson," Lestrade announced. "And I can tell you, Mr. Coopersmith, Mr. Holmes has helped the Yard out of some difficult situations in the past with his sometimes unorthodox ways of doing things. I don't know where his ideas come from, but in my experience they're always sound. If history is any measure, I feel certain things will soon come right."

Coopersmith allowed himself to be mollified, but would exact a price for his troubles.

"I trust you are right, Inspector. In any event, I am certainly prepared to work with you — with all of you — to see this through. I do have one request however. Mrs. Hudson, since you are seen as possessing a sensitivity above your station, I'd like you to undertake a task for which a woman's touch is needed." He proceeded to describe the task he had in mind, looking almost solely to the three men as he spoke.

"We haven't yet had opportunity to inform Lady Sterling's parents of their daughter's death. They're living in a villa in Acharnes, a city north of here. Lady Sterling's father is not in the best of health, so she and the ambassador arranged for Baron and Baroness Martinson to live close by where Lady Sterling could keep a weather eye out — so to speak. I need to send someone to break the news to them, and it strikes me Mrs. Hudson might be helpful in that regard. Of course, I'll assign someone from the embassy to go with her."

Mrs. Hudson offered a single condition in accepting the task. "I'd appreciate it if Nikolos could drive us there. I do want a coachman who can understand me."

Mr. Coopersmith readily agreed, satisfied he had asserted some measure of his authority. Mrs. Hudson was satisfied she was well launched on resolving one of the problems they faced.

Meanwhile, before leaving the embassy, Holmes asked to speak to Miss Pershing, after first confirming his suspicion that the revolver kept in the ambassador's desk drawer was no longer there.

Chapter 3.
The Hazards of Country Roads

After being summoned by Coopersmith and having his task explained to him, Nikolos gave the deputy ambassador his most piteous look, pressed his top hat tight to his chest, and began a desperate, but ultimately doomed effort to disabuse Coopersmith of the course he was proposing.

"Of course, I am happy to oblige, Your Excellency, but it is such a distance to Acharnes, I'm afraid we could not possibly be there and back in a single day. It's not for me I'm concerned, but for the lady (a sympathetic nod to Mrs. Hudson) and my poor wife, who is not at all well and needs me home as soon as I am able."

Had Acharnes been on the other side of the world and Nikolos' wife lay dying, Coopersmith would have proven unyielding. As it was, Acharnes was little more than an hour away, and he knew the coachman to be long separated from his wife. In responding to him, he felt no more obligation to be truthful than had Nikolos.

"Acharnes is no more than 10 kilometers from here, a distance you can cover in less than an hour, even on Greek roads."

Nikolos elected to ignore Coopersmith's underestimate of distance and time. He considered raising the specter of an injury to his horse, but thought the animal's infirmity was unlikely to generate greater sympathy than a dying wife. With no other option available, the coachman risked telling the truth about his concern.

"On each of those trips, Your Excellency, the ambassador provided a guard to accompany the coach. You know that road is traveled by the most vicious thieves and cutthroats in all Greece. I don't worry for myself, but for this poor lady who I would not want to see put in danger."

"I appreciate your concern, Nikolos. For that reason, I have asked Mr. Fitzhugh to accompany you and Mrs. Hudson. He's a strapping young man, quite athletic I believe. I'm sure his presence will prove reassuring." Coopersmith looked to the coachman with the practiced smile of insincerity.

In fact, Mr. Fitzhugh's presence gave no reassurance to Nikolos, who found the term "strapping" confusing, and believed his athleticism would most likely be seen in the speed with which he would run for help while the coachman was left to contend with the assailants. Nonetheless, there was nothing to be done about it. He shrugged compliance and went to see about his horse and coach. While Nikolos readied himself for the journey, Mrs. Hudson excused herself to meet briefly with Holmes and Watson "to work out where and when we would be meetin' up later." An observer, had there been one, would have concluded the schedule was being worked out almost exclusively with Watson, who gave an emphatic nod when she was done.

With Mrs. Hudson safely dispatched for the journey to Acharnes, Watson and Lestrade having excused themselves to assume unspecified responsibilities, and Coopersmith gone to worry and prepare reports, only Holmes remained in the conference room to meet with Cornelia Pershing. Before taking the seat Holmes offered, the receptionist looked to all parts of the room as though unconvinced that she and the detective were truly alone.

Holmes spoke softly but firmly. "Good morning, Miss Pershing. I am Sherlock Holmes. I am here to investigate the morning's tragedy, and identify those responsible. To accomplish that, I need to speak with Lord Sterling. I know that you and Lord Sterling had a certain ... understanding. Is there anything you can tell me that might help me locate the ambassador?"

For a short time the receptionist kept her composure. But soon, her chin began to tremble as she fought an increasingly unsuccessful battle to hold back tears. Finally, the dam broke and with a small shriek she gave in to her hurt and loss, making liberal use of the handkerchief she produced from the sleeve of her blouse. When the small linen square proved unequal to the demands being made on it, she turned to the more substantial handkerchief Holmes offered. He waited until the torrents had turned to sniffles before asking his question again, softening his tone still further.

"I understand this has been an emotional day for you and everyone at the embassy, but it is vital we get on with the work of locating Lord Sterling. I wonder if there is anything he may have told you that could help us find him."

Cornelia Pershing swallowed hard; then swallowed again before responding. "I can't help you find Lord Sterling. I only wish I could." She looked to Holmes, her eyes still filled with tears. "I've heard the stories, Mr. Holmes. I know what people think about my relationship with Lord Sterling. I can tell you there is nothing between us—at least nothing of the sort people want to imagine. I was lost when I came here. I mean, I'd never been away from home and England before, and what no one knows — no one except Lord Sterling — was that before coming here I had a very disappointing experience with the young man I was engaged to. Lord Sterling and my father are old friends, and Lord Sterling took me on as a favor to my father who thought it wise for me to get away. I thought so too until I discovered how difficult life can be when you're alone with only painful memories to occupy your mind. Lord Sterling took me under his wing. He would take me to dinner, and he always made himself available when I needed someone to talk to. We agreed not to tell anyone about my situation so I could avoid embarrassment, but when people saw us together outside the embassy, they came to a terrible misunderstanding. I know it was especially difficult for Lord Sterling. I volunteered to clear the air, but he thought it was still better this way, rather than having me share my life with everyone. I'm sure he's right, but there are many days I wish I had never left England, although Thomas ... Mr. Fitzhugh has always been kind."

There was a moment of quiet reverie before she disappeared briefly back into the handkerchief Holmes hoped she had no intention of returning to him. Righting herself again, she shook her head as if to clear it of any further self-pity before speaking again.

"I do remember Lord Sterling telling me something that may be important." She paused, unsure for the moment about violating a trust, deciding finally it was essential she do so. "You must have heard — it's common knowledge around here — that Lady Sterling may have been cheated on some of the Greek relics she bought. What people don't know is that after Lord Sterling started looking into it, Lady Sterling received a call warning her that if Lord Sterling didn't stop his investigation, his life would be at risk."

Holmes nodded thoughtfully as if he were hearing about the telephone call for the first time. "Did Lord Sterling know who made the call?"

"I'm sure he didn't. He said that Lady Sterling didn't recognize the voice on the telephone. He just said it frightened her a lot."

Holmes nodded his understanding before moving to end the exchange. "Is there anything else you can think of that would be important?"

Cornelia Pershing's forehead wrinkled her concentration, but she could think of nothing else. Holmes stood, thanking her as she gathered herself to become again the embassy's receptionist. He shook off her offer to return his handkerchief; then answered her question before she could pose it.

"I am certain we will find Lord Sterling, and we will find the people responsible for these brutal murders. You have the word of Sherlock Holmes for that."

Nikolos watched from atop his coach as the most junior diplomat at the embassy assisted Mrs. Hudson into her seat. He gave both his passengers the time to get themselves settled, patted the shotgun beneath his seat, and chucked the reins on his bay to begin the journey neither he nor his small horse was anxious to undertake.

Mrs. Hudson recognized her companion as the man who had met her and her colleagues at the Athens train station, and led them to their meeting with Coopersmith. He was clearly the expendable member of the diplomatic team, available for the menial tasks that needed doing by someone bearing the stamp of embassy official, but not yet to be entrusted with significant duties. His sober, nearly haughty demeanor reflected an effort to invest his trivial assignments with the gravity they lacked. Mrs. Hudson knew it to be the behavior of a young man insecure in his new position and likely in himself. He reintroduced himself as Mr. Thomas Fitzhugh, assistant to the deputy ambassador, then stared fixedly at the disappearing countryside, hoping to foreclose any possibility of conversation between them.

Whatever her companion's hopes, Mrs. Hudson felt that the trip to Acharnes would be difficult enough without the further strain of being conducted in silence. Besides, there were things the young man might know or have observed that could be of value.

"I was wonderin', Mr. Fitz'ugh, 'ave you been in Athens long?"

"Not long." A considerable pause followed. It held until good manners, and recognition of his companion's uncanny resemblance to a favorite aunt came into awareness. "It will be five months next week."

"And are you enjoyin' Athens, Mr. Fitz'ugh?"

"I wouldn't say enjoying exactly, Mrs. Hudson. It's like Mr. Coopersmith says. We represent the Queen and our country; we're not here to have a good time." Having paid proper obeisance to his mentor, he relented just a little. "Not that Greece doesn't have its good points, especially with its having so many places where you can walk through the ruins of an ancient civilization. It makes it a very interesting place to be, at least for a while."

"I can't think what it must be like to be so far from 'ome for such a long time." She shook her head in wonder. She was playing off the homesickness she heard in his words and tone in an effort to engage with Fitzhugh, but the truth was Mrs. Hudson was already missing Baker Street.

"Oh, you get used to it. Mr. Coopersmith says some early difficulty is natural, but everybody gets over it. Mr. Coopersmith says when he's back in London, he can't wait for his next posting."

Mrs. Hudson felt certain Mr. Coopersmith's London colleagues shared his sentiment. "Is London where you're from then?"

"No, I'm from Shaftesbury—in Dorset County. My father is the squire there, and I'm his third son. My older brother studied law and it was left to me to study diplomacy. I'm learning a lot and it's been a good career—anyway up to now."

"Up to now?"

"I mean with Lady Sterling being killed and Lord Sterling running off to who knows where. It's 'trial by fire' Mr. Coopersmith says, and he's certain we'll get through it. I'm sure he's right, but I still think it's bloody awful." Fitzhugh blanched his embarrassment. "Pardon my language, Mrs. Hudson."

Mrs. Hudson waved a hand back and forth, signaling her acceptance of the young man's emotional response.

"That's quite alright. It *is* awful. Do you 'ave any thoughts about all that's 'appened."

Thomas Fitzhugh set himself against the back cushion of the coach. He had done some thinking about it and he had his own view of the situation, but he wasn't entirely comfortable sharing that view with a civilian. At the same time, with whom else could he share it? Certainly, no one at the embassy, and he didn't know anyone outside the embassy. Besides, the woman was harmless enough. There was no chance of her talking to Mr. Coopersmith or to anybody at the embassy. He straightened his back, clenched his jaw, and spoke with a sudden conviction.

"I believe there's some who want to push us into war. Mr. Coopersmith thinks it's the Germans. He holds them responsible for the killings and the kidnapping of Lord Sterling. He thinks they want a war with us so they can lay claim to our territory, first in Africa, and then other places in the world." Thomas Fitzhugh paused, readying himself for the heresy he was about to elaborate. "I don't think so. I don't think what's happened has got anything to do with the Germans. And when it comes to coveting territory, I think there's some of our own people who'd like nothing better than a fight so we can take over the part of South Africa we don't own already. I don't know how exactly, but I think our own people could be somehow involved in all that's been going on." His heretical statement now complete, he retreated slightly from the fire of his own rhetoric. "Of course, that's just my opinion."

Mrs. Hudson nodded recognition of her companion's analysis, screwing her face to as earnest a pose as she could manage. "It's all very interestin' I'm sure. Of course, you know a great deal more about these things than I can ever 'ope to know."

Mrs. Hudson paused as if considering all the young man had shared, then moved to yet another view of the tragedy at the ambassador's residence.

"There is, you know, another way of understandin' all that's 'appened that's got nothin' to do with all that international goings-on. I'm not sayin' it's right, but it's somethin' that's bein' talked about. There's people who think Lord Sterling and Miss Pershing might 'ave been sweet on each other, and that's somehow connected to the murders and 'is disappearin'."

Fitzhugh bristled as he rejected any such thinking.

"Balderdash. I don't know who would say that. Certainly no one who knows Miss Pershing. The young lady is much too fine a person to be caught up in any such tawdry goings-on. I do hope you'll straighten out your Mr. Holmes on that score. I would hate to see Miss Pershing subjected to such grossly unfair criticism."

"Are you sayin' she would 'ave resisted the ambassador's advances?"

"Nothing of the kind. I mean, she would have, of course, if she had to. But I'm sure there were no advances. It's nonsense. Total nonsense."

His face was creased in an ugly frown, and Mrs. Hudson felt she had pressed the issue of a romantic relationship with the ambassador as far as she dared. It was apparent to her she had learned nothing more about Lord Sterling's feelings for Miss Pershing, but had had her conclusions about Thomas Fitzhugh's feelings for Miss Pershing vehemently affirmed. It was now time to prepare for their visit to Acharnes.

"Can you tell me what you know about Lady Sterling's parents?"

As it turned out, Thomas Fitzhugh knew very little about Lady Sterling's parents. He repeated the information Coopersmith had shared about Baron Martinson being in failing health, and that Lady Sterling had arranged to have them living close by, but not so close "as to be always underfoot" according to Mr. Coopersmith. In hushed tones Fitzhugh added Coopersmith's further understanding that the Martinsons were entirely dependent on Lord Sterling for their sustenance, although that situation was unknown to the Baron, and Lady Sterling wanted it kept that way. With that very partial description of the Martinsons, Mrs. Hudson suggested it was time to decide on the action they would take when they arrived at the Martinsons' home. To Fitzhugh's great relief, Mrs. Hudson volunteered to assume the brunt of the responsibility for telling them of their daughter's murder, while Fitzhugh would describe the embassy's sympathy and concern. Their strategy made clear, they rode in silence for a while, Mrs. Hudson taking note of how desolate the road was, with farms only occasionally interrupting long lines of forest. It was an observation their driver had already made as, for yet another time, he patted the shotgun that lay hidden under his seat.

The Martinson house stood on a small rise above the town with mountains at its back, and shops and an Orthodox church a street below its front door. Their nearest neighbors were sixty yards farther down the road, their home and stables visible in the near distance. The Martinson house was a mix of brown and gray stone of varying size on the lower level, and weathered timber on the floor above. Mrs. Hudson thought it more house than the couple needed, but it likely gave a place for their daughter to stay overnight, as well as providing room for a housekeeper, perhaps even a cook. Something else caught her attention as she and Fitzhugh climbed down from the coach. Carriage tracks partly on the dirt path, partly on the lawn above the path indicated another driver had preceded them, a driver too excited or too lacking in skill to keep the vehicle on the road. Or perhaps a driver who had come over an unfamiliar road in the dark of night. An outrageous idea began to form in Mrs. Hudson's mind — an idea too outrageous to be ignored.

Mrs. Hudson and Fitzhugh left Nikolos to find stables in town where he could feed and water the bay, and get food and drink for himself. They followed a path that appeared to consist of stones left over from constructing the house. Mrs. Hudson was certain she saw curtains at an upstairs window part for just a moment, and a white-haired woman move away from the window as the curtains fell back together. The woman, who came to the door, however, bore no resemblance to the figure at the window. In the small opening she allowed, she could be seen to be tall and raw-boned, with dark hair drawn back in a tight bun. She stared at the two visitors with a look that suggested disapproval at the interruption to her day. She posed a question to them in a single word of such strong dialect, they were uncertain whether their answer would be understood.

"Yes?"

In responding, Mrs. Hudson extended the length of every syllable of every word in an effort to assure comprehension.

"I am Mrs. 'Udson and this is Mr. Fitz'ugh. We are 'ere to see Baron and Baroness Martinson." She added a smile to establish the innocent intent of their visit.

Without another word being spoken, the white-haired figure replaced the housekeeper without opening the door any wider or appearing any more welcoming in spite of her words.

"I'm Baroness Martinson, may I help you?"

Mrs. Hudson looked to the small slender woman standing ramrod stiff, defiant without seeming cause, in the small space of the narrowly open doorway. Her stance and pallid features supported the idea the carriage tracks had stimulated, and the idea no longer seemed outrageous. The paleness of Lady Martinson's cheeks appeared the result of heavy and hasty application of powder, likely between the time of her appearance at the window and her replacing the housekeeper at the door. That application camouflaged the redness below her eyes, but could do nothing about the small puffiness that had formed there. Two handkerchiefs protruded from the sleeve of the woman's blouse. A single handkerchief would have been appropriate as fashion, two suggested that something other than fashion was being served. The rumpled, but well-tailored outfit of the woman indicated its likely use as night clothes in the course of a sleepless night.

Mrs. Hudson decided she would play act the rest of her visit, but she knew that not only was Lady Martinson aware of her daughter's murder, more than likely a room upstairs housed the man many thought responsible for her daughter's death.

"I'm Mrs. 'Udson. Mr. Fitz'ugh and I are 'ere from the embassy. May we come in to speak to you and Baron Martinson?"

The door came wide, and its one time guardian became a hostess. "Please come in. We can join the Baron in the parlor. Could you prepare tea for our guests, Selena, and a tray of scones, please? Do you eat scones, Mrs. ... Hudson, was it?"

"I do, yes."

The housekeeper left without relinquishing her cheerless expression. Entering a surprisingly spacious parlor, Baroness Martinson pointed them toward a mahogany settee with invitingly plump cushions that stood across a sea of deep carpeting. The arms and legs of the piece seemed so delicate in their carving that both Mrs. Hudson and Fitzhugh felt impelled to keep their hands in their laps, and to take care in the placement of their feet. Baroness Martinson took an easy chair opposite the settee, showing no comparable concern for its richly carved arms and legs. A low table set between them held a cut glass vase of spring flowers. Only the chair beside the Baroness lacked the elegance of the rest of the room's decor. It was an invalid's chair. Its occupant wore a robe over the bedclothes in which he was still dressed. The cause for Lady Sterling's concern about her parent was clear. There was the Baron's obvious frailty, but more striking was the vacant look in his pale blue eyes that raised question about his awareness of the world around him.

"Zachary, these people are from Henry's office and they want to talk to us." She gave no further introduction, the futility of doing so apparent to all.

Baron Martinson looked to Mrs. Hudson, then to Fitzhugh, and finally to his wife, confusion now replacing the emptiness in his eyes.

"Why are these people here?"

While Fitzhugh squirmed his way toward a response to the old man's question, Mrs. Hudson looked earnestly to each of the Martinsons, and softly began to give the report she was certain had been given hours before.

"I'm sorry to tell you, sir, I'm afraid Mr. Fitz'ugh and I 'ave some very sad news. Last night someone entered the ambassador's 'ome, and shot your daughter and a guest. Both of them were killed. I'm very sorry."

Thomas Fitzhugh looked forlornly to his hands, then to the Martinsons with a degree of sympathy it would have been impossible to pretend. "Everyone at the embassy is terribly distraught over this. You have ours and their sincerest condolences."

"Are these people talking about Pamela? Is that what this is about?" The Baron turned to his wife as he tried to make sense of the words and events happening around him. She moved closer to him, taking his hand in both of hers even as tears washed a familiar path down her cheeks.

"They're saying our little girl is gone, Zachary. Pamela ... Pamela is dead."

"Pamela? Our Pamela?" He looked around for meaning, but found none.

"Can you tell me how this thing happened?" the Baroness asked. "What is known about the ... the person who did this?" One well-used handkerchief was put back into service.

"It appears your daughter and 'er guest were surprised by someone. Neither the why of it nor the who is known just yet, but Mr. Sherlock 'Olmes is doin' the investigatin' together with Inspector Lestrade of Scotland Yard, and they will find the person responsible."

"And I can tell you that Mr. Coopersmith and all of us at the embassy are determined to capture this villain and make him pay for this terrible crime." Fitzhugh added.

"Will there be more people coming?" Baron Martinson directed the question to his wife, but Fitzhugh answered.

"There's no one else, Baron Martinson. We're here to represent the embassy. I can assure you that everyone sends their regrets, and I'm certain you'll be hearing from Mr. Coopersmith later."

"Lady Martinson, Lord Sterling 'as gone missin'. Of course, we want to find 'im to tell 'im the sad news. I'm wonderin' if you 'ave any idea where 'e might 'ave gone to?"

The question brought the expected look of surprise from the Baroness. Baron Martinson's forehead wrinkled and he seemed on the verge of saying something when his wife squeezed his hand tightly and spoke for them both.

"I'm afraid I can't help you there, Mrs. Hudson. I'm very grateful to you and Mr. Fitzhugh for coming all this way to give us this dreadful news. But now, I'm afraid the Baron and I will need time to recover ourselves. I don't know if you have children, Mrs. Hudson, but I can tell you there's nothing so terrible as losing a child. And Pamela was our only child. A wonderful girl. Loving and considerate. You know, she found us this place so we could be near to her, and she furnished it herself." The Baroness waved off her housekeeper who had appeared in the doorway bearing a tray holding a pitcher and cups, and plates for the scones she also carried. With a shrug the woman returned to the kitchen.

"We'll come to Athens later to prepare our daughter for travel to England to be buried. I'll answer all your questions then. Now, you must excuse us."

Baroness Martinson pushed to her feet, and stiffened to attention as she waited for her guests to copy her example. Mrs. Hudson and Fitzhugh did so, restating their condolences as they stood. Mrs. Hudson appeared to have a sudden idea. "I didn't see a carriage, might we use ours to get you whatever you might need?"

"What's that?" Baron Martinson looked to his wife. "Is the carriage gone?"

The Baroness looked to Mrs. Hudson with undisguised annoyance; then spoke gently to her husband. "You remember, Zachary, the Zappas allow us to keep our carriage in their stables." She turned back to her guests. "Thank you for your offer. We're just fine. Now, you really must let us have time to mourn our daughter."

"Of course." As they reentered the small hall and reached the foot of the stairs, Mrs. Hudson turned back for a moment, and raising her voice as if becoming suddenly concerned about the Baroness' hearing, she added a last comment. "If you think of anything that might 'elp us find the person who did this terrible thing, I would urge you to contact Mr. Sherlock 'Olmes who's stayin' at the Grand Bretagné in room 318. You might want to write it someplace. Mr. 'Olmes at the Grand Bretagné, room 318." With that, she gave the somewhat mystified Baroness a sad smile, and preceded Fitzhugh out the door to where Nikolos was just returned from town, both he and the little bay refreshed and ready to return home.

The journey back to Athens found Mrs. Hudson looking forward to meeting with her colleagues to share her discovery. She smiled as she envisioned Holmes' skepticism and Watson's surprise. There was, however, one thing that perplexed her. The furnishings at the Martinsons — those she had seen at any rate — were not just tasteful but luxurious. They would have cost someone a considerable sum, and that someone could not have been the Martinsons, but Mrs. Kasiris had suggested Lord Sterling balked at paying for other than serviceable furnishings. Thomas Fitzhugh's voice prevented further consideration of her observation.

"I thought that went well, Mrs. Hudson, very well actually. I do appreciate your coming. I've never been involved in anything like that before, and to tell the truth I would have had some difficulty without you."

Mrs. Hudson smiled her appreciation to the young man. "It's kind of you to say, Mr. Fitz'ugh, but you did just fine. These things take some gettin' used to, although I do 'ope you won't 'ave much opportunity to get used to them."

Thomas Fitzhugh let his shoulders relax against the thin cushion at his back, and allowed his speech to relax the restraint it had been under. For the next twenty minutes, Mrs. Hudson learned more than anyone could want to know of the idyllic village of Shaftesbury, and the countryside adorning, rather than merely surrounding it. She smiled indulgently at each story of home and family, and grimaced thoughtfully as he recounted his entry into the diplomatic service and experiences to date. He told of all he had learned from Mr. Coopersmith, and how impressed he was with the competence and hard work of embassy staff, allowing he was particularly impressed by Miss Pershing's efficiency and sunny disposition, although, like himself, she had only been at the embassy a short time. With that revelation, Fitzhugh quieted, sensing he was in danger of revealing more about himself than might be seemly for the assistant to the deputy ambassador. He looked to Mrs. Hudson to share something of herself, and she felt obliged to respond.

Perhaps stimulated by his example, perhaps too tired from the long ride to be as guarded as she might, she, too, became more forthcoming than she would have anticipated. She shared memories of growing up in London's East End and of her days with Tobias, at times recalling parts of her life she had hidden so far away that hearing them described was nearly as revelatory to her as it was to her audience. She became so caught up in her own reverie she forgot the events planned for the trip back to Athens until those events suddenly began to unfold.

A carriage emerged from a gap in the woods, blocking the road, and forcing Nikolos to pull his bay up short while issuing a stream of Greek obscenities. He bent to reach for the shotgun tucked beneath his seat, but was dissuaded by a pistol shot that whistled past his right ear. Nikolos watched helplessly as the highwayman who had fired at him stepped from the coach with his revolver trained on the coachman. The second highwayman held no weapon, but kept his carriage in front of Nikolos', leaving him and his passengers no escape. Both men wore kerchiefs that covered the whole of their faces beneath their eyes, and floppy workman's caps pulled low that hid nearly all the rest.

Thomas Fitzhugh counted himself a man of action. Moreover, he had been entrusted by Mr. Coopersmith with responsibility for safeguarding the journey to and from Acharnes. Undeterred by the numbers and weapons against him, he started from his seat to fulfill that responsibility. Deterrence came from his companion who placed a restraining hand on his arm and invoked the authority of his mentor in giving cogent argument against immediate action. "Let's see what this is all about. I'm sure Mr. Coopersmith wouldn't want you doin' anythin' rash."

Fitzhugh said nothing, but sat back in his seat, scowling his fury as an alternative to acting on it. For their part, the holdup men took no interest in Fitzhugh or Mrs. Hudson, choosing to deal with Nikolos alone. In an accent that seemed to drift unpredictably between German, Russian, English and several other unidentifiable dialects, the highwayman on the ground demanded Nikolos get down and put his hands in the air, waving his revolver as he did so, thus lending a particular authority to his demand. The coachman was directed to empty out his pockets, and to hand over his coat. The highwayman rejected the soiled handkerchief and pocketbook Nikolos offered, and shook his head to his colleague atop the coach after finding nothing else in Nikolos' coat. As he handed his clothing back to the coachman, the highwayman's kerchief slipped to his chin. It was only an instant before it was replaced over his nose and mouth, but it was long enough to reveal the highwayman to be the possessor of a neatly trimmed, small moustache. One person in the coach recognized the man, but she had known his identity all along.

Nikolos took little note of the slip, consumed as he was with reviewing in his mind the fates of other coachmen stopped by thieves along the same route. Those fates varied in kind, but shared a general theme of dismemberment. Suddenly, the highwayman on the ground appeared to experience an epiphany. Renewing his use of a combination of dialects, he demanded the coachman's top hat. When Nikolos hesitated, the highwayman took to waving his revolver menacingly again, exciting an immediate compliance with his request. As he extracted the prize he found in the lining of the hat his eyes crinkled, suggesting a smile beneath the kerchief. Satisfied with his plunder, he waved Nikolos back to his box; his partner pulled the carriage away from where it blocked Nikolos, and the two highwaymen sent the coach carrying Fitzhugh and Mrs. Hudson on its way.

In spite of the considerable time Mrs. Hudson and Fitzhugh had had to study the two highwaymen, they were in surprising disagreement in the statements they provided the young interpreter who translated their reports to the two Greek police officers who sullenly observed their interrogation. Mrs. Hudson described two men, both tall, both stocky, and both young, almost certainly less than 35, dressed in what appeared to be peasant costumes consisting of loose blouses and work pants. Fitzhugh was certain Mrs. Hudson, being a woman, was flustered by the situation, and her observations or her memory — or both — were understandably flawed. The two men, he said, were, in fact, of moderate height, the one who got down from the coach and waved a revolver at them, was a little bulkier than the one who stayed atop the coach. Their kerchiefs and hats prevented description of their faces, although when the kerchief on one slipped down, he was certain a small moustache became briefly visible. Mrs. Hudson was unsure about the moustache. They agreed the man spoke with a strange accent neither could identify.

"But there was something else that was odd," Fitzhugh reported first to the interpreter and later to Coopersmith. "The man with the revolver, was entirely consumed with Nikolos, and paid no attention to either Mrs. Hudson or myself. He took nothing of value from any of us. He was content with something — I couldn't tell what — that was in Nikolos' top hat."

Nikolos, himself, had disappeared after depositing Mrs. Hudson and Fitzhugh, and his whereabouts were unknown. Faced with widely varying descriptions of thieves who had stopped a coach to obtain something of no apparent value from a victim in no hurry to report the theft, the police informed Fitzhugh and Mrs. Hudson, that they would be concentrating their limited resources elsewhere. It was a decision with which Mrs. Hudson was well satisfied.

While Mrs. Hudson was suffering the hazards of travel on country roads, Holmes had taken a carriage along the far more secure streets of Athens to the Panathenaic Stadium for the official opening of the Games. It was the afternoon of Easter Monday, and with the solemnity of church services hours past, the crowd of spectators had swelled in size to 70,000 in the stadium and 50,000 sprawled across the hills above it. A jubilant Athens was about to begin the Games the doubters — and there had been many — said would never happen. For a week, the city would forget the economic crisis gripping the country, and return to a time when Greece was at the apex of the known world.

Holmes stood with the athletes in a double line on the track as the Greek royal family made its entrance followed by the country's government and military officials. He joined in the thunderous applause that followed the King's pronouncement opening the Olympic Games, and the cheering for the "Cantata of the Olympic Games" performed by a 300 person choir. To the crowd's delight, the choir rightly interpreted the ovation as the call for an éncore, and they reprised the melody that would afterward be known as the "Olympic Hymn" when performed at subsequent Games. Finally, the stadium track and infield were cleared of dignitaries and musicians, and the much anticipated Games could begin.

Mrs. Hudson arrived at the Stadium entrance as the second rendition of the Cantata was ending. Watson and Lestrade were waiting for her as they had promised.

"Another few minutes and we'd have had to go in without you," Watson announced, a broad smile belying any real danger of abandonment.

"I would have waited for you, Mrs. Hudson, regardless of Dr. Watson's action." Lestrade's smile was as broad as Watson's.

"I'm glad you both did. I'm sure I'd never find you in this crowd."

Watson smoothed his small trim moustache. "Perhaps we should take our seats. The competitions should be starting soon. I believe the first events feature running, and something called the hop, skip and jump."

They gave their tickets to the uniformed man at the gate and followed his directions to reach seats high up the eastern side of the stadium. The first of the 100 meter heats had been won by an American Mrs. Hudson recognized from their travels to Athens.

"How was your visit to Acharnes?" Lestrade asked, while they waited for the next 100 meter heat to begin.

"I believe Mr. Fitz'ugh and I got done what 'ad to be done. I'll want to talk to Mr. 'Olmes about it, of course, but I believe things went about the way 'e would've wanted."

"His plan for Dr. Watson and myself also worked well. However, Mr. Holmes should understand that while being on the other side of the law provided an interesting change of pace, it's not something I plan on repeating any time soon — or any time at all come to that."

Watson attempted a mask of mock seriousness, but interrupted himself twice with small giggles. "I felt you were born to the part, Lestrade. Indeed, I suspect it may open up a whole new career for you."

Lestrade gave a dismissive laugh, and the three of them turned back to the track as the second race was getting underway. Again, the winner was an American as was the case with a third race. The crowd acknowledged the victors with the tepid applause they thought appropriate for the accomplishments of athletes from another country.

Then came the hop, skip and jump. It, too, was won by another American, a young man Watson and Mrs. Hudson had seen air pedaling an imaginary bicycle on the boat to Naples. This time, however, there was no restraint in the crowd's display of admiration for the American champion. His victory was so audacious that the numbers claiming to have witnessed it would grow exponentially with each passing year. Before his final jump, the American athlete set his cap a full yard beyond the best mark of the Frenchman leading in the event, then proceeded to jump some distance beyond the cap. The feat was greeted with an initial shocked silence. Then, the applause began, triggered by the spectators nearest the track, and followed in waves until the stadium was engulfed in tribute to the remarkable achievement. American sailors, on leave from their ship in the Piraeus harbor, ran the Stars and Stripes they had had the foresight to bring, to the top of a bare pole at the stadium entrance, setting a precedent that would be adopted in all future Olympic Games.

The remainder of the first day of competition was taken up with 800 meter races, and the discus throw. The latter made for a disappointing end to the day for the Greek spectators as the single American competitor defeated his two Greek rivals, one by only a half foot.

With the first day of the Games complete, Mrs. Hudson believed it was time for the Baker Street trio to review the events of the day and plan for those of the next. She claimed near exhaustion, and asked if Watson would be good enough to see her back to the hotel. Lestrade had informed them — twice — that he was "just a poor public servant who couldn't afford the likes of the Grand Bretagné." His impecunious condition, with which Watson had sympathized — twice — guaranteed the trio could meet in the privacy they sought.

Holmes was already at the hotel when they arrived, having left the stadium early to get ahead of the somewhat deflated crowd, which would have to wait at least one more day for the emergence of a Greek champion. The three detectives found a small conference room at the hotel, and before exchanging a word, set a chair against the door to guard against unwelcome visitors.

The afternoon's highwayman began the discussion with the question he'd been burning to ask since his inspection of Nikolos' top hat. "Mrs. Hudson, how in the world did you know the coachman had the letter from Queen Vickie?"

Mrs. Hudson waved away his suggestion of impressive reasoning on her part before setting about to demonstrate it. "I'm afraid it will all seem terribly obvious after I tell you. You'll remember Mr. Mycroft told us the man who would be bringin' the letter 'ad been instructed to 'ave it on 'im at all times. If, as we've said, the murders of Lady Sterling and 'er German friend are separate from the disappearance of the letter, it would mean the German gentleman would still 'ave it on 'im after bein' shot. Mrs. Kasiris called in Nikolos to look over the bodies. The most she would do with the dead people was to get a blanket to cover 'er mistress, after which she went back upstairs and stayed there. Nikolos could not only get at the German's body without bein' seen, 'e was *the only one* who could get at the body before we got there. That made 'im the only person who could 'ave taken the letter. I'm thinkin' 'e was just lookin' to see if there was somethin' on the man worth takin'—you remember Mr. Coopersmith sayin' Nikolos would take anythin' that wasn't nailed down. 'E would 'ave come across the letter, and what with bein' the regular coachman for Lord Sterling, and bein' around the embassy all the time, 'e may well 'ave known about a letter bein' transmitted, and guessed that a stranger comin' to the ambassador's 'ouse might be carryin' it. With 'is thievin' ways, 'e thought it just might turn 'im a little profit if 'e sold it to the right party."

She paused, adopting a look that invited questions. There were none, and she turned the conversation to the issue she was anxious to address. "Now that we've got the letter we need a way to get it to England and to the Prime Minister before anyone finds out we've got it. And I think I know a way to do that. We'll need to involve Mr. Coopersmith and Inspector Lestrade, and we'll need to put a bit of a spark under a romance that's near ready to catch fire."

Holmes briefly considered pursuing Mrs. Hudson's last comment, but decided instead to pursue the concern that had occupied him from the beginning of their meeting.

"Now that we have the letter in our possession, shouldn't we be concentrating our attention on the murders and Lord Sterling's disappearance before the trails on both grow cold?"

"And we will, Mr. 'Olmes. I don't believe we 'ave to worry about the murderer goin' anywhere in the next few days, and I know we don't 'ave to worry about Lord Sterling goin' anywhere."

Holmes looked warily to Mrs. Hudson, but said nothing. Watson asked the question for both of them. "Why do you say that, Mrs. Hudson?"

"When Mr. Fitz'ugh and I got to the Martinsons' 'ome, I found they already knew about their daughter's death. Bein' as Acharnes is a little over an hour away from Athens, it's only Lord Sterling who could 'ave told them. And I'm sure 'e's still with them, what with 'im not speakin' Greek, and 'avin' no place else to go. Which makes it certain Lord Sterling is not our murderer. I can't imagine anyone goin' to visit the parents of someone they murdered, much less bein' put up by them. There were other things too."

Mrs. Hudson described the Baroness' appearance when she and Fitzhugh arrived, and the Baron's question whether there would be "more people coming," which, combined with the fresh carriage tracks, made clear they were not the first visitors of the day.

"Doesn't that suggest Lestrade may have it right about the murders being tied to the fraudulent sales?" Watson asked. "Lord Sterling might seek sanctuary with his in-laws if he feared himself a target — quite apart from wanting to be the one to break the tragic news to the Martinsons."

"It's a possibility we can't dismiss, Doctor, but I don't think it's very likely. The threat was made to get Lord Sterling to stop 'is investigation. 'E did stop and whoever would know 'e started an investigation would know 'e stopped. Besides, it was the ambassador that was targeted. Why then murder the ambassador's wife and a stranger? There's nothin' to be gained by any of that."

Mrs. Hudson waited for the foreheads of her colleagues to unwrinkle before raising yet another issue for them to consider.

"Shall we go to dinner? I can tell you what I'm thinkin' about 'ow we can get the letter back to England, but I'd like to do it over some of that nice roast lamb they 'ave downstairs."

Chapter 4.
En Garde!

The following morning Holmes and Watson boarded a carriage to the embassy where they were to put into practice the plan developed over dinner the night before. Mrs. Hudson would join them later at the Zappeion where Holmes was scheduled to participate in his first foils competition.

Miss Pershing was again seated behind the reception counter. Her welcoming smile faded to business-like concentration as, without waiting to be asked, she contacted Coopersmith to inform him of his visitors. Coopersmith had her take the visitors to the small conference room where they had met before. Holmes asked that the new security officer join them as well. A short time later the four men were seated around a table, three of them in subdued good humor, and one waiting tensely for their report.

"I have good news for you, Mr. Coopersmith. The letter to the Queen has fallen into our hands." Holmes withdrew a sealed envelope badly the worse for wear from his jacket pocket, and set it on the table. Coopersmith stared at the envelope open-mouthed, lightly fingered it along its length, then withdrew his hand quickly as he remembered he was to know nothing about a letter.

"What letter is that?"

Holmes groaned his response. "We haven't time for that, Coopersmith. It's my understanding that the embassy's janitorial staff knows there is a letter to be received in Athens for transmittal to London."

Coopersmith shrugged, and with an embarrassed smile, gave up the failed pretense.

"How in the world did it come into your possession?"

"That doesn't matter," Holmes replied. "All that's important is that we have the letter, and that we get the letter to the Prime Minister. I have a plan to accomplish that."

The deputy ambassador continued staring at the white envelope that lay between them. As he began to take in the immensity of the windfall that had come his way, his opinion of the man he judged responsible for that windfall underwent a rapid transformation. "However you've done it, Mr. Holmes, you've performed a great service for your country. I can only say your reputation is richly deserved." He looked almost pleadingly to Holmes. "Tell me, if you would, what is your plan?"

Watson sat stone-faced as Holmes recounted the plan he had heard the night before delivered in a female voice and Cockney accent. Lestrade smiled knowingly throughout Holmes' recitation, unsurprised by the cunning of the plan he assumed to be that of the celebrated detective. Only Coopersmith sat in unabashed adulation, nodding at points, whether in agreement or astonishment it was impossible to tell. His occasional questions were no longer expressions of disbelief, but rather respectful requests for elaboration.

"We will need to have a courier," Holmes began. "Someone who will be able to travel without rousing suspicion, and is entirely trustworthy. In this case, two people, both of them from the embassy."

"I don't understand, Mr. Holmes, couldn't I go alone to Whitehall?"

"That would never do, Coopersmith. Your sudden disappearance would be certain to lead to questions — questions we would have great difficulty answering. No, we'd do better with people who wouldn't be well-known, and wouldn't be missed. Junior people who've only been here a short time and haven't established a great many contacts."

Coopersmith nodded an understanding he did not yet possess. "Whom do you have in mind, Mr. Holmes, and why do you believe we need to send two people?"

"We need two people because it takes two to marry and we're sending home two people who plan to be married. Mr. Fitzhugh and Miss Pershing have become engaged after a whirlwind courtship. Which reminds me, Coopersmith, you'll need to see that Miss Pershing has a suitable ring for the occasion."

Holmes steepled his fingers, and gazed heavenward as he described the events destined to befall the happy couple. "As far as anyone is concerned, Miss Pershing and Mr. Fitzhugh are returning home to allow the bride-to-be to be the opportunity to introduce her young man to her parents. Of course, she'll need to be back in England to reserve the church, select bridesmaids, arrange for her dress, and whatever else young women do in this situation. Mr. Fitzhugh may also want to introduce Miss Pershing to his parents, if that's what young men do these days. Isn't there also something about publishing the banns? It's difficult for a bachelor to know about these things, but I'm sure we can work all that out. The important thing is that the ruse will provide an opportunity for Mr. Fitzhugh to carry the letter to London with no one the wiser. I will provide him the details regarding delivery."

"But there's been no reason to suspect any such liaison. If anything, Miss Pershing ... but there's been nothing between the two of them," Coopersmith stammered. "Anyway, nothing I know of." The deputy ambassador's face suddenly clouded, and words came to him slowly. "Although I will say, now that you raise it, Mr. Holmes, I have noticed they seem to look at each other rather oddly at times, and Mr. Fitzhugh becomes even more tongue-tied than usual in Miss Pershing's presence."

"Precisely," Holmes said. "And I guarantee the members of your staff will outdo each other in claiming to have long seen the signs of a budding romance, and not being at all surprised to learn of their engagement."

Coopersmith nodded once again, but a moment later his face clouded once more. "What of the two of them? Will they agree? And can they carry it off?"

"They will be acting for Queen and country; they will certainly agree. As to their play-acting, you're right they will undoubtedly need help in understanding and interpreting their roles."

As planned, Watson waited a beat before urging the action Holmes' comment implied. "There would seem no time to lose. We should get the two of them down here to inform them of their responsibility."

"And to congratulate them on their upcoming nuptials," Lestrade added.

Holmes raised his eyebrows in mock disapproval, but Lestrade focused his attention elsewhere.

Coopersmith ignored them both, and went in search of the soon-to-be affianced couple. Just minutes later he returned with a bemused looking Miss Pershing and the ever somber Thomas Fitzhugh.

The deputy ambassador, having fulfilled his responsibility, turned the proceedings over to Holmes. "Mr. Holmes, I have told Mr. Fitzhugh and Miss Pershing that you are a world famous detective who is working with the embassy on a very delicate matter, which you will be describing to them."

Holmes smiled indulgently, and turned his attention to the young people who had remained standing just inside the doorway.

"Please take seats. I believe you know everyone here." Miss Pershing looked only to Holmes, but nodded her agreement. Fitzhugh looked to each man before nodding his.

"Good. Only the people in this room are to know what I am about to tell you." Holmes paused, heightening the drama to his words, if any such heightening was needed. "I'm pleased to inform you that you have both been chosen to perform certain tasks that are vital to our nation's security. It would be difficult for me to overstate the delicacy or importance of your mission." With the young people now staring at him with the proper degree of dread and wonder, Holmes went on to outline their assignment.

"I want to make clear that we all have the utmost confidence in your ability to carry out this assignment. It involves a letter, a very important letter. None of us know its contents, and you will not know its contents either. You will be returning to England to deliver the letter to a man and at a place of which I will inform you. That man will deliver the letter to the Prime Minister, and he will share it with the Queen."

Holmes paused while Fitzhugh inhaled noisily, and Miss Pershing appeared to have lost the ability to breathe, or move, or speak. Only the blinking of her widened eyes guaranteed the presence of life. "I want to emphasize what I told you earlier, no one outside this room will know of your mission. No one at the embassy, no one you encounter in the travels to London we have planned for you, and with one exception, no one in England other than the Prime Minister. The single exception is someone in Government I will be contacting. He will be the one to receive the letter from you and transmit it to the Prime Minister."

"We come now to what will undoubtedly prove to be the most difficult part of your mission. We need to have a cover story explaining your travel home that is credible on its face, and makes no mention of the letter. Happily, we have developed such a story. It will, however, demand you perform tasks that will seem difficult — certainly at first — and I can only hope may prove less challenging over time. In a word, as far as everyone will know, you will be traveling to England in order to allow Mr. Fitzhugh to meet Miss Pershing's family to discuss with them your forthcoming marriage."

Holmes allowed space for a question or comment from the young people. He received only their very confused stares. "I appreciate the sacrifice I am asking. If it weren't of the utmost urgency, I would never request it. You must, however, understand that to complete the charade, you will have to demonstrate your affection for each other — a rather considerable amount of affection I'm afraid."

Watson acted to soften the blow. "Of course, it need only be for a few days."

Fitzhugh and Miss Pershing looked first to Holmes, then to Watson and finally to Coopersmith, their confusion still evident.

With considerable effort, and only after clearing his throat twice, Fitzhugh finally found his voice. "Is there really no other way?" Then, realizing his question sounded less than gallant, and perhaps unpatriotic as well, he added, "I mean it's a dreadful imposition on Miss Pershing."

Coopersmith had been waiting anxiously to reassert his authority. He seized on the opportunity Fitzhugh's seeming reluctance provided.

"We've considered the options available, Fitzhugh, and this appears the most desirable. As Dr. Watson says, it's only for a short time, and then the two of you can resume acting toward each other the way you really feel."

Holmes nodded gravely in support of Coopersmith's comment, although Watson felt certain he saw the hint of a smile lingering nearby. "If we are all in agreement, I believe it may be useful to have Mr. Fitzhugh and Miss Pershing show us how they plan to demonstrate the proper amount of affection for each other. Merely in the spirit of making certain we can pull off this ruse, of course. If you could both stand please, we might start with the basics. Would you demonstrate how the two of you might hug one another."

Feet set back, the newly ordained lovers leaned into each other and gripped each others' upper arms. Their facial expressions suggested each was greeting a distant relative — in the eyes of the observers, a very distant relative.

Holmes shook his head disapprovingly. "I'm afraid that won't do. Anyone seeing the two of you would assume an arranged marriage rather than a whirlwind courtship. What do you think, Watson?"

Watson agreed, his head shaking slowly side to side like a disappointed pendulum.

"Let's try it again," Holmes requested. "This time you'll want to show you have real feelings for each other."

"It's just a matter of acting," Lestrade encouraged.

"Of course, just acting," Holmes agreed.

This time bodies stayed together a long moment, and hands reached nearly to the backs of their partners' shoulders.

"Better," was Holmes' encouraging assessment, "but it still needs work. No doubt having an audience constrains your behavior. I believe it would be well for you to find what opportunity you can to practice hugs in private. In fact, it would be well for you to have dinner together tonight, just yourselves, to give you the opportunity to become more comfortable with each other. I am certain the embassy can arrange for you to have a private dinner in association with this diplomatic initiative. Would that be so, Mr. Coopersmith?"

The deputy ambassador mouthed agreement, although his face looked at war with his words. Regardless, Holmes was emboldened to continue the educational initiative he had begun.

"You should also become comfortable with kissing each other on the cheek. It's something an affectionate couple would be expected to do, and you are, of course, an affectionate couple. I won't press you to do anything now, but you need to keep it in mind and practice that as well when you can."

Holmes smiled benignly on the young couple. "Do you have any questions?"

There were none.

"Fine, let us then discuss the course we will follow to see that our sweethearts — you must get accustomed to people calling you that — get safely away." Holmes looked brightly to the couple before turning to Coopersmith. "I believe Mr. Fitzhugh and Miss Pershing are too newly established in their relationship to answer questions from staff before leaving Athens. It would be better to have them spend the rest of the day preparing to get away as early as possible tomorrow morning. Coopersmith, you'll need to organize the trip on their behalves. We'll want the two of them in London as soon as possible. I'm afraid you'll need to make all arrangements yourself and inform me promptly of their schedule. Lestrade, if you'll be good enough to leave the schedule for me in a sealed envelope at my hotel, I'll then be able to alert my contact in London as to when to expect them. Inspector, it would also be well for you to be at the station tomorrow to make certain our young people get safely away. Before leaving for my competition, I will write out instructions in terms of the person and the place for their first contact in London, which you can provide to them at the train station. I promise the instructions will not be difficult to follow, but for now," Holmes looked to Fitzhugh and Miss Pershing, "you have enough to do getting ready to leave without having to be concerned with the instructions as well."

"And there's more work for you, Coopersmith. While Fitzhugh and Miss Pershing are boarding the train for Piraeus, you will have to describe the state of affairs — perhaps using a different term — to embassy staff. As a trained diplomat, I'm certain you'll have no difficulty selecting language appropriate to the description of a clandestine, but quite respectable relationship. You might speak of their discovering how much they have in common, and how those common interests and ideas developed gradually — I suppose not too gradually — into affectionate feelings for each other. You'll need to explain that, after they confided in you, you granted them leave to return to England to meet with their families, and you fully expect wedding plans to be announced in the near future."

"Of course, some days later you can report that things didn't work out, and Mr. Fitzhugh and Miss Pershing are no longer in a relationship." The two young people, wide-eyed throughout Holmes' description of their impending nuptials, now simultaneously lost the dreamy look they shared, as their brows crinkled and their mouths pursed.

"I know I leave everything in capable hands," Holmes looked to Coopersmith and Lestrade, "I must go now to prepare for my competition at the Games. I'd appreciate it if someone could locate Nikolos for me. I have some questions for him, and he can answer those when he takes me to the Zappeion."

Coopersmith shook his head mournfully. "I'm afraid no one has seen Nikolos since he was held up on the trip to Acharnes. He appears to have been quite shaken by it, but I'm certain there'll be a coach out front. It should be no problem this time of day. Meanwhile, if you like, I'll find out from embassy staff if anyone knows Nikolos' whereabouts, and let it be known that you want to speak with him."

Holmes grunted appreciation, wrote out the promised instructions and entrusted them to Lestrade, then joined Watson to go in search of a carriage. Before exiting the conference room, he called back to the young couple, "Remember, hugs and kisses, and lots of practice." When he got back to the hotel that night, he would pick up the young people's schedule left by Lestrade, and send Mycroft a telegram giving the day and approximate time an engaged couple would appear at the Diogenes Club carrying the letter he had been sent to obtain. They would wait in the Stranger's Room until he appeared. His telegram to Mycroft would be sent by the hotel's English speaking telegrapher in a code the brothers had created as boys to allow the sharing of ideas without fear of adult discovery. It had never been broken, and he was confident it would not be broken now.

The Zappeion was dramatically changed from Holmes' earlier visit. Two bands at opposite ends of the balcony took turns stirring the crowd with martial music. The spectators at ground level sat on wooden chairs in tiers of uneven rows on either side of the platform on which the athletes would compete. The rows of chairs were interrupted at the center on one side by a trellised barrier encircling two well-cushioned easy chairs on which King George and Crown Prince Constantine sat in full military attire. The royals had chosen to be at the Zappeion lest the prospect of clashing swords alone prove insufficient to draw an audience. Apart from the competitors and referee, the only men who would remain standing throughout the match were top-hatted judges on either side of the platform, their dark formal dress and canes suggesting attendance at a dinner party rather than the observation of an athletic event.

The group of eight foils competitors were divided into two groups of four fencers each, each group scheduled for a round-robin series of matches to determine the four fencers who would face off two days later in semi-finals contests. Holmes learned that his first opponent was one of the four Greek participants, a man whose flaring black moustaches appeared designed to draw attention away from his small thin frame. As Holmes and Watson walked to a changing room to dress in the protective jacket and pants that had traveled with them from Baker Street, Holmes became aware of a carefully groomed man in the crowd with carrot-red hair and beard. He had seen the man before, in this same arena, skulking in the night shadows while he accustomed himself to the venue. Several rows behind the man he caught Mrs. Hudson's eye. She nodded her understanding, and smiled encouragement for Holmes' success.

Holmes entered the arena for the second contest of the day, appearing after a French competitor had dispatched his Greek rival. That, at least in part, explained the restrained applause he received and the thunderous applause that greeted his opponent. Holmes remembered, not for the first time, that he hadn't faced a man in competition since his days at university. The call came for each man to slip on his mask in preparation for the match. They stood opposite each other waiting the referee's commands. The instructions came in Greek, but Holmes had no difficulty making translation.

"On Guard."

Each man stiffened his left leg and bent his right, at the same time tossing his left hand in the air and flexing the hand that gripped the foil.

"Ready."

Holmes tensed, aware there would be only a second or two until the next command, and he meant to make full use of the element of surprise.

"Fence!"

Before the referee had completed the word Holmes had curled his blade beneath that of his opponent, lunged, and struck home just below his competitor's heart.

One point to Holmes with two more needed. For a moment the crowd was silent, as stunned by Holmes' action as was the Greek swordsman they were supporting. There followed a low grumbling that grew louder, and threatened to become something more until the referee called once again.

"On Guard."

The crowd quieted as the two men assumed the required stance. Holmes knew the element of surprise was gone, and he would have to rely on a more traditional strategy to gain the additional points needed to win the contest.

"Ready."

"Fence!"

The second exchange lasted only a few seconds longer than the first, but had a dramatically different outcome. The Greek fencer made as if he was replicating Holmes' strategy, He curled his blade below Holmes, but only faked an attack. Holmes parried the apparent thrust, and rocked back in retreat. It was the opening his opponent was seeking. He again curled his blade beneath Holmes', but this time carried through his lunge, the blade point catching Holmes below his right shoulder.

The next two points were divided between competitors. In the first, Holmes was not fooled by a second feint attempt or by a third, but when each man simultaneously attacked the other, the Greek fencer's touch was made with the tip of his blade while Holmes' touch was made with the side of the blade resulting in the point going to the Greek combatant. Holmes took the next point when his opponent slipped, parrying Holmes' straight thrust, and thrown off balance, was at the mercy of Holmes' follow-up lunge.

The crowd was now in full-throated support of their countryman, believing Holmes to have gotten both his points under questionable conditions. With the call of "Fence!" the local favorite laid his blade across Holmes' blade, momentarily applying pressure to get a response from Holmes, then thrust home, but Holmes recovered sufficiently to parry his opponent's attack, then made his own lunge just a second too slowly, and had his thrust successfully parried as his opponent retreated.

Fortified by the crowd's noisy appreciation for his successful defense, the Greek fencer mounted a second attack, employing a feint toward the left side of Holmes' body before lunging to his right. Holmes was ready for the strategy. He parried his opponent's thrust and made a straight lunge of his own, employing speed with no effort at deception. Whether the result of surprise at Holmes' move or fatigue from the competition's length, the point of Holmes' foil found its target. The match was over. Holmes was declared the winner to groans of disappointment from all but Watson, Mrs. Hudson, and a handful of British spectators. His victory guaranteed he would be in the next round of the foils elimination to be held later that same day. After the obligatory nods of recognition to his opponent, the referee, and judges, a weary, but exhilarated Holmes joined Watson in returning to the changing room to collect himself before his second match. The red-haired spectator, who was observed by Mrs. Hudson to cheer neither fencer, followed Holmes' every step until he passed from view.

Holmes and Watson had barely settled themselves in the changing room when they were joined by one of the top-hatted men who seemed oblivious to how out of place he appeared in a room of half-dressed men. The top-hatted man's speech suited his dress, and appeared equally out of place.

"Monsieur Holmes, a moment if I might."

Holmes brushed back a lock of hair that had fallen across his forehead and he had been too tired until now to replace. "Sir."

"I fear I have .. nouvelles décevantes ... how you say, unhappy news."

The man looked genuinely pained, and Holmes envisioned the worst. A rule had been violated and he was not, as first declared, the winner of his match, or, worse yet, his second match was to start immediately, giving him no time to recuperate.

"Your next adversair cannot compete. He became hurt in combat and cannot go on. You will have to be ... vainqueur par forfait. I haven't words in English."

Watson did. "Winner by forfeit."

Holmes did his best to appear disappointed with his compromised victory, only to fail badly in the effort.

Dinner at the hotel was interrupted by well-wishers who had witnessed Holmes' triumph, or had had it described to them. Launceston Elliot led the singing proclaiming him "a jolly good fellow," in which virtually all diners joined. Several had no idea who Holmes was, or why he was believed to be a jolly good fellow, but allowed themselves to be caught up in the celebration. When the last verse had been sung and nobody had denied, Elliot informed the room that Holmes was not the only contestant to bring glory to Queen and country that day; Durand Ramsay had advanced on the pistol range and would be competing for a medal later that week, and Edwin Flack had won the 1500 meter race. In the spirit of good will, Elliot neglected to indicate that the country to which both men brought glory was, in fact, two colonies on an island nearly 10,000 miles from Great Britain, and Ramsay and Flack elected not to correct him. Good will was so bountiful that even the reclusive Oswald Benton came by to mumble his congratulations before returning to the table at which he sat alone. The day's excitement led the trio to forego the evening stroll around Athens each had planned, and, instead, to linger over dinner before returning to their rooms. They would meet the next morning to learn if Fitzhugh and Miss Pershing got off as scheduled, and to search for Nikolos. But now, they were ready for a respite from the several challenges thrown at them that day.

Holmes had already spread his nightshirt across the bed, and was about to change out of his daytime dress when there was a loud knock at his door, then unintelligible voices, and finally a series of soft knocks. Opening the door he found himself facing a grinning Edward Battel, late of the British embassy kitchen staff, recently become a member of the British Olympic cycling team. Beside him, a slightly built young lady with a longish, but attractive face, and a wealth of straight black hair running well beyond her shoulders, tried to smile away her discomfort at finding herself late at night on a stranger's doorstep.

"Mr. Holmes, it's good to see you again, and to have a chance to give proper thanks on behalf of myself and Fred — Mr. Keeping, that is — for standing up for us to Mr. Coopersmith. And I hear tell you had your own win today, so congratulations from the two of us on that as well. Let me introduce my very good friend, Miss Alexandra Kannapolis, who's another part of the reason I wanted to see you. Actually, Alex is maybe the biggest part." The grin impossibly widened as he looked from Holmes to the threshold he had yet to cross.

Holmes acceded to Battel's unspoken request. "Mr. Battel, Miss Kannapolis, won't you please come in and have seats. I appreciate your coming all this way to express your gratitude, but there was really no need."

The grin reduced itself to a broad smile. "Mr. Holmes, I'm not here just to say thank you — although that alone would be worth the trip. I'm also here to return the favor you did me. Mr. Coopersmith was asking everyone—well, everyone except me and Fred, and the rest of the serving staff — if they knew where to find Nikolos, that you wanted to talk to him."

Holmes gave a cautious nod.

"Well, that's where Alex comes in. Except I'll ask you to please keep quiet about me and Alex. The embassy has a strict rule about fraternizing with the locals, and if it got out about us seeing each other, I could lose my job, and Alex could get in trouble too. See, we're not just friends, we mean to get married if I can ever convince her father that being

English isn't a disease. Anyway, Alex speaks English pretty good, I mostly taught her myself, and she knows a way to find Nikolos."

Holmes looked to the silent Miss Kannapolis with more skepticism than he intended, and waited for her first words. She spoke only four.

"I can find him."

Holmes looked to Battel for greater explanation, but he had turned to grinning as his sole form of communication.

As it turned out, Miss Kannapolis' initial statement was a mere prelude to all she had to report in what turned out to be heavily accented, but surprisingly good English. "Athens is small town, Mr. Holmes. People know each other, especially people in same job of work. My uncle, Spiros, he drives carriage. He learns little bit German, so he can drive for German embassy like Nikolos drive for English. My uncle doesn't like Nikolos, but will help find him. He thinks Nikolos belong in jail. He's a ... nkan'nkster ... a bad man, very bad. You want good help, you tell my uncle you put Nikolos in jail, but he make help either way. I make arrange for you to see my uncle. You be at Taki's before seven tomorrow. Taki's where drivers meet for breakfast. My uncle is there every morning."

"I will be there, Miss Kannapolis. Thank you — thank you both — for doing this."

Battel waved off Holmes' gratitude, while Miss Kannapolis wrote out the name of the café in Greek, at the same time assuring him that every carriage driver in Athens would know Taki's.

His mission accomplished, Battel clapped his hands as he rose to leave. At the door, he paused to toss a question back to Holmes. "Is Mr. Lockhart here to see you?"

Holmes screwed his face into a question. "Mr. Lockhart?"

"Mr. Carter Lockhart. The red-headed bloke. You can't miss him. He looks like his head is on fire. I knew him in South Africa. Well, not 'knew' exactly. He's got ways like Mr. Coopersmith, and probably doesn't know I was there the same time he was. He's one of those muckamucks who looks past the people he don't think are worth seein'. He's with the Colonial Office so I can't think why he'd be in Athens unless he's taking time to see the Games, but even so you'd think he would've announced himself at the embassy. Anyway, he's downstairs with a newspaper in front of his face, but I can tell you he gave me the once over when I came in, and it looked to me like he was doing that with everyone."

Holmes thanked Battel for his information, and assured him he'd look into it. Holmes knew he'd have a red-headed shadow at least until the letter reached London. Worse yet, this Lockhart might learn enough to try to intercept the letter himself or have people in London do so. After all, Coopersmith and the young people they were relying on were amateurs at subterfuge. They could easily let something slip that would undo everything. Holmes needed to get rid of the red-headed man before his nosing around led anywhere. There was no time to consult with his colleagues on a plan, nor did he feel any need to.

In the small hours of morning, when he was certain Lockhart would no longer be on watch, he had hotel staff wake the English speaking telegrapher to send a second telegram to his brother. He didn't take the time to put it into code, feeling certain he had worded it in a way that would be misinterpreted by all but Mycroft.

His telegram read: "Making progress. Ran into colleague of yours from the Colonial Office. Hope you are able to recall Carter Lockhart. A dedicated man deserving your attention. SH" Holmes received no reply from his brother, but he never saw the red-headed man again. He learned later the Prime Minister had been seized with a sudden need for an eyewitness account of progress in the Sudan Campaign by someone senior in the Office of the Colonial Secretary. Through sheer good fortune the PM had learned the Colonial Office had such a man visiting Athens, less than four days from the battlefield.

Not long after sending his telegram, Holmes roused Watson to appraise him of the evening's activity, and arrange for the Doctor to accompany him to see Miss Kannapolis' uncle and, hopefully, to find Nikolos. They decided it would be best to leave a note for Mrs. Hudson, rather than wake her, and left a message with reception to be delivered to her in the morning. It told her they had "gone to find a coachman knowledgeable about dealers in Greek antiquities," and they would see her for dinner.

Chapter 5.
Theodore Bikelas' Revelation

The café was crowded with groups of men who seemed to overwhelm the small tables at which they sat nursing cups of dark coffee and filling the room with cigarette smoke. Arguments, laughter, and the earnest exchange of ideas spilled across adjacent and more distant tables among men who yesterday shared their tables with someone across the room or someone a few feet away, and tomorrow would do the same.

Holmes and Watson had no difficulty locating Miss Kannapolis and her uncle, Miss Kannapolis being the only woman in the café. They drew curious glances as they made their way to the table against the back wall where she and her uncle sat, but the patrons soon found their coffee and conversations of greater interest and turned back to both.

"Miss Kannapolis, it's good to see you again. I've brought with me my friend and colleague, Dr. John Watson. And this, I take it, is your uncle, Spiros."

At the mention of his name, the man in question looked up from the coffee cup his huge hands encircled, made a guttural sound that might have signaled acknowledgement or dismissal, then found a thread on his pant leg that required immediate attention. The brief moment of eye contact was enough to chasten the two detectives. The glowering look, over moustaches so thick he appeared without benefit of an upper lip, made them wonder if their early rising had been for nothing. His niece provided reassurance it had not.

"My uncle help you, but he wants you put Nikolos Meskipoulos in jail where my uncle say he belongs."

Holmes cleared his throat; then directed his comment to the man who had yet to speak, and now seemed to have discovered something of interest on his other pant leg. "We intend to question Nikolos about his role in certain activities that may be criminal. If we do not get the right answers, we will turn him over to the authorities." Holmes added an emphatic nod to his declaration, and set his face to look as vindictive as he could manage.

Miss Kannapolis put into Greek Holmes' response. Throughout her report, Spiros, finding nothing of further interest on his pant legs, stared blankly at a distant part of the room. Even after Miss Kannapolis had finished, Spiros continued to stare ahead, as if considering whether Holmes' statement merited any kind of reply. Holmes and Watson would later swear the room itself quieted. The coachman's silence ended with the same guttural sound he had employed in greeting the detectives. This time the unintelligible sound was followed by a brief spate of words equally obscure to Holmes and Watson. Miss Kannapolis translated his message.

"My uncle doesn't think English can put Nikolos in Greek jail, but help you anyway."

As if Spiros' decision had brought a sudden end to their morning, the café began to empty. Miss Kannapolis explained it was seven o'clock and time for the drivers to go to work. Soon, they were the only ones in the café except for one man with curly dark hair spilling out from a workman's cap pulled low on his forehead. He called for another coffee as he leaned back against the wall where he sat. Spiros gave him a curt nod as he led his niece and guests from the café after tossing two drachma on his table. The workman's cap jerked up long enough to allow the man to make his own stone-faced nod in return. Once outside, Spiros explained as his niece translated.

"Nikolos' cousin. Not so bad. Not like Nikolos. Not so good either."

The information stimulated Watson's curiosity, and led to a series of questions that Spiros answered through Miss Kannapolis. "Is the man a driver?"

"He is, most of the time."

"Why didn't he go with the rest?"

"He rented his carriage. The drivers do sometimes if the price is good. Aristedies — that's his name — rented his two or three days ago."

"To whom would he rent a carriage?"

"He never say, and it is not wise to ask. It can be for illegal acts."

Remembering Mrs. Hudson's report of fresh carriage tracks outside the Martinsons' home, Holmes thought he knew to whom Aristedies had rented his carriage.

Miss Kannapolis left them as Holmes and Watson climbed into Spiros' coach. He drove them a short distance to a small cottage to which he pointed as he spoke a single word, "Nikolos."

As they stepped down from the coach, he spoke once more, this time without need of an interpreter. "You put in jail." And then, roaring with laughter, he drove on leaving Holmes and Watson staring after him with wonder.

Apart from the white paint peeling from its wooden boards, the cottage was indistinguishable from the others that lined a street of broken pavement regularly interrupted by small clumps of green making a doomed effort to take back the street. Their knock was answered by Nikolos who, upon seeing his visitors, did his best to bar the door, but was no match for the combined force of the two men. They had interrupted the coachman's meal; pita bread and sections of orange were on a table in a space that served as both parlor and dining room.

Nikolos guessed at the reason for their visit. "I do nothing wrong. I have nothing to do with stealing. It's not like Mr. Fitzhugh says, the letter has nothing to do with me. I only take it to give to Mr. Coopersmith. I do nothing wrong."

"Nikolos," Holmes said, "we know all about the letter. We know you meant to sell it. But we can put the letter aside.

It's not why we're here. We need your help with something. It's very important to us, and to the embassy, and you are in a unique position to be of assistance. But I have to warn you if we don't get your help, we may remember the letter, and ask the Greek police to learn how it came to be stolen from a dead man at the ambassador's home."

Nikolos' eyes widened and his lips parted. He recovered sufficiently to stare sullenly at the two men, but fooled no one, least of all himself. He gave in to the inevitable.

"What is it you want me to do?"

"You drove Lady Sterling to see the dealer — the man who arranged for the sales of Greek antiquities. A man named Theodore Bikelas. I want you to take us to him."

"If I do this, no more talk about police?

"Our interest is in finding Bikelas. The police are very busy. I see no reason to add to their work."

"Will Bikelas know it's me that sent you?"

"Only if you tell him."

Nikolos made a trip to the table and took up a section of orange. He spoke in the moment before stuffing it into his mouth. "Alright. I take you."

He led them to the stables in back of his house and began to hitch his small bay to the carriage. As he fit the bridle over the horse's head, Holmes asked a seemingly off-hand question. "When did you arrange for Lord Sterling to rent your cousin's carriage?"

If the detective expected Nikolos to respond with guilty surprise, he was sorely disappointed. The coachman continuing attaching the harness to his little horse. When he had finished, he looked blankly to Holmes. "My cousin. I don't see my cousin for months. I don't know what he does with his carriage and I don't care. If you want to see Bikelas before he goes out, we get started now." Nikolos led the horse and carriage out of the stable to make his point.

Reading the note brought her by the bellboy, Mrs. Hudson chuckled at Holmes' description of his intent to find a coachman knowledgeable about antiquities dealers. Anyone seeing that would conclude they were off on a typical tourist expedition to search for bargains in Greek relics. She knew they were on a search for first Nikolos, and then Theodore Bikelas. The cryptic nature of his note made clear how far Holmes had come over the years. He could still, at times, grab the wrong end of the stick, but all in all, he could now very nearly justify the unflagging self-confidence he had shown from their very first meeting; and she had come to feel increasingly comfortable with his exercising an ever larger measure of independence in the consulting detective agency's investigations.

She had only just taken her seat in the hotel's restaurant and begun studying the menu when she was approached by the outsize figure of Launceston Elliot.

"May I join you, Mrs. Hudson?" The request was accompanied by a smile so irresistibly congenial, she would have been hard pressed to refuse even had she been so inclined — which she was not.

"Please do, Mr. Elliot. It's good to 'ave you."

"Will your Mr. Holmes or Doctor Watson be joining us?"

"I'm afraid not, Mr. Elliot. They've 'ad an early breakfast and gone on."

"Well then, I have you all too myself." There was again the engaging smile, accompanied by Mrs. Hudson's sudden interest in the napkin on her lap. "But please do remember me to them both."

"I will indeed, and I'm sorry I missed your event yesterday, Mr. Elliot. I was at the swordsplay at the same time you were liftin' weights. May I ask 'ow things went for you."

"It was a bit of a mix, Mrs. Hudson. In the first event, Mr. Jensen, the Danish competitor, and I lifted the same weight, but it was ruled that Mr. Jensen showed greater style and he was given first place. However, it was a costly victory for Mr. Jensen. He injured himself and was unable to give his best in the second event, which was a one hand lift. Since he was my major competition, I was able to win the event, although I'd have to say my victory was a wee bit tainted."

"I'm sure the men you defeated didn't see your win as tainted. But don't I remember you'll be doin' some wrestlin' as well."

"I am, Mrs. Hudson, but that's two days off, so I'm free as a bird today. Might I convince you to join me in a small walk around Athens?"

"I'd like nothin' better, Mr. Elliot, but I'm feelin' badly about Mrs. Kasiris, the ambassador's 'ousekeeper. She was very upset when I left 'er after the terrible tragedy, and I'm thinkin' I should go see 'ow she's gettin' along."

"I'll not see an attractive woman like yourself going unescorted in a strange city. Unless you have an objection, I'll accompany you to the ambassador's house. I can stroll around the neighborhood while you finish your business. That way I can get in my morning's walk with the added bonus of enjoying your good company."

At another time Mrs. Hudson would have welcomed the attention of the handsome Scotsman — to say nothing of the envious looks she was bound to receive from the members of Athens' female population they passed. On this occasion, however, Launceston Elliot's presence threatened to complicate the investigation she planned. Nonetheless, she saw no alternative to accepting his gracious invitation and whatever risk went with it. "I'd be delighted for the company, Mr. Elliot."

The agreement struck, they gave the hovering waiter their orders and discussed areas of each other's life over the breakfasts they ordered. Mrs. Hudson learned that Elliot had been born in India, and lived there several years in spite of the pride he took in his Scottish heritage, and the Scottish brogue that seemed carefully cultivated. At his urging, she walked through some of the cases of which he had heard, carefully eliminating any discussion of her own role in their resolution. She wondered about his interest in the consulting detective agency's cases, but dismissed it for the moment as simple curiosity, and fairly customary behavior when people learned of her association with Holmes. When breakfast was done, they had the doorman hale a carriage for the short ride to the ambassador's residence.

To Mrs. Hudson's surprise, helmeted policemen, white-gloved and wearing button down tunics overhanging baggy trousers, were positioned on every side of the building. She walked to the front entrance only to be challenged by the policeman stationed at that post. Although unable to understand his words, she found his gestures unambiguous. She was at a loss as to how to proceed when the looming presence behind her stepped forward to assert an authority he had learned long ago his size permitted. He made competing gestures, pointing toward the house that the policeman pointed away from, complementing his gestures with his own tirade delivered from a half foot above the top of the policeman's helmet. In the end, however, it was not Elliot's size, gestures, or torrent of words that turned the tide. Rather, it was a name.

To convince the policeman, and the two of his colleagues who joined him, that Mrs. Hudson should be allowed entry into the ambassador's residence, Elliot twice invoked the name, "Sherlock Holmes." The first time it was for clarification. He pointed to Mrs. Hudson, then clasped hands together as he voiced the name of the detective to make clear her connection to Holmes. The gasps of recognition that greeted the name led him to repeat it a second time, louder and with a still firmer clasp of his hands. Unwittingly, instead of providing clarification, Elliot had produced an extraordinarily useful obfuscation. The policemen understood Elliot to be identifying himself as the detective they knew only in legend, although they were aware he was someplace in their city. With a broad sweep of his arm, the policeman, who had refused entry to Mrs. Hudson, now invited admission to the ambassador's residence to the man he believed to be the world's foremost consulting detective. They all but ignored the diminutive woman accompanying him, whose significance they didn't understand, but whom the detective seemed to think should enter with him.

Once inside, Elliot discovered Lord Sterling's library where he promised to remain. Mrs. Hudson, meanwhile, reacquainted herself with the Sterlings' housekeeper who, true to her word, remained waiting the return of her master. This time they met in the downstairs parlor, where, as before, the housekeeper sat at the edge of the least comfortable chair.

"'Ow have you been gettin' on, Mrs. Kasiris?" Mrs. Hudson made the obligatory good will query, although it was clear to her the housekeeper was getting on quite well. She was a good deal more composed with the two bodies removed, and no more consumed with sorrow than she had been at their first meeting.

"I'm doing well, Mrs. Hudson. I thank you for your concern. May I ask if there's anything learned about Lord Sterling?"

"I'm sorry to say there isn't, Mrs. Kasiris." The woman nodded at the expected response. "I 'ad some questions for you. It's to find out some things Mr. 'Olmes wants to know." Mrs. Kasiris blinked acknowledgment. "'Ave there been any calls to the 'ouse in the last two days?"

"There has not. Except Mr. Coopersmith, of course. He called two times to know if I hear anything from the master—which I do not."

"Anyone else?"

Mrs. Kasiris seemed to suddenly discover the discomfort of the chair she had chosen. She adjusted her position once, then a second time before responding. "I also receive calls from my friend, Mr. Seropopoulos. He is calling to ask how I am." A small blush and glance to the room's carpet made clear to Mrs. Hudson that Mr. Seropopoulos was more than a friend. It put her in mind of the lost key Mrs. Kasiris had reported at their last meeting. She gently probed for more information.

"Mr. Seropopoulos sounds like a good soul."

"He is good soul."

When the housekeeper said no more about either Mr. Seropopoulos' soul or corporeal being, Mrs. Hudson chose to let a silence take hold and grow. Pursed lips and a deeply furrowed brow reflected the difficulty the silence was causing Mrs. Kasiris. The outcome of the struggle with herself was inevitable.

"Mr. Seropopoulos and I have been what you people call 'keeping company'. We go for walks, sometimes we eat together, and sometimes he comes to the house for me after work."

Mrs. Hudson smiled at the revelation she had already guessed, and pressed to learn more about Mrs. Kasiris' "friend."

"Does Mr. Seropopoulos live nearby?"

"Not so far, on Metaxes Street."

Mrs. Hudson would have liked to have had Dr. Watson along to record the unfamiliar names, but she knew if she were to write down what Mrs. Kasiris told her, it would appear more like an interrogation than a conversation, and would likely lead the woman to speak less. She would need to store the names in her memory until she could write them down later. Fortunately, Mrs. Hudson was a student of Professor von Feinaigle, and from his work, *The New Art of Memory*, she knew to form associations of unfamiliar names with more familiar words and names. Mrs. Kasiris' suitor and the street he lived on were reversed in order, and became "me taxes serve a populous." She smiled at the idea that the income tax she paid each year provided her an unexpected benefit.

With the phrase filed for later use, Mrs Hudson turned to a second concern. "Tell me please, did you always answer the telephone for Lady Sterling?"

"Yes, of course, that was part of my job."

"And thinkin' back to a week, or maybe ten days ago, do you remember there bein' a call for Lady Sterling from a man whose voice you didn't know? I'm thinkin' it would 'ave been a call that upset Lady Sterling?"

Mrs. Kasiris pursed her lips and squinted an effort to travel the distance back to the time requested by Mrs. Hudson. "I can't think of calls like that. There's been calls, of course. Mostly lady friends of my mistress, and two from her dressmaker, but that's another woman. The bookseller called — he's a man — but my lady wasn't upset after. And I'm sure Mr. Bikelas called. He called nearly every week, but those calls never upset her either."

Mrs. Hudson waited while Mrs. Kasiris searched her memory for any other telephone calls. When none seemed to come to mind, Mrs. Hudson pressed the issue, "There were no other telephone calls you can remember, you're sure?"

Mrs. Kasiris face no longer showed a frown of concentration. "I'm sure that's all."

"Thank you, Mrs. Kasiris, I'll leave you to get your work done. I appreciate your takin' the time to talk to me."

Mrs. Hudson got up to leave, smiling her good-bye as she did. She was stopped by a final comment from Mrs. Kasiris. "You ask more questions than man from the embassy. Not Mr. Coopersmith, man who works with Mr. Coopersmith. He wanted to know about telephone calls too, especially ones from Mr. Bikelas. And he had me show him things Mr.

Bikelas help my lady buy. He very interested in those. Does your Mr. Holmes work with Mr. Benton?"

Mrs. Hudson did not respond to the housekeeper's question. She had a question of her own. "Did Mr. Benton come to visit you?"

"Yes ma'am."

"I thought the Greek police kept everybody away from the ambassador's residence."

"Yes, that's right, ma'am, except Mr. Benton come the same day you and Mr. Holmes come, and before police was keeping everyone out. Besides that, he said he had Mr. Coopersmith's permission to be here, and I was to tell him everything I know."

Mrs. Hudson grimaced an effort at a smile. "I thank you again for your time, Mrs. Kasiris."

Mrs. Hudson had gone to see Mrs. Kasiris to inquire about telephone calls, more particularly, the threatening phone call that she now knew had never occurred. She found the unexpected findings about Oswald Benton overshadowing that report as well as what she had learned about Mrs. Kasiris' friend, Mr. Seropopoulos.

Benton's association with the Foreign Office and interest in Lady Sterling's purchases, taken together with his departure from London, indicated the Foreign Office was not content with Scotland Yard being the sole investigator of those purchases, and had arranged to have its own man on the scene. It explained Benton's interest in Holmes on board the ship from Liverpool, and his break-in to Holmes' cabin during their voyage. Doubtless, he wanted to confirm his suspicion that Holmes was working with Scotland Yard — knowing that he often did — to aid in their investigation of Lady Sterling's purchases. Since he, himself, was traveling incognito as an Olympic athlete, it would be natural for him to believe Holmes was doing the same. Finally, it explained his absence from the ambassador's reception for the Olympians using the weak excuse of having to meet a friend. No doubt he wanted to avoid the possibility, if not likelihood of one or more of the embassy staff recognizing him as a colleague, and exposing his Foreign Office connection.

Her conversation with Mrs. Kasiris led Mrs. Hudson to feel an increased sense of urgency about the investigation of Lady Sterling's purchases. She also found herself with some curiosity about Oswald Benton's tennis skills. Those skills, or their absence, would be on display that afternoon, but Mrs. Hudson's plans did not include witnessing them. She went to collect Launceston Elliot, and apologized for doing him out of his walk. He waved off her concern, and the two of them left the residence to get on with the activities each had planned for the day.

Unaware of a competing investigation, Holmes and Watson relaxed in Nikolos' carriage as they traveled to see Theodore Bikelas. The coachman took them to the outer limits of the city, slowing as he approached a house on a small rise, then guiding the carriage along the semi-circular drive that fronted it. The house gave no sign of being a place of business, rather it gave every sign of being the home of a successful man of business. A gently sloping slate roof topped two stories of fieldstone reflecting every imaginable shade of brown. Six windows topped by elaborately molded cornices were to the left of the door on each level, and a seventh smaller window with a faux balcony fronted by impressive latticework stood above the door.

"This is where I take her ladyship to see Mr. Bikelas," Nikolos reported.

"Thank you Nikolos. Wait here for our return. I don't imagine we'll be long."

Holmes and Watson proceeded up a stone path, lifted the knocker from its position in the lion's mouth, and let it fall loudly against the door. A voice answered their knock with a question in Greek. While they considered how to answer, the door was opened wide revealing a man in his mid- to late-thirties, a little above middle height with an athletic build made apparent by leaving several buttons of his white shirt unfastened. The carefully crafted image was furthered by a great quantity of dark hair slicked back in small waves, thick eyebrows over dark eyes, and a prominent cleft chin. He was, as Watson later described to Mrs. Hudson, "a lady's man," who might well have been found attractive by Lady Sterling, and whose presence in his home might well have been resented by Lord Sterling.

He looked first to Holmes, then to Watson, then back again to Holmes before repeating the question he had called through the closed door. Holmes assumed the question asked by a Greek of strangers on his doorstep would be the same as that asked by an Englishman in the same situation, and answered accordingly.

"My name is Holmes, Sherlock Holmes, and this is my friend and colleague, Dr. John Watson. I believe I am speaking to Theodore Bikelas, and that you speak English."

"I am Theodore Bikelas. Is there some way I can help you?"

"There is indeed. We have an interest in Greek antiquities. May we come in to discuss our interest with you."

Theodore Bikelas looked critically to each man before stepping back to allow their entrance.

Holmes and Watson found the center hall cluttered with statues, some with arms or legs missing, two of them headless; as well as bowls and urns in similarly complete and incomplete states. Boxes and straw were stacked in a separate area at the back of the hall. All in all, the room gave more the impression of a warehouse than the elegant home suggested from its outside.

Bikelas led them to the front parlor which quickly recaptured the luxury the building's exterior had promised. At its windows, ceiling to floor brocade curtains were drawn to half hide the outdoors, while pale white French Provincial furniture was strewn with seeming haphazardness throughout the room, inspiring expressions of admiration more often than comments about comfort. On either side of a stone fireplace were portraits of a man and woman whose period dress and haughty demeanor suggested their earlier ownership of the mansion, and their pride in that achievement. Holmes smiled greeting to the couple without noticeable effect, then settled himself on the parlor's settee while Watson chose one of the three matching easy chairs. Bikelas, holding fast to a cautious smile, sat across from them on another of the easy chairs.

"You have me by surprise, gentlemen; I wasn't expecting visitors. Tell me what it is I can do for you. Are you interested in any particular type of antiquities? I can give you a good price on replicas of important art objects."

"Replicas only?" Holmes asked. "What if I wanted to purchase genuine objects?"

Theodore Bikelas' forehead furrowed in consideration of the prospect raised by Holmes. "That's possible of course, but might take time. What kind of objects are you interested in?"

"I was impressed with the objects you procured for Lady Sterling."

The cautious smile returned. "Are you a friend of Lady Sterling?"

"I wouldn't say a friend exactly, I have, however, visited her home."

Bikelas nodded thoughtfully as if Holmes had just shared a particularly profound observation. "I did help Lady Sterling with several purchases. What exactly are you looking for?"

"My first concern is with the authenticity of items I purchase."

"I'm not sure I follow you. What is your issue regarding authenticity?"

"I want to be confident the items I buy from you are genuine. For example, can you tell me that the items Lady Sterling bought from you were genuine?"

The cautious smile disappeared, never to return. "You're not here to buy antiquities, are you, Mr. Sherlock Holmes?"

"No, we are here to understand how Lady Sterling came to purchase copies of antiquities when she paid the price of the originals. I trust you'll not dispute that you sold copies and charged Lady Sterling for the originals. We have the report of a reputable archaeologist that the items on display at the ambassador's residence — items you purchased for her — are fakes. That means that you, and whoever you are working with, cheated the British Government out of hundreds of pounds. And it may mean even more. Lady Sterling is dead — murdered in her home, a home to which you were a welcome and frequent guest, a home to which you might have been admitted on the evening of her murder."

"I'm thinking Lady Sterling found out she was being cheated and contacted you to demand an explanation. Knowing her schedule, you went to the ambassador's residence at a time when the ambassador would not yet be home, and the housekeeper would have already left for the day. You expected to find her alone and planned to murder her before she could identify you to the authorities, but you found someone with her, so you had to murder the two of them. Of course, for the moment, those are only my suspicions. But I believe the Greek police will find them persuasive, and will likely want to take steps to pursue them, particularly with the pressures they're getting from the Greek and British Governments."

Holmes looked his piercing best at the man he had accused of murder, while Watson scowled his contempt. The hostile stares, and bombastic talk were intended to achieve what a dearth of evidence could not, and lead the man to stumble into the confession of a capital crime of which he might be guilty, while forcing his admission of fraud, a crime of which he was surely guilty.

For a moment it seemed to be working. Bikelas shook his head vigorously as Holmes began, and ran his fingers through his hair, threatening its carefully fashioned undulations. He bounced from his chair when Holmes was done, and paced the small part of the room near where he had been sitting. The whole of the strange performance was over in a matter of seconds. Reclaiming his seat, Bikelas adopted an oddly conciliatory tone as he again faced his accusers. It was as though he felt himself unsnarling a difficult problem for an uncomprehending audience, as indeed he was.

"I knew I should never do what Lady Sterling ask. I knew it from beginning."

Watson gave voice to the confusion his face showed. "What is it you're saying?"

"You've got everything wrong way around. The buying copies and pretending they originals was Lady Sterling's wish, not mine. I only take cost of copies, she keep the difference between my price and the price of originals. I can show you receipts. I keep very careful records with Lady Sterling. I am reputable agent. I sell copies when I say I sell copies, and originals when I say I sell originals. I have very good friend at the Archaeological Museum. A big expert. He checks for me anytime there is a question about originals and copies. But there was no question with Lady Sterling."

Watson managed to recover his voice without having lost his skepticism about Bikelas' innocence.

"Your records prove nothing. You could have created a false listing of sales as part of your plan to defraud Lady Sterling and the British Government. Your charge against Lady Sterling is ridiculous on its face. Lady Sterling is ... was

... a wealthy woman. Why would she concoct a fraudulent scheme — risking her position — just to steal a few hundred pounds?"

"I don't know this word 'concoct.' If you are asking why she did this thing, it is simple to answer. She did it for her family — her mother and father. She tell me all about it. They have no money, but they once have lot of money. Her father thinks they still do. She told me about his problems, about him living in the past when things were better for him. She tell me she has to take care of her mother and father, and about having to ask Lord Sterling for everything. Lord Sterling pay for them to come to Athens, for house and food, but not for nice things in the house. So she fix."

Bikelas looked to two bemused faces and shrugged. "What can I do? Women tell me things. She asks me to get her copies of Greek relics — good copies for her house. She don't tell me she means to cheat her government. Anyway, she don't tell me at first. Later, she say it not matter, she find a way to pay back the government. I tell her I have to give her receipt showing just what she paid me. She no care. So that's what I do. I never take more money than the cost of the copies I sell, and I always give her receipt."

"And how do you explain about this house, and these handsome furnishings if you are charging such modest amounts?" Holmes asked.

Bikelas shrugged a second time. "It is a house I borrow. I make agreement with this man who has business in Patras. He is in trade, and has to be there many months of the year. A fine house that is empty is target for thieves. He needs someone to stay in his house, I need a house customers can see is house of respectable businessman. I am respectable businessman, but my house needs to show it. Big house, nice things makes people feel good about me. I help my business friend, he helps me. It is all very by the law.

Holmes was not yet ready to swallow Bikelas' story or his innocence. "Can you tell us where you were three nights ago — the night Lady Sterling was killed?"

"Three nights ago." Bikelas squinted his way to the past, his eyes returning to normal as he arrived at his destination. "I was here. With customer. He arrange to buy relics ... genuine relics. Some of them are in the hall. I need to pack them to send to him in England. And don't ask how long I was with customer. I only know it was dark when he left. You may know my customer. He is very smart about Greek relics. Mr. Albert Needham." Theodore Bikelas looked to Holmes and Watson, who did their best to maintain the impassive expressions they had adopted at the beginning of Bikelas' explanation.

"We do indeed know Mr. Needham ... know him quite well, and we will be checking your story with him," Watson replied.

"I invite it, thank you." Bikelas rose from his chair. "If there's nothing else, gentlemen, I do have business to run."

Neither of the two men had another question, and they rose as well to follow him back to the cluttered entrance hall. Holmes stopped at the open door and turned to Bikelas.

"We will need to speak again. Will you be at this address?"

Bikelas smiled ruefully. "Where should I go? My business is here."

Outside, Nikolos sat atop the box of his carriage exactly as they had left him except for a cigarette now dangling from a corner of his lips. He never looked to Holmes and Watson as they climbed again into his carriage, but chucked the reins on the bay and started for the embassy.

The two men sat quietly, each one considering the claim made by Theodore Bikelas. At last, Watson broke the silence.

"What do you think, Holmes? It seems outlandish to believe that Lady Sterling would use her position at the embassy to commit a massive fraud, but there are things Bikelas said that are consistent with what we know. Mrs. Hudson told us that Lady Sterling's parents lived in a surprisingly well-appointed house, and that her mother described her as a good daughter who provided for her parents. If she had to find a way to pay for luxurious furnishings, the scheme to use her household allowance would certainly be a way to do it — maybe the only way if Lord Sterling adamantly opposed giving such support."

"And," Watson continued, "his claim to have been with Needham the night of the murder is too easily checked for him to lie about it. Moreover, as I recall, Needham did claim to be too tired to attend the ambassador's reception the afternoon of our arrival in Athens. Doubtless, he had made some sort of arrangement to see Bikelas before leaving London, and didn't want to break his appointment. It also supports Bikelas' claim that he is, in fact, a reputable businessman if someone as knowledgeable as Needham is willing to use him as an agent. I suspect, Holmes, we've eliminated a murder suspect, but gained a credible explanation for Lady Sterling's purchases."

"That may well be, Watson, but I believe there's need for caution before we proceed too far. We don't know what time Bikelas' session with Needham ended, only that it was dark. Bikelas, or for that matter, Needham, could well have had time to get to the ambassador's residence. Indeed, Watson, if you recall all of our Olympic colleagues appeared to be having early dinners, and any one of them could have made the short walk to the residence when done eating. It all merits a pipe and further consideration. For the moment, I suggest we return to the embassy to see Lestrade and make certain our young friends got off alright before we consider our next steps."

Watson nodded agreement. He recognized the need to "consider our next steps" would necessitate involving the missing member of their consulting detective agency, but decided it was neither necessary nor politic to state the obvious.

News of Oswald Benton's dual role changed Mrs. Hudson's timetable. She would meet with her two colleagues when they returned from seeing Bikelas. With nothing to be accomplished until then, she resolved to fill the time available by attending the bicycle races at the Velodrome. She feared that, lacking the support of the embassy, the two service workers, whose participation Holmes and Watson had made possible, might find themselves without a friendly face in the crowd. She parted from Launceston Elliot, who apologized for not joining her, citing a need to practice for his wrestling competition.

The newly built Velodrome seated 7,000 spectators in tiers surrounding a third of a kilometer banked track. Once again, the King was in attendance in the hope that the royal presence would help fill the stadium. However, the strategy that had succeeded handsomely at the Zappeion failed badly at the Velodrome. The reason for the sparse attendance became readily apparent. The race involved 300 turns around the track, a dizzying affair that taxed the endurance of participant and spectator alike, and a substantial percentage of both disappeared well before the 300th turn.

One spectator took her by surprise. Catching her eye, Albert Needham waved and smiled from his seat nearly a quarter of a turn away. After a moment's hesitation, he crossed the many rows and tiers that separated them; then stood expectantly over Mrs. Hudson trying to recapture both his breath and his smile after completing the laborious journey.

"May I join you, Mrs. Hudson?"

"Please do, Mr. Needham."

While the small man continued to work at catching his breath, Mrs. Hudson sought to satisfy her curiosity about his presence at the bicycle race. "I'll admit I'm a bit surprised to see you 'ere, Mr. Need'am. It was my understandin' you'd be spendin' all your time at the archaeological museum lookin' at all those statues and things from thousands of years ago."

"That was certainly my intention, Mrs. Hudson, but I discovered that between this being Easter week, and the city's concern about clogging the streets with carriages because of the Games, the Museum of Archaeology is closed for the week. And, while you wouldn't know it to see me today," he said, patting his considerable paunch, "I was something of a devotee of bicycle racing as a young man—even participated in some races at the university. When I learned about the Olympic racing, I thought I'd come to see what it was like, although I won't be able to stay to the end. But what brings you to see a bicycle race, Mrs. Hudson? You're not going to tell me you're here because you competed as a young woman." He followed up his remark with a series of noises Mrs. Hudson took to be laughter, although they sounded as though the man was trying to bring a gagging reflex under control.

Mrs. Hudson smiled politely, uncertain about the humor in Needham's comment, and waited until certain of the archaeologist's survival before explaining her intent to provide the two embassy staff with some semblance of a rooting section. For the time Needham remained in the stadium, their talk ranged over a variety of topics without ever touching on Lady Sterling's purchases. Not long after Needham had smiled his leave taking, Battel joined the six riders who had already dropped out of the competition. It was her cue to leave as well. Exiting the Velodrome, Mrs. Hudson overheard the conversation of two Americans, one of whom was recounting the victory of "this Oswald Benton chap" who had defeated his opponent in a tennis match. This Oswald Benton chap, she thought, was emerging as a man full of surprises.

Miss Osterkos, Miss Pershing's replacement in reception, was a plump cheerful woman, nearing fifty, but attempting, through the liberal application of cosmetics, to forestall its arrival. She arranged for Holmes and Watson to see Lestrade, her breezy manner suggesting they might all be going on a picnic together.

In fact, they met in the same small conference room in which they had met twice before, leading Watson to wonder aloud whether there was another conference room. Lestrade assured him there was one, a larger room used chiefly for what Coopersmith called "all hands meetings." A young man appeared with tea and biscuits, at the request, he explained of Miss Osterkos. He set the tray in the center of the table, and poured tea for all three amidst overwhelming silence. He then backed slowly from the room, eyeing each man as he did, as if fearing an assault by one or all of them if he dared turn his back. When their server had left, Lestrade answered his guests' unspoken question.

"The young people got off on the first train to Piraeus. Coopersmith has organized their travels to get them to London in just three days. And I must say, Holmes, you were on the right track in encouraging them to have dinner together. They were a good deal more comfortable with the plan and with each other this morning. I suspect they'll have little trouble pretending affection on their trip."

"There was one interesting development while you were gone. This fellow from the Office of the Colonial Secretary, red-headed bloke named Lockhart, was at the embassy first thing in the morning, wanting to see Coopersmith and raising quite a fuss about it. He let everyone within shouting distance know he'd gotten a directive sending him to the Sudan, and he was certain it was Coopersmith's doing. He finally stormed out when Coopersmith refused to see him."

Holmes shook his head in bewilderment. "I suppose that's life in Her Majesty's service. Meanwhile, is there anything new regarding the murders at the ambassador's home or concerning Lord Sterling's disappearance?"

"Nothing, I'm afraid. It does appear, however, I will be able to get back to the investigation into Lady Sterling's purchases very soon. The Greek police have informed us that they will no longer restrict movement in the area of the ambassador's home, and I will finally be able to have Needham accompany me to clarify the authenticity of Lady Sterling's purchases, or, as everyone suspects, their lack of authenticity." Lestrade paused in his report, recognizing the incomprehension in the faces of his audience. "I forget that you haven't been at the embassy for a while. It seems the Greek authorities were quite upset when they found the embassy had chosen not to inform them of the two murders until several hours after their discovery. They retaliated by closing the street for a time to foot and carriage traffic supposedly to allow them to carry out their own investigation. It appears only Mrs. Kasiris is permitted to cross their barrier, probably because she's seen as one of theirs rather than one of ours."

"But surely the house can be considered British property," Watson protested.

"That was pointed out to the Greeks, but they responded that the house was only leased to our government. The truth is they felt quite strongly about not being informed or involved in an investigation in their own city, and had the capacity to enforce their displeasure. It's my understanding that only your Mrs. Hudson managed to get through their cordon when she went to see how the Sterlings' housekeeper was doing. And she was only let in because she was with that weightlifter bloke who they thought was you, Mr. Holmes, and they wouldn't deny access to a man of your reputation. I suppose you should be complimented that you — even if it wasn't you — was the only person for whom they broke their rules. In any event, they've decided we've now been sufficiently punished, and I'll be able to get into the residence as soon as tomorrow and resume the investigation. After that, assuming the items are fake, it will just be a matter of picking up the man who sold the items to her and determining if he's the one who was making threats, as I suspect will be the case. Curious thing about that, the man who was arranging the purchases for Lady Sterling — this fellow, Bikelas—turns out to be the same person Needham contacted to make purchases for the museum in London. It appears he's either got them fooled too, or he is running a more complicated business than anyone might have expected. Anyway, as soon as we sort that situation, we will be better able to sort the murders."

Holmes frowned his response to Lestrade. He was not yet aware of Mrs. Hudson's conversation with Mrs. Kasiris, but his own meeting with Bikelas had made him less suspicious of the antiquities agent.

"As you say, Lestrade, this may be a more complicated business than it appears. Frankly, I'm not convinced that Bikelas is our man."

Lestrade looked hard at Holmes, but said nothing.

Watson tried to pour oil on waters that were threatening to become troubled. "There's still much to do, and we will need to remain in close touch as we explore different avenues."

"Of course you're right, Doctor. And we'll see where the evidence takes us, Mr. Holmes. Please do give regards to your Mrs. Hudson, and let her know I sorely miss her raisin scones. I always believed her baking was an important contribution to our investigations."

"Yes," Holmes said, "I suppose one makes what contribution one can."

Dinner that night involved a sharing of all that had been learned during the day. Mrs. Hudson chewed thoughtfully on the roast lamb she had ordered, while Holmes and Watson took turns reporting what they had been told by Theodore Bikelas, and what Lestrade had planned for Bikelas.

"All that you learned gives us a better understandin' about the expensive furnishings I saw at the Martinsons. Knowin' that Lord Sterling wasn't willin' to pay for them, I am certain that Mr. Bikelas was tellin' the truth, and it was Lady Sterling, not Bikelas, who was runnin' the deception. It also fits with Mrs. Kasiris not knowin' of any telephone call for Lady Sterling from a man threatenin' Lord Sterling. There never was a telephone call. Lady Sterling only pretended there was to get 'im to stop investigatin' before 'e could discover 'er deception. It's also why Lord Sterling didn't 'ave Mr. Bikelas' proper address. Lady Sterling gave 'im the wrong address, and 'e never thought to check it with Nikolos."

She went on to report the rest of her meeting with Mrs. Kasiris, omitting mention of Launceston Elliot, which she was certain would only trigger weak attempts at adolescent humor.

"There's two more things I learned from Mrs. Kasiris. First, she 'as a very close friend, a Mr. Seropopoulos who lives on Metaxes Street." Mrs. Hudson smiled at her successful use of von Feinaigle's memory aids. I'm thinkin' 'e's got the key to the ambassador's 'ome Mrs. Kasiris says has gone missin', and it might be worth payin' 'im a visit to get to know what 'e's been doin' with that key, and whether 'e 'ad reason to use that key the night of the murders. I'm thinkin' that's somethin' you might follow up on, Dr. Watson."

Watson nodded and jotted down his best guess at the spelling of the man's name, not having read von Feinaigle, he would be dependent on the written word to remember the man's name.

"And we know that Oswald Benton 'as been sent by the Foreign Office to conduct an investigation of Lady Sterling's purchases on their be'alf. It's for certain that Mr. Benton will be joinin' with the Inspector and Mr. Needham when they go to see the things Lady Sterling bought. With that able to 'appen as soon as tomorrow, it means we need to 'ave a plan for keepin them out of the 'ouse for at least a day and for us gettin' into it as soon as tomorrow night, and I 'ave some ideas about that."

Mrs. Hudson shared her ideas with her colleagues, prompting a spirited exchange and the development of a plan on which all three ultimately agreed. They recognized there were some holes needing to be filled in, but decided they had done all they could do for the day. They would sleep on it and see what tomorrow would bring. As it turned out, tomorrow would bring a great deal.

Chapter 6.
Lord Sterling Returns

At first, the dream had Holmes' full attention. He was in a fencing match, but wore no protection and carried a sword that was little more than an elongated knife. His opponent was in full protective gear and wielded a thick broadsword. A mask kept hidden his opponent's identity. He only knew the person was short, and spoke to him in a strange dialect when the person spoke at all. The platform on which they competed was surrounded by water. Across the water on either side of the platform stood each of a set of twins, their faces an indistinct blur except for trim moustaches. One cheered loudly for Holmes, the other decorously for his competitor. For a time the clash of swords obscured any other sound. The knocking finally broke through his slumbers, and he called sleepily to the sound, "Is somebody there?" He got no answer. He pulled on his robe, pushed his hair back from his forehead, and called again to the door, receiving the same response.

He looked to the pocket watch he had set on the table next to his bed. It was nearly three in the morning. He considered the revolver on the shelf of the wardrobe, and rejected it in favor of the umbrella he had left by the door. The man in the doorway required neither precaution. He was a little past fifty, not much above middle height, but thickset with a full beard that had once been black and now held gray streaks. Another time his burly presence might have appeared menacing, now he seemed to slink beneath the cap pulled low to cover much of his face. Holmes recognized him from the brief exchange they'd had a few days earlier.

"Please come in and have a seat, ambassador, I know you've had a long trip."

Lord Sterling nodded his appreciation, but said nothing as he accepted Holmes' invitation, selecting what looked to be the more comfortable of the room's two easy chairs. For a while, he maintained his silence while Holmes tried to shake off the drowsiness he felt from being awakened a few hours into a sound sleep. Holmes was about to give Lord Sterling the option of either speaking or making use of the couch while he went back to sleep, when the ambassador began an explanation for appearing at his door.

"I believe you're a man who can be trusted to be discreet, Mr. Holmes. You're the only person in Athens who knows I'm here. I got your hotel and room number from the visit a Mrs. Hudson made to my in-laws, Baron and Lady Martinson, and I came up the backstairs to avoid anyone seeing me. I hope you can understand, Mr. Holmes, I needed time to deal with all that happened that night. I came home to find my wife dead, and a man I'd never seen before lying dead with her. I tell you, Mr. Holmes, I felt miserable and confused, both at the same time. I know I shouldn't have run off, or stayed away as long as I have, but I had to work these things through and I knew I couldn't do it here, not with the newspapers and the Foreign Office and my own staff all wanting to probe me or sympathize with me, and all the time wondering what I had done, and what I wasn't telling. In any event, I'm back now and ready to answer all questions."

"Why are you here, Lord Sterling? Why come to see me?"

"I'm not a fool, Mr. Holmes. I know it's customary to blame the husband in these situations. I want to share with you what I know and what I've been doing, and if I can, I want to engage you to find my wife's murderer. I'll pay any amount you require, but, whether you accept my offer or not, I want you to hear me out."

Holmes had taken his pipe from where it lay on a table, and began an elaborate show of filling and lighting it

143

before speaking to Lord Sterling's request. "I can't accept your proposition, ambassador. I'm already involved in the investigation, and, as you say, the husband is always counted a suspect in these cases. You should know, in that regard, that the man found dead with Lady Sterling was, to the best of our knowledge, someone she knew from her days at Girton College, whose reason for being in Athens had nothing to do with Lady Sterling. In terms of the investigation, which is already well under way, I promise to be fair, but I must go wherever it leads me."

Lord Sterling grimaced his understanding of Holmes' position. Now fully awake, Holmes moved the conversation to another concern.

"I must also tell you I located the man who arranged the sales of antiquities to Lady Sterling, and the situation is not what it seemed." Lord Sterling edged forward in his seat. "The purchases were indeed fraudulent, but the fraud appears to have been Lady Sterling's idea. There is reason to believe Lady Sterling knew she was buying copies, and that she kept the difference between her purchase price and the price of the originals. It appears that Lady Sterling used the funds she obtained to help her parents maintain the appearances the Baron thought were their true state."

Lord Sterling sank back against the cushion of his chair, all the color drained from his face. "This is my fault. I told Pamela — Lady Sterling — her family would need to become accustomed to living more modestly. You do know, I arranged for them to come to Greece, and I put them in a nice little cottage, but I did draw the line at perpetuating the Baron's fantasy of their continuing great wealth. I should have known Pamela would find a way around my prohibition."

Lord Sterling quieted and Holmes could find nothing more to say. For a while they sat together in silence, Lord Sterling struggling to take in this latest heaping of tragedy on top of tragedy. At last the ambassador spoke. "I suppose there's no way to keep all of this secret. Not for me, I've been through this sort of thing before. But I hate the thought of Lady Sterling's reputation being sullied or her parents being held up to ridicule. The Baron probably won't understand all that's happening, but the Baroness has been through so much and doesn't deserve this."

Holmes drummed his fingers on the arm of his chair before exhaling a small stream of smoke and taking his pipe in hand. "There might be a way, Lord Sterling. Two questions before we begin. Are you in a position to make restitution to the government for Lady Sterling's purchases."

"Of course, anything that will help."

"And do you still have the key to your residence?"

"Yes, it's never been out of my possession."

"In that case, Lord Sterling, I believe there may be a way to avoid unnecessary embarrassment."

Lord Sterling spent the night maneuvering his considerable bulk into the narrow confines of the couch in Holmes' room. It was, nonetheless, the most satisfactory night's sleep he'd had in nearly a week. Holmes, on the other hand, spent a nearly sleepless night in the broad confines of the room's bed. He finally gave up any expectation of sleep, and at half six he dressed and summoned his colleagues to breakfast with him at seven.

Once seated, Watson asked the question that reflected the distress on both his and Mrs. Hudson's face.

"Holmes, you look awful. Did you get any sleep last night?"

Holmes smiled weakly. "I had a rather active night. At about three I was visited by Lord Sterling who is, as we speak, asleep in my room." He paused to allow for small gasps of astonishment, but found only intense concentration.

"He has emerged from hiding, and reports himself prepared to face whatever consequences there may be. He, of course, insists on his own innocence in the double murder, states that he does not know the man found with his wife, and greatly regrets withholding the money that would have made Lady Sterling's fraudulent behavior unnecessary. I believe he is truly remorseful on that score. More than that, he holds himself entirely responsible for her crime. He is quite willing to reimburse the government, and is anxious to do anything that might salvage his wife's reputation and protect his in-laws."

"Well done, Holmes," Watson called.

"Yes, Mr. 'Olmes, it was truly well done."

Holmes nodded acknowledgment of his colleagues' accolades. He raised a hand for them to desist shortly after they had finished voicing their tributes.

Only then did Watson feel he'd spotted a problem. "But wait a moment, won't the return of funds be obvious? Won't it trigger additional questions?"

Holmes had already considered the difficulty Watson raised.

"The money is in the ambassador's household account. It's entirely under his control, and need be seen by no one until a final accounting is made, which almost certainly will not occur before the end of the year."

Mrs. Hudson looked to her colleagues with a broad smile. "The 'oles in our plan are now filled in. There is just one thing more. Mr. 'Olmes, you'll 'ave to convince Lord Sterling 'is life is in danger, and that 'e can't go back to work — or worse yet, go 'ome — until you tell 'im it's safe to do so. In fact, we don't want anyone to recognize 'im for the next couple of days. You'll need to get 'im to do the play actin' you're so fond of if 'e's to leave the 'otel room. I assume you brought a carpetbag full of surprises." She got the expected sober nod from Holmes.

"Good, for now, we'll need 'early enough breakfasts to get us through a long day and an active night. After breakfast we start." She turned her attention to the menu and her colleagues did the same, joining her, as well, in broad smiles of satisfaction.

Holmes returned to his room to find Lord Sterling still curled up in sound sleep. He was loathe to wake the man; however, there was simply too much to do for him to remain asleep.

"Lord Sterling." Then louder, "Lord Sterling," at the same time gently rolling the ambassador from side to side. His efforts were rewarded with a pair of half open eyes, followed by the ambassador slowly folding himself into a sitting position. He looked around the room, taking stock of the unfamiliar surroundings before speaking.

"Thank you again for letting me stay with you. Can you tell me, what is the time? And I wonder, would there be a way for me to get something to eat? I've hardly eaten anything the last two days."

"It's nearing half eight. As for getting something to eat, we can arrange for that, but you'll need to remain out of sight, or, more accurately, unrecognizable for two more days."

Holmes' guest was now wide awake, and had become again the ambassador. "That's impossible. As I say, I appreciate your accommodating me — I appreciate it a great deal — but I must now do what I can to resume my life and duties."

Holmes was prepared for Lord Sterling's rejection. "I don't think you fully appreciate the situation. It is imperative that you do not return to the embassy or to your residence until it is safe to do so. The murderer is still out there, and you may be a target. Since I cannot keep you locked in a room — much as that would make good sense — I must insist you disguise yourself. That will allow you to leave the hotel. However, even with that, you should not go anywhere near your home or office. We simply cannot chance your being recognized by someone."

There followed a great deal of harrumphing and throat clearing, but the ambassador saw something in Holmes' eyes that told him his objection was fruitless, and quite possibly against his best interests. "Very well then, you're the expert, and for a while at least I'll put myself in your hands, but only for a while. Threat or no, I have a job to do, and frankly I have a need to immerse myself in it not only to serve my country, but to take my mind off of Pamela." The look the ambassador gave him made Holmes regret having once suspected the man of his wife's murder. "Where would you have me go, and what did you mean about making me unrecognizable?"

"You can take a room at this hotel if you will do so in disguise, and make it a habit to eat in the dining room at times when it is unlikely to be much frequented, or better still eat at nearby restaurants. For now, let us see what we can do about a proper disguise. I don't suppose you'd agree to shaving your beard."

The man's agitated look told Holmes the accuracy of his supposition.

"No, well I didn't really expect you would. I do have some applications we can employ to change your appearance, but I didn't bring many of my makeup materials and, if you don't mind my saying so, you do present a challenge; however, let us see what we can do. I wonder, do you know any Hebrew?"

A half hour later, the ambassador, heretofore a devout member of the Anglican Church, had become an elderly gentleman of the Hebrew faith, white bearded, with rimless glasses, a soft homburg which he was instructed to wear at all times, and a dark coat. After much practice, he perfected a stooped walk to complement his advanced age. To Holmes' surprise, after studying himself in a mirror, Lord Sterling found the idea of passing himself off as someone he wasn't, an exciting proposition and one he was anxious to try.

Holmes, however, ruled against his going immediately to the hotel lobby, suggesting instead a more circuitous route. "You must leave this room at fifty minutes past nine. You should again take the back stairs rather than the lift. You will arrive in reception ten minutes later where you will exit the hotel using the side entrance. At exactly that same time, an older woman will suddenly collapse at the opposite end of reception capturing everyone's attention, and allowing you to leave without being detected. You will then turn the corner and return, entering through the front entrance, to request a room in the name of Mr. Absalom Tublin, telling the person at the desk your luggage will follow."

"I have to leave now. You can order food from the kitchen to be charged to the room. I would like you to leave the door unlocked, and when the boy knocks, go into the lavatory, and call for the boy to leave the food."

"My goodness, Mr. Holmes, you are a caution. You think of everything."

"Not everyone would agree with you," Holmes observed drily. "Now, I will need the key to your residence." Pocketing the key, Holmes made one last plea for compliance with the stricture he thought essential. "Remember, you must be certain to use your disguise whenever you leave the hotel room."

"I shall, Mr. Holmes, and I can't thank you enough for your assistance."

"It's nothing, nothing at all," Holmes shrugged off his small lie. "I'll be back this evening to learn how things have gone. By the way, do you have a revolver?"

"For my protection, yes. Ever since Pamela received a threatening telephone call, I've carried the embassy revolver with me."

Holmes allowed himself a self-satisfied smile. "I thought as much." And with a nod to Lord Sterling, Holmes took his leave to begin his tasks for the day, stopping first to inform the older woman in room 428 of her impending collapse.

While Holmes was transforming Lord Sterling into Absalom Tublin, and Mrs. Hudson was resting in her room, Watson decided to use the short time available to enjoy a pipe and another cup of tea. His relaxed moment was dispelled by the entrance of four Olympic athletes with whom he was by now well-acquainted. They directed the head waiter to seat them at a table near to Watson, then insisted he join them. Watson tried to demur, noting that their table was already full, and his addition would put them in tight and uncomfortable quarters, but all four men declared his concern unwarranted, and proceeded to pull a chair from an adjoining table and fit it between Edwin Flack and Grantley Goulding, and across from Durand Ramsay and Launceston Elliot.

"We needed an Englishman at the table, Dr. Watson," Elliot said, with a grin a little too sly to be solely welcoming. "We have been discussing issues faced by those of us who are citizens of the Empire, but are not English, and we can benefit from the perspective of someone who is both a citizen and English. Of course, Grantley is nominally an Englishman, but his heart is in South Africa where he plans to resettle shortly — in spite of all we've been telling him."

After ordering a pot of tea from the waiter who materialized suddenly at his elbow, Watson squinted his confusion, and asked Elliot what he meant. His question prompted broad grins from all and snickering from Flack.

Elliot sought to explain. "It would be difficult for you to understand. As an Englishman, you quite naturally see yourself as placed at the very center of the universe, and see all of us as inhabiting space somewhere on its periphery. You mean no harm, it's what you're taught as a boy and hear over and over for the rest of your life. England is the land of Shakespeare, Keats, Shelley and Milton. Scotland is a land of sheep."

"And Australia is a place fit for felons," Flack added. "The colonies are untamed and exotic, or are, at best, not as civilized or as fit a place to live as England. What we are fit for is to provide the resources to make you great, or to take the refuse that detracts from your greatness. Either way, England is the hub, and all of us not fortunate enough to be English, have only the honor to be called 'subjects of the Crown'."

"I really must object." Watson had stopped puffing on his pipe and his face was turning an unbecoming shade of crimson. "I believe we honor all those who make contribution regardless of where they're from." He turned to Elliot, whose broad smile he now recognized as reflecting something other than good fellowship. "We certainly honor the poetry of Robert Burns."

"Do you now. In truth, I've long wondered whether it isn't the case that what's found attractive about Bobby Burrrrns is his fracturing of the English language, confirming the view that Scotsmen speak an inferior, although amusing form of English. Frankly, Doctor, I don't know a Scotsman who speaks as poorly as Burns would have us believe all Scotsmen speak."

"Is this the way all of you think?" Watson made no effort to mask his exasperation.

Goulding looked up from where he'd been studying his hands folded on the table. "I been telling them right along they've got it wrong, Doctor. I ran some races down in South Africa — where I intend to be going as Mr. Elliot said — and I was treated as good as anyone could want, maybe because I won every race I was in. Anyway, whatever these blokes say won't be true for me. When I get to South Africa, I'll be as English as if I were still in Piccadilly."

"What about you, Mr. Ramsay," Elliot challenged the only person who hadn't yet spoken.

Ramsay looked around the table, then beyond it as if hoping to be called away. "I hadn't given it much thought. I guess when you put it like that, I'd have to say I can see the difficulty with our situations."

"Difficulty is right!" Flack pounded a fist on the table, signaling his transfer of relatively good-natured taunting of Watson to less good-natured criticism of Ramsay's insufficiently caustic response. "My God, man, we're in the midst of a struggle back home over federation and maybe even forming a republic like they have in America. I'm all for the colonies coming together under a federal government, but only if it's like Mr. Dibbs says and we become a republic. It's not that I've got anything against the Queen. It's just that if we're going to be our own country, we should make it our own. What do you say, Ramsay?"

Although no one else at the table had any idea what was involved in achieving either federation or republic, let alone who Mr. Dibbs was, all eyes turned to Ramsay to learn whether he stood with Flack on those issues. For his part, Ramsay looked still more anxious to be summoned somewhere, anywhere else.

"I'm just not a political person," he said sheepishly. "Frankly, my home-building business takes up nearly all my time. I leave the politics to others."

"Well, we'll all be involved soon enough," said an only somewhat subdued Flack. "Federation is almost here — by here, I mean Australia of course."

"There's somewhat similar discussion going on in Scotland," Elliot added. "It's a minority opinion, of course, but there's been talk of home rule — similar to what was talked about, but never happened in Ireland."

"You see, Doctor Watson," Flack said, "in spite of my friend Ramsay, there's movement toward separation. There's lots of us want our own country. There's change coming, Dr. Watson. Maybe not tomorrow, but it's coming."

"Sometime indeed, but right now is the time for all of us to be getting to the Games," Elliot said. "Or if you prefer, Dr. Watson, we should a' be gang away."

Watson considered the revolutionary conversation of the morning, then dismissed it as offering scenarios too unlikely to be of concern. He took a carriage to the embassy, intending to arrive shortly after its opening, knowing Lestrade would already be there. Lestrade was always punctual. The Inspector came out to the reception area to collect Watson and bring him to his office.

Watson politely refused Lestrade's offer to have tea brought in, explaining that he had another stop to make before getting to the Zappeion to see Holmes' match. The Inspector grunted understanding.

"I'm here to ask a small favor on behalf of Holmes."

Lestrade took a pencil from his desk, and began turning it slowly between his fingers as he waited the Doctor's request.

"I know you and Needham are planning a visit to the ambassador's residence now that the Greek authorities are no longer blocking entry. I know, Inspector, you're not one to postpone until tomorrow what can be accomplished today. In this one instance, however, I am asking you to do just that — to put off your visit for one day. I can't tell you the reason for doing so. I can only tell you the reason is sound."

The pencil's rotation came to a brief halt. "Dr. Watson, you want me to delay by a day the investigation I was sent here to conduct as expeditiously as possible."

"Quite right."

"And you can't tell me the reason for my doing so."

"To do so would make impossible the success of the action, and could, I fear, have an adverse effect on people's career and status."

Lestrade's eyes widened as he studied Watson's impassive expression. There was only one person whose career and status could be affected, and the only reason it could be affected had to do with the propriety of the action Holmes would be taking. Had anyone else suggested he turn a blind eye to an action that was questionable at the very least, and quite possibly illegal, he would have turned him out of his office with instructions to staff to bar the door against his return. This was not, however, anyone else. From their long history together, Lestrade knew whatever the action Holmes planned, it would almost certainly lead to a worthwhile outcome. He knew, too, ignorance of the action would allow him to sleep more soundly that night, and to answer fewer questions in the days to follow.

"You and Mr. Holmes can have your day, Dr. Watson, but I can only give you one. You have until tomorrow to do what is necessary in accord with your 'sound reason'."

Lestrade rose. Watson followed, solemnly extending his hand to seal their pact. With equal gravity Lestrade shook the hand offered. The mask of correctness did little to hide the regard each man held for the other.

Finding Holmes on his doorstep for the second time in as many days, Theodore Bikelas was more confused than upset, and he was quite upset. His invitation to Holmes to enter his borrowed home was polite, but nothing more. Holmes commented on the fact that the entrance hall was now cleared of paraphernalia and boxes, and was told by Bikelas that the artworks had been packaged for delivery. Removing a watch from his pocket, he added that he had an appointment to see customers shortly. Holmes noted he did not volunteer a definition of "shortly," and Holmes did not request one.

As on his last visit, Holmes took a seat on the settee in the parlor to which he was led, and Bikelas took an easy chair opposite.

"I am, of course, pleased to see you again, Mr. Holmes, but may I ask the reason for your visit? Have you perhaps decided you would like to purchase some art objects — perhaps something to remember your visit to Athens? I can give you an excellent price." Bikelas smiled at his own pretense, and waited to hear the detective's reason for this second visit.

Holmes returned the smile before answering Bikelas' question. "I fear that nothing you have would go with the decor of my flat, which might best be described as Early Chaos. I am here to enlist your assistance in making right a situation that has gone terribly wrong. First though, am I correct that the Archaeological Museum is still closed in recognition of Easter week?"

A deep nod.

"And can I assume that your friend from the Museum — the one you said you sometimes call on for advice — is still in Athens?"

A second deep nod.

"Good. Then, we can proceed."

Holmes went on to outline the scenario developed the prior evening, and finalized hours earlier. As he did so, the antiquities trader became increasingly pale and his chair appeared to become increasingly confining. When Holmes was done, he adamantly refused to play the part designated for him — exactly as Holmes knew he would. Holmes then told him of his certainty that the authorities — both Greek and British — would show great interest in his complicity in perpetrating a fraud on the British Government.

"But that's blackmail," Bikelas stammered.

"Oh, it is very definitely. I'm glad you recognize that. It saves a great deal of pointless discussion."

Aware now that moral suasion would not prove successful, the antiquities trader tried a second strategy. "I don't think I can get done what you ask of me."

A strategy of coercion, having proven successful once, was put back in use. "I would urge you to try. Think what will happen if you don't."

Bikelas sagged in his chair, convinced that further resistance would prove futile. "What time tonight do you want me?"

Taking no chance on a slip-up or misunderstanding, Holmes reviewed the plan, this time to a more receptive, if still essentially captive, audience. When he was done and Bikelas had asked his last question, Holmes excused himself, reporting his need to return to the Olympic Games for his event. Bikelas neither wished him well nor asked about the event. They parted with only a curt nod of acknowledgment to each other. It was sufficient to its purpose. The plot was unfolding exactly as planned.

Chapter 7.
Mrs. Kasiris' Friend

Watson prayed the name Seropopoulos would be as unusual on Metaxes Street as it would have been on Baker Street. He had no guidance beyond the name and the street. Mrs. Hudson had not wanted to rouse suspicion about her interest in Mrs. Kasiris' friend, and so had not pressed the housekeeper for more information. As it turned out, Metaxes Street was more alley than street and extended only a short, winding distance before running into a cement wall. There was a café at the corner where Watson planned to make use of two of the few Greek words he had acquired in hopes they might pave the way to discovery of Seropopoulos' house. He took an outside table on the Metaxes Street side of the café. When the waiter approached, Watson spoke as authoritatively as he could, "Kafé, parakaló." The waiter left without making response or changing expression, and for a moment Watson wondered if he had gotten the order right. When the waiter returned with his coffee, Watson was sufficiently reassured to try a third word in Greek, this time a name, "Seropopoulos?"

The waiter repeated the name slowly as if it stirred a distant memory. "Seropopoulos."

Watson made his eyes grow big, and raised a hand, palm up, to signal his wish to find the man. The waiter grunted, and said the name "Seropopoulos" again, this time sounding as though the memory had been recalled. He walked out to the street, beckoning Watson to follow. He pointed to either the fifth or sixth door in the terraced housing across the street. Watson first held up five fingers, then six, and shrugged his question. The waiter tucked the tray he still held under one arm and with his free hand he held up first five, then a single finger. Watson smiled and used up the remainder of his Greek vocabulary to thank the man. "Efcharistó."

Without relinquishing his dour expression, the waiter said something back to Watson. Having no idea what the waiter had said, Watson widened his eyes and again raised a hand, palm up, having decided the gesture might serve as a multi-purpose expression of ignorance. The waiter shrugged his inability or unwillingness to prolong the non-conversation, and left Watson to finish his cup of strong Greek coffee, which the doctor thought capable of bracing him for at least the day, and likely some part of the evening.

Like all those coming before and after, the sixth house down was two stories of whitewashed stone with outsize windows on both levels to catch what breeze there might be as spring faded and summer began. The second floor windows held balconies of a size that would admit a small child, assuming parents sufficiently irresponsible to allow a small child to explore them. Their purely decorative purpose was confirmed by the elaborately curved wrought iron fences bordering them.

Watson pressed the button beside a wooden door whose bright red color clashed dramatically with the house's white masonry. The bell sounded two harmonious tones, and was answered by a tall slender man with thinning hair that was changing from the brown it had once been to the gray it was fast becoming. His moustache, and the neatly trimmed goatee it joined, already showed the color his remaining hair would soon match.

Before he could speak, Watson asked, "Mr. Seropopoulos? I am Dr. Watson. Dr. John Watson."

"Seropopoulos," the man corrected, putting emphasis on the third syllable of his name. "English?" Seropopoulos asked, cocking his head to the side. Without waiting for Watson's response, he raised a second question, "Something you want?"

Watson ignored both questions to put one of his own. "You have English?"

"Little English, yes."

Watson had not yet been invited into Seropopoulos' home, and was concerned that either his entire inquiry would take place on the doorstep or, worse yet, Seropopoulos would grow tired of the exchange and shut the door on him. He decided to eliminate both possibilities.

"Would it be alright if we spoke inside?"

Seropopoulos looked hard at Watson as if judging what danger might attach to admitting him. After a moment, he decided to assume the risk. "Yes, pardon, please to come in."

Watson was led from the small foyer containing only an empty umbrella stand to Seropopoulos' parlor. His host motioned him to a chair that was more functional than fashionable, mirroring the furniture in the rest of the room. However, it was neither the furniture, nor the framed copies of well-recognized art masterpieces prominently displayed on the walls of the room, that captured his and every other visitor's attention. Rather, it was the stuffed brown bear standing in full growl on its hind legs in a corner of the room between two sets of low bookcases. On the two shelves of those bookcases were positioned a red fox, marten, badger, ground squirrel, hare, wolverine, and weasel in place of the expected book collections. Watson thought it best not to comment on the bear and small mammals, and to go directly to his prepared script.

"I understand you are a friend of Mrs. Kasiris," Watson's inflection made it clear he was posing a question. It was as much to get confirmation as to clarify the extent of Seropopoulos' command of English.

"We are friends, yes." Seropopoulos smiled his response. "Maybe little more than friends. Why you ask?"

"My associate, Sherlock Holmes, and I are investigating ... looking into the deaths where Mrs. Kasiris works."

At the mention of the deaths, Seropopoulos threw his hands in the air, looked away from Watson, then turned back to glare at him. Watson was momentarily taken aback. He was now reconsidering his first impression of his host as reserved, if not timid, and taking greater note of the multiple cadavers in the far corner of the room.

"What should I care? People die in ugly world. Gaia ... Mrs. Kasiris safe. She good woman. Sterlings not know how good." The glare lingered even as his small tirade ended. Watson decided to give in to the curiosity that had become overwhelming.

"All these animals, Mr. Seropopoulos, were they shot by you?"

"All. I very good shot."

"I see that, and did you stuff them as well?"

Seropopoulos gave the question a dismissive wave. "I shoot, do not stuff animals. I am school headmaster, before that I teach mathematics. I teach for .... " He winced at his inability to report the number, then showed it by flashing his fingers to a total of 26 "... years."

Watson looked properly impressed. "And is there no school this week, Mr. Seropopoulos?"

Seropopoulos nodded. "Easter ... and Games."

"Have you been to the Games, Mr. Seropopoulos?"

Again, a nod. "I see King George, and I see big people picking up ... heavy things, and I go see shooting. Not like my shooting." He gestured to the corner of the room where his collection of kills stood.

Watson followed his direction, this time attending more closely to the stuffed animals. When he did, he became aware of a telephone between the red fox and wolverine.

"You have one of those new telephones?"

Seropopoulos looked to the instrument disdainfully. "They insist I have one. If they need me for, how you say, a bad thing at school."

Watson nodded sympathetically. He thought it might now be safe to return to a discussion of the murders at the ambassador's residence, but that it would be prudent to begin as innocuously as possible.

"Did you know Lord and Lady Sterling?"

Seropopoulos screwed his face in concentration as he searched for words. "Not know. I meet. I go to get Gaia from house, I see Sterlings, say hello. That's all."

"Did you see the Sterlings the night Lady Sterling was killed?"

"Why you want know? I know nothing about dyings."

"We just need to know as much as we can about all that happened that night. Were you at the Sterlings' house that night?"

"I go to get Gaia that night. I have friend lets me take his carriage sometimes."

"Did you see anything odd that night — anything that was different from other nights?"

"I go back door. By kitchen. I see nothing; I hear nothing. I come for Gaia. That's all."

Seropopoulos rose at this last question, and waited for Watson to do the same. "No more questions. I know nothing, I have nothing for saying."

At the door of Seropopoulos' house, Watson wished his host well. Seropopoulos made no response.

Mrs. Hudson had a visit to make that morning as well. Mrs. Kasiris had a role to play in the activity planned for that evening — a very significant role — and the housekeeper needed to be informed what it was.

As expected, she found the police had given up their blockade of the ambassador's residence. However, Mrs. Kasiris appeared intent on making herself as great an obstacle to her getting inside the front door as the Greek police could have hoped to provide. Gaining entrance would require a ploy.

"Mrs. Hudson, I answered all questions. I have no time for more."

"I don't 'ave questions, Mrs. Kasiris, I 'ave news about Lord Sterling."

With that revelation, the door was pulled wide, and the housekeeper became as open and welcoming as she had been obstinate and discouraging a moment before. Wordlessly, she led Mrs. Hudson to the kitchen at the far end of the hall. She took a seat on one side of the room's small table, and Mrs. Hudson took a chair opposite. "What can you tell me about my master's return, Mrs. Hudson?"

"First, Mrs. Kasiris, you must promise that what I tell you will remain secret." Mrs. Hudson paused, waiting to get the woman's promise of confidentiality, knowing that, whatever the promise made, the secret would be too precious not to share with someone. Someone she viewed as entirely trustworthy, someone to whom she felt especially close. And that would be fine, that someone was essential to the success of the night's work.

"Yes, of course. I tell no one."

"Lord Sterling is well and will be returnin' in a very few days."

"But where has the master been? Why won't he be here sooner?"

"There's reason for 'is not comin' just yet." Mrs. Hudson paused, and stared intently at the housekeeper before continuing, her voice now as somber as her expression. "But there's somethin' else, somethin' very important we 'ave to talk about. It's got to do with protectin' the good name of this 'ouse."

The housekeeper's stare made clear her earlier reluctance was gone. Mrs. Hudson felt certain she was ready to assume her role.

"Mrs. Kasiris, I believe you told me that Mr. Seropopoulos is a good friend of yours." Mrs. Hudson received a tentative nod. It was all she expected and as much as she needed.

"And you believe him to be an 'onorable man?"

No nod, instead a question. "What are you getting at, Mrs. Hudson? Mr. Seropopoulos is as good a man as I know. Why are you asking me these things?"

"I 'ave a special request to make of you and Mr. Seropopoulos. It is somethin' that will involve Mr. 'Olmes and Dr. Watson, and two other people, one you know and one you don't. I 'ave to tell you there could be some danger involved. But if we succeed there'll be nobody to say a bad word about Lady Sterling or any in this 'ouse ever again."

For a long moment Mrs. Kasiris gave no reply. Just as Mrs. Hudson was beginning to think she might have misjudged the situation, the woman came straight out of her chair, went wordlessly to the larder adjoining the kitchen, and reemerged with a bottle and two glasses. She set those on the table, still without speaking, and went again to the larder, this time returning with two plates holding tidbits of food. She set one plate in front of Mrs. Hudson and the other at her own place. She filled half of Mrs. Hudson's glass and half of her own with the bottle's clear liquid, added a little water to each, set the bottle down, and raised her glass to Mrs. Hudson.

"Ouzo. Drink slow. Is strong. Mezedes," she said, pointing to the plate of food. "You eat with ouzo. We will drink, we will eat. You will tell me what I should do, and I will tell Mr. Seropopoulos what he should do."

Mrs. Hudson clinked Mrs. Kasiris' glass with her own, and downed a substantial part of her first taste of alcohol since New Year's Eve. She found it was not the sherry she expected. It triggered a fit of coughing from Mrs. Hudson, a round of laughter from Mrs. Kasiris, and a camaraderie that surprised and pleased both women.

"Before we start, I must know one thing. I am correct, am I not, Mrs. Kasiris, the missin' key you mentioned—it's with Mr. Seropopoulos?"

Perhaps fortified by the ouzo, or perhaps by the matter-of-fact questioning of her new found co-conspirator, Mrs. Kasiris did not shrink from her response.

"It is key I lend to Mr. Seropopoulos to use sometimes."

"Good. That may be important in the future. Now, I will share my thinkin' with you — that is, mine and Mr. 'Olmes."

Between sips of ouzo, and bites of a dish she enjoyed without learning its chief component was squid, Mrs. Hudson outlined a series of activities whose careful coordination would be necessary to the evening's success.

When she was done, and she'd had Mrs. Kasiris repeat back to her the actions she would be taking, and the actions Mr. Seropopoulos would be asked to take, she thanked Mrs. Kasiris for her hospitality. She rose to take her leave, only to find herself afflicted with a sudden and surprising unsteadiness. She paused a long moment to gather herself, then followed Mrs. Kasiris to the door on a course that appeared somewhat more challenging than it had when she had entered the ambassador's home earlier. The two women shook hands at the door, each of them knowing they were sealing their agreement to join forces in an intrigue whose end they could not wholly foresee.

As she went in search of a cab to the Zappeion where Holmes would soon be competing, Mrs. Hudson was feeling well-pleased with the situation, and not from the ouzo alone. The evening was as well organized as was possible. Moreover, she now felt certain she knew the identity of the murderer of Lady Sterling and the German courier. Confirmation was lacking, but she had a plan for obtaining that.

The semi-finals of the fencing events were sufficiently an attraction to make King George's presence unnecessary. A capacity crowd was in attendance by the time it came Holmes' turn to compete. He had drawn the Frenchman, Henri Callot, who had easily dispatched his earlier challengers.

Mrs. Hudson took a seat in the third row and was joined by a grim-faced Watson, who was unable to report more than that he had seen Seropopoulos before Lestrade took a seat on the other side of Mrs. Hudson. The Inspector told them of the latest crisis at the embassy. A telegram had arrived informing Mr. Coopersmith of the planned visit by the Queen's youngest daughter, Princess Beatrice. The trip was notable for its poignancy. The Princess would be visiting Athens in the course of her first foreign travel since the death of her husband, Prince Henry.

Watson wagged his head in sympathy for the beleaguered deputy ambassador; then, all settled back for the first of the foils semi-finals. Either Henri Callot or Holmes would be going on to the medal round. The crowd felt the tension of the match and quieted as the contestants were introduced. The members of the Baker Street trio alone were aware that if Holmes were to be the one moving to the medal round, he would need luck—luck and a dramatic surge of energy. A night of little sleep and morning of intense activity would, Dr. Watson had told Mrs. Hudson, surely dull Holmes' senses and slow his reactions.

At the call, "Fence," Holmes tried for the quick strike that had been successful against his earlier opponent. But Callot had watched Holmes' match with his Greek rival, and was not taken by surprise. He parried Holmes' thrust with a swift lateral move of his weapon, the thick back of his blade deflecting the thin front of Holmes'. Without delay, the Frenchman initiated a riposte, taking two quick steps forward. Holmes tried to retreat, parrying as he did, but was too slow and the tip of Callot's foil touched his left shoulder. First point to the Frenchman.

The second call, "Fence," elicited a changed strategy by both men. Holmes was content to play defense as Callot became the aggressor. The Frenchman feinted with his weapon, stopping short of an attack. Holmes started to parry Callot's thrust, recognized the deception, and drew back into a defensive position. Having failed to draw Holmes into a parry that might leave him open to a line of attack, Callot began a conversation between blades, leading the two men to strike foils with neither gaining advantage. Now, it was Holmes' turn to initiate a line of attack. He feinted toward a point above the Frenchman's heart and found the downside of Callot's preparation. Holmes had not needed to use feints in the match with the Greek fencer that Callot had witnessed. He acted to parry the feint, believing it to be part of a genuine attack, and recognized his mistake too late. Holmes brought his foil beneath Callot's and thrust its tip to the Frenchman's abdomen. Point to Holmes.

Callot angrily tore off his mask as he prepared for the next point, making clear his disgust with his recent performance, and determination not to make the same mistake again. At the word, "Fence," he again initiated a feint, this time at a point lower to minimize the risk of a parry leading to a thrust below his weapon. As he expected, Holmes easily parried his thrust. When he did, Callot pressed his blade against that of Holmes, both weapons pointing to the arena's ceiling. Callot took a step toward Holmes intending to force the issue. As he did so, his feet became entangled with Holmes' feet, causing the detective to stumble and fall backward to the ground. With his opponent prostrate before him, Callot touched the tip of his foil again to Holmes' abdomen. One judge immediately awarded the point to Callot, but his decision was quickly challenged by the other judge. At that point, the two judges huddled with the referee to conduct a very public debate to determine the appropriate scoring. Burdened by language differences, discussion evolved into arm waving, hand wringing, an effort by one judge to demonstrate tripping, and a mimicry of swordplay by the other. In the end, the first judge's decision was upheld. There were groans from several of the spectators, and shouts of disapproval in Greek to the judges, but it was point to Callot.

Both men again assumed the on-guard position, Holmes determined to prolong the match, Callot to end it with a third touch. As they began, it was now Holmes who first thrust his foil forward, holding it parallel to the ground, then lunging, drawing the expected and successful parry from Callot. Withdrawing his weapon from Callot's, he reset himself to thrust and lunge at the opening his initial feint had created. Callot, however, had guessed his intent and moved forward to catch the upper, thinner part of Holmes' foil with the lower, thicker part of his own weapon. With the blades locked together for a moment, Holmes thrust up joining the thick part of his weapon to that of his opponent, pushing hard as he did and dislodging the foil from the Frenchman's hand. It fell between the men, leaving Callot defenseless. Without hesitation, Holmes picked up his adversary's weapon and extended its handle to Callot. With small bows to each other, the two men again assumed the on-guard position. This time it was Callot who thrust first, but before he could initiate a lunge, Holmes engaged his weapon, moving forward to press it to a side and open up a line for his own attack. He was only partly successful, Callot moved sideways to escape and Holmes' touch was to the upper part of his opponent's right arm, inches outside the scoring area. Worse yet for Holmes, he came just enough off balance to leave himself vulnerable as Callot now assumed position to thrust and lunge, Holmes' effort to parry only deflected Callot's foil enough to force the touch from going to his heart, where it was aimed, to his left side. Still a point, the third, and the match to Callot.

The men removed their masks, bowed to each other, then to the judges and referee, and shook each other's hand, but there the Frenchman departed from prescribed routine. He embraced Holmes, surprising him, and leaving him momentarily terrified he was about to be kissed on both cheeks. The Frenchman, however, had something else in mind. He turned to face the crowd, raising Holmes' hand high in the air as he did and turning both men in a slow circle, repeatedly shouting, "Magnifique! Magnifique!" loudly enough to make certain all in attendance could share his admiration for Holmes' effort. For what Watson and Mrs. Hudson were certain was the first time in their colleague's life, Holmes blushed and looked to the ground, too overwhelmed by the tribute from his competitor and the audience to face either.

When the applause had subsided, and Lestrade and Watson regained their seats, Mrs. Hudson was anxious to turn their attention to the murder investigation. Neither man was, however, quite ready to shift attention away from the exhibition just witnessed. They carried out frenzied congratulations of each other as the nearest, best substitute to congratulating Holmes. On her third try she was able to interrupt Lestrade's recounting the events of the match all had witnessed to focus him on the investigation in which they were joined. She explained that, in accord with Holmes' request — a request of which she would later inform Holmes — she was to send a telegram to his brother, Mycroft, a secret telegram that had to be sent from the Athens post office, away from the prying eyes of people at the embassy or the hotel. She told him she would need a friend of Mr. Battel's, a Miss Kannapolis, to help her with the translation. She wanted the Inspector to find Mr. Battel when he returned to the embassy, and have him ask Miss Kannapolis to meet her at the central post office at one o'clock the next day. She felt reasonably certain he grasped the assignment after she had repeated it two more times.

There were more accolades for Holmes when he returned to the hotel with Watson and Mrs. Hudson, and even requests for his autograph from guests who knew nothing of Holmes, the consulting detective, but had been impressed by Holmes the skillful fencer. Even at that, Holmes found himself sharing the spotlight with Oswald Benton, who appeared to be as surprised as everyone else at his win that day, allowing him to advance to the medal round in tennis the next day. Indeed, by deciding to team with one of the men from the German team he had defeated, he had positioned himself to compete in the tennis doubles match on the same day. It was not a decision that met with widespread approval from his British teammates.

Flack, too, was all smiles as he and Ramsay joined the group for dinner, Flack had won the 800 meters run, his second victory as he now set his sights on the upcoming marathon. Ramsay's competition, the shooter explained, was scheduled for the next day where he would be firing the military pistol at targets 25 meters distant. Only Launceston Elliot was disappointed with his day, as the rope climbing event, for which he was fully prepared, had been unexpectedly postponed to the following morning. Nonetheless, Elliot gamely led the cheering for those who had met with success, as well as for Holmes, whom he described "as having lost a competition, but nae a loser."

The good feelings led to the unusual sight of Benton joining Flack, Ramsay and Elliot at one table while the members of the Baker Street consulting detective agency sat at an adjoining table. The physical distance proved no impediment to a cheerful banter between tables. Finally, after all had eaten their desserts and drunk their coffee, Holmes rose from his seat, and looked with something close to affection to teammates who had become friends.

"I must beg you, gentlemen ... and lady," he gave Mrs. Hudson a small bow, "to excuse me, it's been a long and exhausting day. And as thoroughly as I have enjoyed your company, I find myself in need of rest and an early evening. I want to wish all those competing tomorrow the greatest success in your events, and everyone a very good evening." He gave a tired smile and left the dining room with a host of good wishes trailing after him.

A short time later, Watson yawned his way to his own departure. Mrs. Hudson followed after him without feeling the need for a comparable display of theatrics. The truth was the night was just beginning for Holmes and Watson, and Mrs. Hudson's plans for the next day called for a sound sleep.

Chapter 8.
A Good Night's Work

Once in his room, Holmes lit a pipe and turned his attention to his notes on bicycle tire treads. Or, at any rate, tried to. He made a start on an introductory paragraph, but found his mind wandering from the empty page to consideration of the work to be undertaken later that evening and, more particularly, to the several things that could go wrong in carrying out that work. He would have to rely on several people of questionable ability and uncertain motivation. There was Bikelas, whose actions would be motivated solely by fear of being exposed as a participant in fraud, and Bikelas' friend, who was participating as a favor to the antiquities dealer. Holmes would be counting, as well, on Nikolos, whom he knew to be a conniver and thief, and Seropopoulos, who would have to conduct tasks far removed from those of a mathematics teacher turned headmaster. He was anxious for night to fall, and to learn how well this rag-tag group would perform. For now, there was nothing to do but wait for the hours to crawl by.

Watson shared his colleague's plight. He had brought two copies of *Lancet* on the chance there would be quiet periods during which he could delve into the latest findings in the medical literature. He lit a pipe, and turned to an article by Dr. J. Hopkins Walters titled, "Death under Chloroform." In spite of its intriguing title, it proved to be no more compelling for Watson than bicycle treads had for Holmes.

At half two in the morning Watson joined Holmes in his room. At two fifty they left the hotel and walked to where Nikolos had parked his coach a short distance beyond the entrance to the Grand Bretagné. Without speaking, Holmes and Watson entered the coach, Nikolos chucked the reins, called a soft word of encouragement to his small bay, and drove to the residence of the ambassador.

At three o'clock the coach pulled up to the front of the residence where Bikelas, and a man neither Holmes or Watson recognized, were waiting on the front seat of a wagon. As Holmes and Watson climbed down from their carriage, an anonymous call was being made to alert the Greek police to a disturbance on Metaxes Street. The caller insisted on remaining anonymous. While all area police converged on a non-existent disturbance, Holmes, Watson and Bikelas unloaded two small crates from the back of the wagon under the watchful eye of the man accompanying Bikelas. The antiquities dealer never introduced the man, but all knew him as Bikelas' friend from the Museum of Archaeology. Using the key given him by Lord Sterling, Holmes opened the door to the ambassador's residence. Twenty minutes later their work was finished. At about the same time, the police ended a thorough search of Metaxes and surrounding streets, and concluded someone had played a trick on them. With a mix of epithets directed at the telephone, its inventor, and an unknown user, the police returned to their posts around the city.

For the third and last time, Holmes cautioned Bikelas about keeping secret the evening's activities, and promised the anonymous museum archaeologist all would be set right before the Museum reopened. Nothing was needed beyond a sharp look to give final warning to Nikolos. He grunted understanding, and climbed atop the carriage to return his passengers to their hotel. The whole of the evening's activity had taken less than forty minutes.

The reception area of the Grand Bretagné Hotel, bustling during the day with guests, porters and reception staff, was now populated by a single clerk who made effort to give them the cheery greeting expected of him, a greeting they made no effort to reciprocate. They wanted only their beds, and risked no diversion from their goal.

The day Lestrade had promised Watson having passed, at nine in the morning of the following day he made ready to visit the ambassador's home in company with Albert Needham. A somewhat red-faced Oswald Benton announced that he would join them, revealing that the Foreign Office had asked him to investigate Lady Sterling's purchases as well — not, he assured Lestrade, as any criticism of him, but just to get another pair of eyes on the situation. Lestrade was little mollified, feeling that his own vision was more than sufficient.

The Inspector maintained a stony silence during their carriage ride. Benton recognized Lestrade's resentment, and maintained an interest in Athens' scenery throughout the ride. Only Needham made an effort to fill the silence his fellow passengers created, advising them of his unexpected delight with the Olympic Games. He explained that, since the Museum of Archaeology remained closed throughout Easter week, he found himself at a different sporting venue almost every day. Without waiting for an expression of interest in his activities, Needham rattled on to describe them.

"I don't know if you've seen him, but our Mr. Flack seems to have wings on his heels. He simply left his fellow runners in the dust — as the man next to me said. A very colorful expression I must say, and very descriptive of Mr. Flack's efforts."

"And Mr. Elliot is quite an impressive man. He did very well with the lifting of weights, although I believe he was treated most unfairly in one of his events. Our side had entered a protest, but the judge insisted the Danish gentleman won."

"And if you missed seeing Mr. Holmes with his sword play, you really missed a treat. He was a regular D'Artagnan out there. Stabbing at his opponent, jumping back, then coming forward again. A great clashing of swords by both men. It was as exciting as anything I've seen. And I will tell you, even though Mr. Holmes lost his match, he was a credit to the country."

Needham paused to allow for comments from his fellow travelers. None was forthcoming. Their absence slowed, but did not stop his continuing effort to talk his way to a level of comity among the three men.

"Of course, I'm still hoping to get to the Museum, It would be a terrible shame to come to Athens and never get to it. I did get to the major archaeological sites — the Acropolis and the Parthenon of course, and a great many of the lesser known sites as well. I could never forgive myself if I missed seeing those." Needham spent the rest of the trip recounting his impressions of the historic sites he had seen, those impressions running the gamut from ecstasy to awe-struck, with an occasional smiling acknowledgment from his companions the only exchange he was able to stimulate.

Upon their arrival at the ambassador's residence, Needham dropped the role of affable companion, and became the sober-minded expert on Greek antiquities he had been commissioned by the Foreign Office to be. Lestrade and Benton remained grim-faced and independent, while intent on fulfilling identical responsibilities.

Mrs. Kasiris greeted them at the door, her impassive expression suggesting she was unsurprised by their visit. Benton pretended ignorance of the housekeeper, and all three men took turns introducing themselves to Mrs. Kasiris. She lent herself to Benton's deception although she couldn't prevent the beginnings of a smile on greeting him.

"We're here to see the Greek antiquities Lady Sterling recently purchased for the house," Benton reported. "It's part of an inventory we're conducting for the British Foreign

Office. Nothing that need concern you. If you could just show us where the pieces are located."

Mrs. Kasiris nodded her understanding and led them to the parlor where she did her best to melt into the background. Benton and Lestrade looked around the room as if assessing the worth of its contents. Needham walked straight to a piece of pottery depicting orange-colored dancing men, most nude, some with folds of drapery trailing behind, all set against a black background. He stopped just short of the piece as if an invisible wall kept him from getting any closer. He spoke to the two men, but continued staring at the pottery.

"It's a Euthymides." He was breathless. "I've only seen one other Euthymides in my life. There are only eight. Anyway, there are only eight we know of. It's a glorious piece. What's called an amphora. It's five hundred BC, maybe five hundred fifty."

"What's a Euthermides?" Benton asked.

"Euthymides. And it's not a what; it's a who. Euthymides was a potter, a very great potter."

"Then, it has some value?"

Needham made a noise sounding alarmingly like a gagging reflex that Mrs. Hudson could have told them was the archaeologist's best approximation of laughter. "I'd say so. It's almost priceless."

He turned to look at a small statue of a nude boy with one arm chipped off. He never moved from the spot, even as color seemed to drain from his face.

"Unbelievable. It's magnificent. It's by Phidias or perhaps someone from the Phidias school. A great piece. I don't know how Lady Sterling did it. She has managed to secure wonderful artwork."

"You mean the statue is also valuable?" Benton made no effort to contain his bewilderment.

"Extremely."

175

Benton felt he had no choice but to reveal he was not a stranger to the ambassador's residence. "I don't recognize these pieces from when I was here a few days ago. Mrs. Kasiris, have these items always been here?"

Mrs. Kasiris screwed her face into a mask of confusion, English having suddenly become an obscure language. "What does this mean, 'these items'?"

Benton scowled. "The statues and things. Were they here when I came to see you?"

Mrs. Kasiris shook her head slowly back and forth, the mask firmly in place. "Always have old things in parlor."

Lestrade recalled Watson's request that he postpone the visit to the ambassador's residence by a day, and his admonition that knowing the reason for the postponement could jeopardize his career. For once in his life, he was content to be uninformed. He was certain Benton's recollection was correct, Mrs. Kasiris' confusion was a sham, and Holmes and Watson had had a busy night involving activities that were very likely in violation of one if not several laws.

Needham was unconcerned about Benton's frustration, indeed was unaware of it. His focus was on the unexpected discovery of a treasure trove of antiquities. "Mrs. Kasiris, are there more items Lady Sterling purchased?"

The meaning of "items" having become suddenly clear, the housekeeper led the group to the dining room where Needham swooned anew over a vase depicting two figures the archaeologist identified as Achilles and Ajax at play. He identified the artist as Exekias, and again wondered at Lady Sterling's astoundingly astute purchases. The last piece available, a drinking vessel in the shape of a horse's head by an artist Needham identified as Brygos, excited a final shriek of excitement from the archaeologist.

"I am delighted to have had the opportunity to see this magnificent art which is uniformly of museum quality —

provided we are speaking of a first-class museum. Frankly, I see no reason for my having come all this distance to report the obvious. The man who questioned the authenticity of these pieces was obviously appallingly ignorant of Greek antiquities. Lady Sterling — may she rest in peace — was clearly a fine judge of art and managed to acquire an astounding collection with whatever money she was provided."

"I will be reporting Mr. Needham's findings to the Yard and to Whitehall," Lestrade stated. "I presume you will be doing the same, Mr. Benton."

Benton threw his hands in the air. "If that's Mr. Needham's judgment, I will, of course. I'll tell you frankly. I simply don't understand it. I could swear things were different when I was here earlier." He pursed his lips and shrugged. "In any event my assignment is complete. Now, if we can get on back to the embassy I have a tennis match to prepare for — actually two matches."

With that, they took their leave of Mrs. Kasiris, later to write reports that would close the book in the matter of alleged fraudulent purchases of Greek artifacts. There would be left only the middle of the night return of the museum quality antiquities to the museum from which they had come, Mrs. Kasiris' return of the copies of relics, temporarily housed in the attic, to their places in the parlor and dining room, and Lord Sterling's return of the money diverted by Lady Sterling to meet her parents' needs. In Acharnes, the Baron and Lady Martinson had slept soundly through the nighttime machinations undertaken on their behalf, and awakened to take pleasure in the luxurious furnishings those machinations guaranteed them.

The ride back to the embassy was again dominated by an exuberant Albert Needham, now consumed with a new enthusiasm. The Greek artifacts he had seen at the ambassador's residence had banished from his mind the

177

Olympic achievements that entirely occupied it earlier. Nominally addressing his two companions, his speech consisted chiefly of a variety of superlatives loosely connected to an occasional noun, by which he described the amazing, exciting, wonderful, beautiful, exquisite, unmatched, astounding and extraordinary artworks he had been privileged to see. His soliloquy relieved Lestrade and Benton of any need to deviate from their barely maintained tolerance of each other. At the journey's end, the two men achieved a single moment of cooperation. Before exiting the coach, and during a momentary lull in Needham's explanation as to why Exekias was the finest exponent of black figure art, Benton observed that it would be well for the two of them to present reports that were without conflict on key points. Lestrade granted Benton's point, and they set about determining the broad outlines, and some of the specific language of the reports each would be sending to their superiors. With that, the three men exited the coach together before entering the embassy separately.

The Inspector was now free to give his full attention to the double murder the Yard had instructed him to investigate, and he was anxious to do so. The man with whom he would be coordinating those efforts was, however, only just waking from a long and active night; and the woman, with whom that man would be collaborating, was traveling to the central Athens post office to send a telegram, whose response she was confident would affirm the results of her own investigation.

She couldn't chance sending the telegram through the hotel and its bilingual operator, and she couldn't be certain the operator at the central post office would have sufficient English to work with her. Mrs. Hudson needed an intermediary who was trustworthy, and although they hadn't yet met, she felt certain from the reports of her colleagues,

Miss Kannapolis would fill that role. More to the point, she knew no one other than Miss Kannapolis who could fill that role. Arriving at the post office she searched for the person Holmes had described as "a small, slim woman with long black hair, attractive in a nervously twitchy way." As it turned out, the person in question found Mrs. Hudson.

Emerging from the doorway of a tailor's shop a few doors down from the post office, a soft voice sounded hesitantly at Mrs. Hudson's back.

"Excuse, please. Are you Mrs. Hudson?"

Turning to the voice, she found a woman who fit perfectly Holmes' description. "I am Mrs. 'Udson, and I thank you for comin', Miss Kannapolis. I 'ope I'm not causin' you to miss your lunch by meetin' at this time." Mrs. Hudson smiled her apology.

"No, of course not, Mrs. Hudson, I'm happy to help. Edward didn't tell me what it is you want me to do, only that it's for Mr. Holmes." At the last she lowered her voice further, becoming nearly inaudible, and looked to either side of Mrs. Hudson as if to make certain there would be no one to overhear the illegal act she was certain she would be asked to perform.

Mrs. Hudson acted to allay Miss Kannapolis' fears. "I simply need your help with translation, Miss Kannapolis. I 'ave to send a very important telegram for Mr. 'Olmes, and I am afraid the telegraph operator won't 'ave English."

Miss Kannapolis nodded several times to make clear her understanding, although her troubled expression remained firmly in place.

Entering the post office, they walked to a standing desk just vacated by a self-important looking businessman. Mrs. Hudson withdrew from her purse two sheets of paper, one covered with writing and the other blank. She found a pencil as well, and handed the blank sheet and pencil to Miss

Kannapolis, then used the desk to smooth out the sheet with writing.

"I will read to you in English what you need to copy down in Greek for givin' to the man who does the telegraphin'."

Miss Kannapolis took the pencil in hand, fixed a fierce look of concentration on her face, and declared herself ready. For the next few minutes Mrs. Hudson dictated the English version of the telegram that would be sent in Greek, addressed — with unintended appropriateness — to London's Diogenes Club. She was unconcerned about its arrival at Mycroft's door in Greek. He would have all of the Foreign Office available to him for translation — indeed all of the government. She added instructions for him to send his response from a post office rather than a government office, and address it to her at the hotel. It would, she was certain, appear sufficiently pedestrian to avoid prying eyes. She had Miss Kannapolis read the message back to her translated from the Greek in which she had taken it down, made two alterations, then had her read it back again. Satisfied finally that they had it right, she let Miss Kannapolis lead her past a row of caged windows until they came to one with what she was told was the word tilegrăfima above the cage.

The man behind the bars was just finishing up with an older man with deep-set sad eyes wearing a somewhat frayed dark jacket. From the dirt beneath the fingernails of his calloused hands, Mrs. Hudson knew him to be a man still engaged in manual labor in spite of his age. His careful handling of the papers returned to him by the telegrapher, the jacket he wore in the warm weather, and his subservient manner as he bent to the task of thanking the telegrapher, indicated both the importance of his mission and the infrequency with which it was conducted. Mrs. Hudson was struck, as well, and far less sympathetically by the telegrapher's supercilious air as he accepted the old man's gratitude as though it were his by right.

The old man bowed his way from the telegrapher's cage, creating a space quickly filled by Mrs. Hudson and Miss Kannapolis. Mr. Akiros, as a small sign in Greek and English at a corner of his window identified him, asked a question Mrs. Hudson inferred to be a version of, "What can I do for you ladies?" Although spoken in Greek, his condescending tone transcended language.

More accustomed to such behavior than Mrs. Hudson believed anyone should be, Miss Kannapolis smiled and nodded before timorously requesting his assistance, showing him the paper she had transcribed and gesturing to Mrs. Hudson as she spoke.

Mr. Akiros looked doubtfully from Miss Kannapolis to Mrs. Hudson as if finding it unimaginable that the two women could produce a coherent message. From that point on, Mrs. Hudson became an increasingly exasperated observer of the exchange between Miss Kannapolis and Mr. Akiros. The telegrapher appeared to call for frequent clarifications of Miss Kannapolis' writings, pretending to barely controlled anguish over the difficulty she was creating for him. Miss Kannapolis smiled piteously, spoke in tones that sounded to Mrs. Hudson far too deferential, and was altogether far too accommodating of the officious bully. Twice she questioned Mrs. Hudson about a requested change in wording; twice Mrs. Hudson was adamant that her version be the one transmitted. Each time Miss Kannapolis explained Mrs. Hudson's intransigence to Mr. Akiros in penitent tones only to have the telegrapher sneer his acquiescence before continuing.

He read the document a final time, and sharing a last dark scowl with his two customers, he threw a hand in the air, issued a very audible groan, and turned to tap out the message. When he was done, he looked to Mrs. Hudson and tossed off another few words. Speaking as though sharing a secret, Miss Kannapolis informed Mrs. Hudson that Mr. Akiros wanted six drachmas. She set the money in the small valley beneath the bars of the telegrapher's window, then scraped Miss Kannapolis' notes, and what she assumed was a receipt from the same cavity. Even before she had recovered the materials, Mr. Akiros was looking past her to the young woman next in line, and asking her business in the arrogant tone to which he believed himself entitled.

There was now nothing more for Mrs. Hudson to do until she received a response from Mycroft Holmes. She was certain she would then have in hand the evidence to support her conclusion about the murderer of Lady Sterling and the German courier. Until then, there was the Olympics and some unfinished business.

After taking Miss Kannapolis back to the drapery shop where she was employed, Mrs. Hudson directed the coachman to return her to the hotel where she planned to reunite with colleagues she hoped would be rested from their nighttime adventures. She found them in the dining room, where they had completed late and prosaic breakfasts of eggs, bacon, toast, and tea they had convinced a reluctant kitchen staff to prepare. They were barely speaking, instead puffing contentedly on pipes. Everything pointed to the success of their mission.

"I see everythin' went well at the ambassador's 'ome."

"Better than well, Mrs. Hudson," said a smiling Watson. "Lestrade stopped by earlier to confirm that Mr. Needham sent a telegram to the Foreign Office expressing his satisfaction that the artifacts in the ambassador's residence are clearly genuine and of the highest quality. He and Benton have already sent telegrams that are less flowery, but carry the same message. Lestrade also requested that he not be told where those antiquities had come from, but expressed the hope they find their way back." Both Watson and Holmes made gurgling noises deep in their throats in an effort to stifle the laughter that threatened to explode past their defenses.

"And what have you been up to, Mrs. Hudson?," Holmes asked after sending forth a stream of white smoke in the direction of the room's high ceiling.

"I 'ad some questions for Mr. Mycroft, and sent off a telegram just before comin' to see you."

Holmes' eyes widened as he removed the briar from between his teeth; Watson grunted his understanding of the message Mrs. Hudson was delivering. Sending a telegram to Mycroft signaled that Mrs. Hudson was putting the last pieces together before identifying the killer.

"And what is it you wanted to learn from my brother?"

"I'm not ready to say just yet. Not until I'm sure I'm not a ways off base. But I'll tell you everythin' as soon as I hear from Mr. Mycroft. For now, I'm thinkin' we might do well to support our boys at the Games."

Neither man expected Mrs. Hudson to be any distance off base. Nor, indeed, did Mrs. Hudson. However, both men knew it would be pointless to press the issue, and decided instead that supporting "our boys" was their wiser course. Having learned that one of their boys, Durand Ramsay, had competed that morning in the military pistol event and failed to advance, they were feeling an urgency about becoming a visible source of support for the remaining athletes.

The afternoon would see swimming in the Mediterranean, shooting with the military rifle and free rifle, and the finals of the tennis tournament, but the events that would capture their attention would be wrestling and bicycle races. Mrs. Hudson would take a carriage to the Panathenaic Stadium, the site of the opening day ceremony, to cheer for Launceston Elliot.

Holmes and Watson felt obliged to cheer for Keeping and Battel, having championed their participation in the Olympic Games. At the Velodrome three bicycle races were scheduled, with two additional races to be held the following two days. Before going their separate ways, they agreed to meet for dinner and to invite Lestrade to join them.

Chapter 9.
Battel's Race

At both athletic venues, the detectives found the Greek audiences boisterously ebullient. The day before, Spiridon Loues, a runner about whom virtually nothing was known, had won the marathon, defeating Edwin Flack among others. The one thing that was known about Loues was the only thing of real consequence to the Greek populace. Spiridon Loues was one of them. His was the first victory by a Greek athlete, and it came in the event created to replicate the mythical run from Marathon to Athens by Phiddipides to announce a great military victory more than 2400 years earlier. That the messenger dropped dead immediately after his arrival had done nothing to dampen the resolve of the seventeen men who began the race, or the interest of the thousands who followed its progress. Having a Greek runner the victor, in perhaps the most iconic of Olympic events, restored national pride, and made the youngster more than a hero, it made him a national treasure.

At the Panathenaic Stadium, the crowd settled back to enjoy the wrestling matches that included two Greek competitors, a Hungarian and a German, as well as Elliot. In spite of marked differences in the weights of the contestants, there was to be a single winner, and the crowd was confident that man would be one of the two Greeks. The crowd's cheerful complacency did not last beyond the first round of matches. Both Greek athletes advanced, but found themselves pitted against each other in the semi-finals. The winner's opponent would be the five foot, four inch German wrestler, who had easily and inexplicably dispatched the six foot, four inch Elliot, who had himself easily dispatched the Hungarian in a preliminary round. Hours later, when the finals match between the victorious Greek and his German competitor was called due to darkness, the crowd was more exhausted than exhilarated, and many were resigned to their champion's defeat the following day. Mrs. Hudson reflected the crowd's disappointment as her own champion was nowhere to be found, having dressed and returned to the hotel. It was just as well, she had no words of comfort to offer that would be adequate to the situation.

Holmes and Watson were equally unsuccessful in their efforts to root to victory their British colleagues. Two races were run: a single lap time trial, and a 2,000 meter sprint. The crowd of 7,000 saw their Greek champion do no better than second in both races, finishing behind Paul Masson, a lanky Frenchman with close cropped dark curly hair and a trim moustache, who rode his bicycle with his nose to the handlebars and his bottom the highest point of his body. Whatever the aesthetics, he was clearly the best of the day's racers. The two riders who had spent the early part of the day completing chores in the kitchen of the British embassy, finished fourth and fifth in the single lap time trial. As the day wore on, the damp, chilly air combined with the losses suffered by the Greek cyclists served to create a gradual, but persistent exodus from the Velodrome.

One man countered the trend and pushed his way through the exiting crowd. Lestrade, too, had come to give support to his countrymen. Spotting familiar faces, he settled himself beside Holmes and Watson to prepare for the third and last race of the day. It was the 10,000 meter bicycle race. As it turned out, neither British cyclist was entered, and no Greek finished in the top three. Again, Masson with his unorthodox riding style was the victor, this time followed by one of his countrymen.

"There's still tomorrow," Watson observed, but there was no enthusiasm in his voice.

"And the day after that," added Holmes with only slightly more spirit.

"Are you saying there are still more cycling contests scheduled?" Lestrade asked.

"Two," Watson informed him. "They're both distance events and very demanding. Tomorrow is the cycling marathon. It follows the same course as the running marathon although it doubles the distance. The day after is the last event of the Olympics. It's a twelve hour race. Whoever has gone the greatest distance around the track in a twelve hour period is the winner."

"That's extraordinary," Lestrade said. "I'm exhausted just thinking about it. Will our English boys be competing?"

"That's our understanding," Holmes said.

"Then we must be here to cheer them on — at least some of the time," Lestrade urged, and Holmes and Watson readily agreed, although neither they nor Lestrade sought to give meaning to "some of the time." As planned, Holmes and Watson invited Lestrade to join them at dinner to review where things stood in their joint investigation. Lestrade enthusiastically agreed, volunteering a restaurant he had heard about from Battel where they could get more authentically Greek food than their hotel restaurant offered. Lestrade's parting words before returning to the embassy were to encourage Holmes and Watson to bring Mrs. Hudson with them to dinner.

"I appreciate that your Mrs. Hudson will have little to add to our discussion, but I should hate to think of her eating by herself in a strange city."

Holmes promised to bring her with them, regretting only that the poor woman would be bored to tears by an exchange that would be so far removed from her interest or understanding. Watson grunted what Lestrade took to be agreement, and Holmes knew to be something else.

Nearly a dozen tables spilled out onto the narrow street outside Damigos. Two men, well into their 50's, sat at one, ignoring the plates before them in favor of a heated argument, flailing arms and pointed fingers accompanying their raised voices. As one man filled the glass of the other from the half full wine bottle, it became apparent these were old friends engaged in argument as familiar as it was turbulent. A second table was taken by a neatly, but not finely dressed young woman who closed her eyes after a first taste of the dish before her, while the man with her smiled his satisfaction. He reached across the table to take her left hand, and reverently stroked the wedding band she wore. That drew a smile from Mrs. Hudson, who recognized the couple as newly married, their modest dress and the absence of an engagement ring to go with her wedding band indicated they were enjoying a celebratory dinner somewhat beyond their means. At a third table a bearded man with rimless glasses sat alone reading a newspaper. The chalk on the right sleeve of his coat and the collection of workbooks protruding from his well stuffed briefcase identified him as an educator. None of the people who had undergone Mrs. Hudson's brief study paid any attention to the middle-aged woman and her two male companions as they entered the restaurant.

Lestrade was already waiting for them. He had taken a table near the kitchen, normally an undesirable location, but one where disturbance from other diners would be unlikely. He stood until Mrs. Hudson was seated, then passed around the menus the waiter had left at his instruction.

"I hope you like this place. They call it a taverna. Mr. Battel wrote down some things he recommended we try. In particular, he suggested the saganaki as a starter and the pastitsio for our entree." Lestrade enunciated the two dishes slowly, reading from the slip of paper he had brought.

The Inspector's reading earned him tolerant smiles from Watson and Mrs. Hudson, neither of whom had any intention of straying from the baked lamb and chicken dishes that had become staples of both their diets, and were pictured on the menus prepared for non-Greek speaking customers. Holmes, not to be outdone in willingness to brave the unknown, acted in concert with Lestrade in ordering both dishes Battel had suggested. A short time later two small dishes of a yellowish-white block of cheese were brought to the table where the waiter first drenched them in ouzo, then set them afire, shouting "Opa" in unison with the few other diners scattered around the room. Handing each dish to Holmes and Lestrade, he spoke the single word, "saganaki." Holmes clapped his hands in delight while Lestrade grinned broadly. Watson and Mrs. Hudson maintained their reserve, the Doctor's only response was to permit his eyebrows to venture a short distance into his forehead before quickly recalling them to their accustomed position.

Taking a sip of the Retsina wine he had ordered for the table — again on Battel's recommendation—Lestrade asked, "Have you heard about Benton winning the singles tennis competition, then teaming with a German player to win the doubles? There was some feeling about that at the embassy I can tell you — I mean, his teaming with a German — and I wasn't too thrilled myself. It won't surprise me if our people refuse the award, and I wouldn't blame them a bit."

"Well said, Lestrade," Watson brought a fist down on the table threatening the glasses of wine. "It's clearly bad form on Benton's part."

Holmes' face wrinkled in disapproval. "I'm not sure I agree, Watson. One doesn't get many chances in life to win medals." Holmes looked absently to an empty place on the far wall before continuing. "If there's the chance for one, I say take it. Not at all costs to be sure. But it's not as if we're at war with the Germans."

While Watson harrumphed his disagreement, Lestrade acted to calm waters that threatened to become roiled. "Perhaps at this point we should move to a discussion of our joint investigation and leave to later a consideration of

Benton's behavior. I know you'll be pleased with the success of one part of our investigation." Whatever discord might have been brewing moments earlier was gone as Holmes and Watson leaned in toward the Inspector in anticipation of his news. Mrs. Hudson alone sat back in her chair, although she was no less interested in the Inspector's report.

"I had a meeting with Coopersmith late this afternoon after I got back from the bicycle races, and he gave me leave to share with you what he told me. Mind you, it's all very hush, hush, but Coopersmith thought it only right I tell you the contents of the two telegrams he got from the Foreign Office, what with your involvement with all that's gone before."

"First, you'll be pleased to learn the Yard and the Foreign Office were greatly relieved to learn that the relics purchased by Lady Sterling are genuine. That finding very likely averted a nasty crisis — it certainly saved Lord Sterling's career — anyway, the issue is now considered closed." Lestrade took another small sip of his wine before continuing. "Officially, that removes Bikelas from our list of suspects. He would have no reason to threaten or harm anyone over the sale of authentic relics." Lestrade's raised eyebrow reflected his awareness that he was venturing into waters whose depth was unknown to him, but was well understood by his fellow diners. "It doesn't explain the threatening telephone call, but perhaps there is no explanation — at least none we need be concerned about."

Lestrade looked across the table to Holmes and Watson and found two sphinxes, two uncomfortable sphinxes, unhappy with having to keep from Lestrade the truth about the threatening telephone call. Both knew if that truth were spoken, Lestrade would have no choice but to conduct the thorough investigation he would see as his responsibility. That would ultimately reveal the nighttime activities undertaken on behalf of the Sterlings and Martinsons. There was the danger that the altruistic nature of those activities might not be appreciated by Lestrade's colleagues to whom he would be duty bound to make report. And so, all remained silent until the Inspector spoke again.

"By the way, there was word of a disturbance in a street not far from the ambassador's residence the night before we visited. It seems that police from all over the area were summoned, only to find there was no disturbance. I'd call that a strange coincidence, wouldn't you, Mr. Holmes?"

Holmes had finished the saganaki, and pushed his plate away to make room for the next course. He patted the napkin to his mouth before responding. "I don't think it's all that strange, Lestrade. Now that you have people using these telephone things, it seems to me inevitable the police will receive a great many calls from people who think they see something when there's really been nothing at all."

Lestrade smiled indulgently at Holmes' suggestion, choosing to ignore the fact that he hadn't mentioned the use of a telephone to alert the police. "Perhaps so. At any rate, everyone is pleased with the outcome, and maybe that's all that's important. And there's more good news."

Before he could continue, their waiter arrived, his face reflecting the strain of delivering a tray overflowing with the four main courses to be served his table. Everyone at the table watched in silence as each course was set before its recipient. When he was done, the waiter refilled the wine glasses of the three men and Mrs. Hudson's water glass, gave the table a small part of a bow and returned to the kitchen. For the moment, the Inspector's second topic was tabled as each of them took a tentative taste of their dishes. All came away satisfied, and there was a round of hearty congratulations for Lestrade, and appreciation to Battel for the choice of restaurant.

The Inspector smilingly acknowledged their compliments before returning to the good news he had promised. Once again, he paused to warn them of the confidential nature of the information he was about to share.

"A second telegram came while I was still with Coopersmith. It seems our two young messengers made excellent time getting to London, and the letter they were carrying has, by now, made its way to the Prime Minister, and we can presume to the Queen."

"Excellent," pronounced Holmes, and he took an extra large bite of his multi-layered dish.

"Did Coopersmith reveal what was in the letter?" Watson asked.

"As much as they revealed to him, or maybe somewhat less. As I say, it's all very hush-hush."

In spite of his claim of only modest knowledge, Lestrade lowered his voice in answering Watson. "What I was told is that the letter makes clear there is no immediate threat of German aggression. Those were the words Coopersmith used: 'no immediate threat.'"

Watson broke the silence that followed Lestrade's report. "I suppose one could describe it as hopeful, in that there is still time to explore a rapprochement between countries."

"Or for each side to develop armaments," Holmes observed drily.

"You've been very quiet, Mrs. Hudson, I wonder, is there a woman's point of view?" Lestrade felt obliged to draw the woman he knew only as Holmes' landlady into the conversation.

Mrs. Hudson looked down modestly, and her response was initially directed to the baked lamb and potatoes on her plate. "Well, of course, I know it's all most complicated, and I'm sure there's parts beyond my understandin', but it seems to me that what with these Dutchmen — the ones they're callin' Boers — findin' diamonds and gold in their country, they're likely to fight, if it comes to that, to 'old on to their land.

When you add to that there bein' lots of Englishmen workin' for them, and them not always havin' the best of it accordin' to the papers, I'm afraid we could be in for it sometime soon. But, like you say, Inspector, it's just a woman's point of view."

While Mrs. Hudson sipped her water, Lestrade looked to her with eyes wide. He missed seeing the small smile on Watson's face, and the look of studied disinterest on Holmes'. "Most interesting, Mrs. Hudson. Most interesting."

Lestrade affirmed his words with several nods, then moved the conversation in a new direction. "There was something else Coopersmith told me that I can also share with you. The Foreign Office reported to the embassy that Mr. Fitzhugh and Miss Pershing will be delayed in returning to Athens. It seems they will be visiting Miss Pershing's family — not as part of the pretense we organized — a real visit to Miss Pershing's family, and there's expected to be a posting of the banns not long after. A rather surprising development, wouldn't you say?" Lestrade looked to his fellow diners.

Watson answered for all of them. "Let's say we're not entirely surprised." There were small smiles from the three representatives of the consulting detective agency. "Was there anything else in the telegrams we should know?"

"Nothing more in the telegrams, but Coopersmith wanted to be certain I understood that concern is mounting about the murders at the ambassador's home and Lord Sterling's disappearance. Parliament, in particular, is growing restive. 'Restive' was his term, and it sounds like a word that would come from Whitehall. Parliament, he told me, is being pressured by the public, and the public by the papers. In a word, Coopersmith is anxious for us to move as quickly as we can, especially with the Olympics coming to an end soon. He raised the possibility of our staying beyond that. I don't know what you would choose to do, Holmes; the Yard will almost certainly ask me to stay."

Lestrade swallowed the last of his pastitsio before continuing. "I confess I still feel I'm in the early stages of the investigation." He ran his napkin across his mouth, then tossed it beside his plate. "Things just aren't adding up for me. Looking at all the possibilities, the murders could even be the result of a botched robbery. Someone shows up at the house — maybe he's been watching it for a while and knows Lady Sterling is home alone at a certain hour — he unexpectedly runs into the German who challenges him. He kills him, and then Lady Sterling, maybe because he runs into her when he's looking for things to steal. Nothing's been stolen, but he could have simply panicked after the murders and run off."

"And, of course, you can't entirely rule out Lord Sterling as a suspect. He comes home unexpectedly early and finds his wife with another man. It's certainly a motive for murder even if you don't add in the gossip about the Sterlings' marriage. On top of which we have his running away, which we know is often the mark of a guilty man."

"Or of one who is terribly bereaved," Watson volunteered.

"Or bereaved," Lestrade granted. "Then there's the coachman, Nikolos. We know he stole the Dowager Empress' letter. But I'm inclined to look beyond him for the murders. Nikolos is a sneak thief, a petty criminal who's more likely to take advantage of a situation than to organize one, and unlikely, in any event, to kill two people to achieve his ends."

"So what then? If not robbery or jealousy, what reason can there be for the murders? As I say, things just aren't adding up for me. How do you see it, Mr. Holmes?"

Holmes smiled indulgently, acknowledging the Inspector's confusion as he sought to reduce his own.

"You've put your finger on the problem, Inspector." The smile deepened and was accompanied by a small, but knowing nod. "I don't want to keep you in the dark, Lestrade, but I also don't want to be premature. I can only assure you things are moving in the right direction."

"Mr. Holmes, is it possible you'll have an answer as soon as the next three days?"

Mrs. Hudson's eyes closed, and her head dipped ever so slightly.

"I'm sure of it," Holmes responded.

Buoyed by Holmes' reassurance, Lestrade drank the last of his wine, then turned his attention to the plate of kataifi that had been ordered for the table at the Inspector's insistence, arguing they had to try something other than baklava before returning home. After agreeing the choice was a good one, discussion turned to the bicycle marathon scheduled the next day. Seven men were known to have entered, but the talk around the table centered on Edward Battel, and his chances in the grueling event. Before leaving for their hotels and welcome sleep, all vowed once more to be on hand at the finish of the race regardless of the pressures they faced in having only three days to solve a double murder and locate the missing ambassador.

At first, Lord Sterling found to his surprise he rather enjoyed his masquerade as a member of the Hebrew faith. The assumption of the new identity each day, as instructed by Holmes, allowed him to disappear into another person, and to avoid, for a while at least, the weighty responsibility of being Lord Henry Edwin Sterling.

He found it easy enough to view himself as Absalom Tublin; the problem, he found, was the view of others toward Absalom Tublin. More particularly, it was the unevenness of that view and of never being certain of public reaction to Absalom Tublin. Most, to be sure, simply regarded the full-bearded figure in the long dark coat and hat with momentary curiosity and nothing more. A few smiled or nodded their respects. He thought they might be fellow Jews until he remembered that he wasn't himself Jewish. At least as many, however, looked at him askance, if not with hostility, one muttering, "Christ-killer," as he went past.

Places of business were equally uneven in their reactions. When he checked into his hotel, the clerk was pleasant, efficient and altogether exactly what Lord Sterling might have expected if he had been Lord Sterling checking in. Similarly, most restaurants were more interested in his business than in making a scene, but twice he was told he couldn't be seated without a reservation in spite of a sea of empty tables. Both times he restrained himself from demanding to see their reservations list, knowing it was unlikely any such list existed. When he was seated, it was typically at a less desirable table in the back, or one close to the kitchen or the washrooms. Waiters were sometimes abrupt or absent for long periods. Most reacted with surprise at the generous tips he was accustomed to leaving, and it occurred to him that they likely regarded it as an effort to combat a stereotype, rather than the gracious gesture he meant it to be.

Quite simply, the weight of the new identity was exceeding both his wishes and his expectations. Increasingly, he felt himself prepared to confront whatever danger Holmes believed threatened him — as long as he could again become Lord Sterling. In any event, Holmes had stipulated that the charade would not go beyond Wednesday, the day King George was scheduled to make presentations to the winners of the Olympic events. All the foreign dignitaries would be expected to be present. It would provide the proper stage for him to reemerge on the diplomatic scene. Secure in that thought, Lord Sterling was soon fast asleep.

With the new day, Mrs. Hudson readied herself for another trip to the Velodrome. Unlike her dinner partners, she would be present at the start of the day's bicycle race as well as its conclusion. She had given her word to Miss Kannapolis that together they would see the cyclists off, or, more accurately, they would see one particular cyclist off.

An unsurprisingly sparse crowd was gathered in the early morning to watch and cheer for the riders who would attempt the 87 kilometer race. Battel stood beside his bicycle, searching the crowd while waiting the two Greek words he had carefully rehearsed. He spotted Alexandra Kannapolis about the same time Mrs. Hudson did. He grinned broadly to her and made a half circle greeting with his right arm. He mouthed something that Mrs. Hudson could not divine, but whatever it was made Miss Kannapolis smile wistfully. Then came the words: Étoimos — Ready. And a beat later: Archi — Start. And the seven men were off.

Mrs. Hudson made her way around the Velodrome bleachers as the racers, hunched over their bicycles, circled the oval track before leaving the stadium to make their way over the rutted and pock-marked road to the town of Marathon. Miss Kannapolis had eyes for Edward Battel alone and was unaware of the short, somewhat stocky middle-aged woman making her away to where she stood. When the last of the men had disappeared into the tunnel headed for Athens' streets, Miss Kannapolis crumpled into a seat, the tears she could no longer contain streaming down her cheeks. Mrs. Hudson reached her just as the breakdown began. She took the empty seat beside her, and cradled her in her arms. For several minutes their conversation was reduced to Mrs. Hudson repeating "there, there" every few seconds, and Miss Kannapolis interrupting her dialogue with words in Greek, and an occasional, "Oh, Mrs. Hudson," and, "What am I to do?" All the while, people who had been sitting near Miss Kannapolis, having seen the racers off, edged their way to the stadium's exit, looking back frequently to the couple with mixed expressions of sympathy and curiosity.

Mrs. Hudson could guess at the reason for the outburst. Holmes had made her aware of Mr. Kannapolis' opposition to Battel as his daughter's suitor, as it had been reported to him when the two young people visited his hotel room. Undoubtedly, talk of the young man's fitness as a son-in-law had arisen again when she told her father of her intention to see his race, and the conversation had not gone well. As the tears began to subside, Mrs. Hudson had her suspicions confirmed.

"I don't know what to do, Mrs. Hudson. I don't want to live without Edward, and my father refuses us to marry. Edward wants me to go away with him, to Canada or Australia. He says someplace where we make a new life. He means someplace away from my father, but I can't do that." She wiped her eyes with her fists and took a deep breath before continuing.

"I could never leave father. Not after all he's done. My mother died when I was born. My father was mother and father to my sister and me. He was becoming important man, working in bank, and had to stop and become lower, a clerk, to spend more time with us. My sister left home and marry. She lives in Thessaloniki, and we see her only sometimes. My father says it's okay, she should have her own life, but I know it hurts him. If I left, I don't know what it might do to him, but I won't do such thing, Mrs. Hudson. And still, I can't leave Edward either."

"Why does your father object to Mr. Battel?"

There was again a wistful smile. "My father is very traditional man, Mrs. Hudson. He want me to marry nice Greek boy. And he thinks Edward will not be able to take care of me. I tell him Edward will not always be servant, but he doesn't listen. Edward is fine cook, and is saving to open his own restaurant. I help."

Mrs. Hudson had been listening intently as Miss Kannapolis reported Battel's and her litany of problems, and now asked a seemingly irrelevant question. "Tell me, Miss Kannapolis, what does your father think of King George?"

The young woman was perplexed by the question, but only hesitated a moment before answering. "He's like all of us. We love our King. The King, Queen Olga, and the Princes, Constantine and George. Why do you ask?"

Mrs. Hudson uncharacteristically ignored Miss Kannapolis' question. "This is very important. If you ask 'im, will your father go with you to the awards ceremony the day after tomorrow?"

"Yes, definitely he will go. King George will be giving a medal to Spiridon Loues. His win in marathon means all of Athens will be at awards ceremony."

Miss Kannapolis looked to Mrs. Hudson for further explanation, but found only a blank stare. "You come to the ceremony with your father, and if Mr. Battel only does 'is part, I believe things will work out." Mrs. Hudson held the young woman's hands in hers and smiled broadly. The two of them sat like that for several seconds before Mrs. Hudson released her.

"For now, I must get back to my 'otel. I will be back later, and we can watch the end of the race together."

At the hotel Mrs. Hudson learned there was still no telegram from Mycroft. She considered, then quickly dismissed the idea of sending a second telegram. It was unnecessary. Mycroft was well aware of the time constraints they were under. He would send word. She was sure of it.

Three hours later with midday still more than an hour off, Mrs. Hudson was again in the Velodrome, this time accompanied by Holmes, Watson, and Lestrade, as well as a reluctant Coopersmith. The deputy ambassador had decided it would be unseemly not to show support for a member of embassy staff, no matter the man's status. Miss Kannapolis came to the edge of the group to stand beside Mrs. Hudson. She held fast to a brave smile while accepting introductions to all but Holmes, the only person she had met before.

There were brief snatches of conversation interrupted by lengthy periods of silence. Mrs. Hudson and Miss Kannapolis shared the lengthy silences, but did not participate in the conversations. Across the arena, their Olympic colleagues, all their contests now completed, occupied two rows midway up the stadium seating. Elliot, Flack, Ramsay, and Benton were there, as well as Albert Needham. Only Goulding and Keeping were absent. Goulding, upset about his loss in the hurdles after promising certain victory, had left for England. Coopersmith had ruled that with Battel at the Olympics, it was essential Keeping remain in the kitchen.

Forty-five minutes after they were seated, the lead cyclist emerged from the dark of the tunnel, his face contorted with the pain he felt, his mouth open and his breathing coming in great gulps. Dirt covered one side of his uniform where he had fallen somewhere along the way, leading to his favoring the arm on his other side. The victoriously disheveled figure was not Edward Battel. When the crowd recognized the rider was Greek, there began an ovation that swelled to a size belying its sparse number. When it was done, facing an unknown, but almost certainly lengthy wait for additional finishers, the overwhelmingly Greek audience began a rapid exodus from the Velodrome. Miss Kannapolis had long since determined to wait forever for the man she hoped to make her fiancé, Mrs. Hudson would wait with her in hopes it would prove a considerably shorter time than Miss Kannapolis was prepared to endure; and Holmes, Watson and Lestrade would wait with Mrs. Hudson. Coopersmith would wait as well, unable to devise an acceptable justification for leaving.

It was another twenty minutes before the second finisher arrived looking every bit as bedraggled and exhausted as the man who had beaten him. His appearance spelled a second disappointment for Miss Kannapolis and all who had hoped to celebrate with her. The athletes across the way began to slowly exit the arena, making apologetic waves as they did. Only Elliot came to join them in their vigil which was now beginning to resemble a death watch. Battel, if he finished the race, would not be eligible for a medal as only first and second place were to receive that recognition. Even the weather was conspiring against the hopes of those remaining. The temperature was turning quickly from cold to frigid. Although no one spoke of it, all but Mrs. Hudson and Miss Kannapolis were pondering how to leave the arena with a modicum of grace if Battel was not the next finisher.

And then it became frighteningly apparent there would be no need to develop such a strategy. Bloodied from the scrapes of several falls, and grime-covered from the need to twice repair his bicycle, Battel circled the Velodrome oval in a glassy daze before collapsing at race's finish. Miss Kannapolis ran down the arena steps at an alarming speed to be at his side. Those who had been waiting with her hurried behind at an only slightly less reckless rate. Even Coopersmith jogged behind his more fit colleagues, his face showing the strain of either worry or his sudden exertions. Mrs. Hudson proceeded at a still more measured pace, although with a concern equal to those preceding her.

Battel gave Miss Kannapolis a weak smile; it seemed a struggle to work himself into anything more substantial. She simply spoke his name over and over again. The men lifted him gently to his feet, and standing on his either side, guided Battel's slow progress from the track to a bench in the infield. When he was seated with Miss Kannapolis beside him wiping blood and dirt from his face with the handkerchiefs volunteered by each of the men, he haltingly told the story of his race.

"The first half ... the ride to Marathon ... really hard ... so many holes ... stones. Had to be so careful." Battel looked around as if discovering his rescuers for the first time. "Is there water ... does anyone have water?"

All eyes turned to Coopersmith. He grimaced his unhappiness with the role thrust on him, but hurried off to fulfill its demands.

"It was the coming back that was a killer.... I don't know how many riders dropped out. ... I passed two I know ... maybe three. You know I was actually in the lead for a while.... The Greek rider ... he probably won ... had to fix his bike and I got past him." Battel's face crinkled into a near smile at the memory. "I think he got a new bike from someone. Anyway, it looked like a different bike when he went past me.... Which happened when I fell. I think it was the stones that finally got me. That's where I got most of this." He slowly raised an arm to point toward the blood on his face. "I don't think I broke anything, but my bike had to be fixed as best I could. That's when another rider passed me. I knew I couldn't win, but I had to finish. Nothing was gonna keep me from doing that." Battel looked defiantly around, as if daring someone to deny him that victory, before again making clear his frailty. "Is that water here?"

"It's almost here, darling," Miss Kannapolis reassured him, as Coopersmith came toward them as quickly as he dared without spilling the contents of the jug he carried. When Battel had refreshed himself sufficiently, he started toward the showers and changing room, leaning at times on Elliot who walked by his side. Holmes, Watson and Lestrade trailed behind, speaking words of support and encouragement. When Battel returned from the changing room somewhat cleaner and a great deal more refreshed, the men and Mrs. Hudson felt they could safely take their leave. All but Miss Kannapolis and Coopersmith left, the deputy ambassador explaining sheepishly he would see to it Miss Kannapolis and Battel got home safely, unexpectedly adding, "Mr. Battel's courage deserves at least that."

Mrs. Hudson had hoped for a higher finish from Battel. As it turned out, he was not only ineligible for a medal, but coming in third placed him last, as no other rider completed the 87 kilometer endurance test. Nonetheless, if Mr. Coopersmith could come to recognize his performance as courageous, she could hope that the person critical to her plans might see things the same way.

Walking through the hotel lobby, she was still thinking about what might be done to further Battel's heroic image when she was recognized by one of the reception clerks. He called to her that a telegram had arrived less than an hour earlier. With the precious envelope in hand, she led Holmes and Watson to the lift and then to her room. She took a seat on one of the two easy chairs, the men ignored the other chair and the chaise, and hovered over her as she eagerly tore open the telegram. She read it through, her head bobbing up and down as she finished each line. When she was done, she read it a second time, then handed the paper to Holmes, her face wreathed in a self-satisfied smile, making clear it was the news she expected. Holmes grunted his acknowledgment of the telegram's contents before handing it to Watson. When the Doctor was finished, he issued a long and solemn groan as he handed the single page back to Mrs. Hudson.

"You knew of this, Mrs. Hudson?"

"It's what I suspected, Dr. Watson. Now we know our man, it's time to talk about 'ow we plan to capture 'im. I 'ave some thoughts about that."

Thirty minutes later they were decided on a strategy. It was a little past one and there was a good deal to be done, but Mrs. Hudson turned the conversation to Battel and his bicycle race. She was surprised, but pleased to find both her colleagues had used the word "heroic" to characterize the cyclist and his performance. Watson went so far as to say Battel's race was heroic precisely because he lost, and knew he had lost while still on the course, but insisted on finishing in spite of the pain, the blood and the injuries — an observation that drew Holmes' vigorous assent. Mrs. Hudson now felt certain that if such disparate men as Mr. Coopersmith and her colleagues could hold the same view of Battel, that portion of her plan could definitely work. She also decided that she would never understand men and their sports.

They quickly reviewed the remaining events in the Games. Tomorrow, there would be the twelve hour bicycle race involving Frederick Keeping, the other kitchen staff member turned Olympic athlete. It would be the last competition of the Games, and be followed the next day with the King's awards. King George, himself, would present the medals to those finishing first and second in their events. It was understood there would be some special awards as well which the royal family was keeping a surprise. And then it was time to take up the tasks that would spell the success or failure of their efforts. With nods of understanding, and without further discussion, Holmes left to see Lord Sterling, while Watson went to the embassy to meet with Coopersmith and Lestrade. Mrs. Hudson would go to the ambassador's residence to visit again with Mrs. Kasiris. If there was time, they just might reward themselves with slices of baklava when they were done.

Chapter 10.
The Return of Lord Sterling

Holmes pounded three quick raps on the door of Absalom Tublin's room, then took a half step back, looking to his right and left while he waited impatiently for a response. The voice from behind the door was less questioning than demanding.

"Yes."

"It is I, Sherlock Holmes."

The door was opened by a figure who had shed the outer trappings of Absalom Tublin and become again Lord Sterling, British Envoy Extraordinary and Minister Plenipotentiary to Greece.

"Have you news, Mr. Holmes?"

"Good news, Lord Sterling. As we agreed, tomorrow your charade as Absalom Tublin will be over. More particularly, you can again take up your official duties at the embassy as of tomorrow morning, and move back into the ambassador's residence at the end of the work day. There will be scheduled a breakfast gathering for your staff and the Olympic athletes, and you can make clear your intent to resume your duties at that time. You'll need to let people know you can now be reached at home whenever necessary, although on that first day you expect to be so busy getting caught up on your work, you're not planning on leaving the office before seven."

"I don't understand. Does that mean you are near to catching the killer? Is it the case that I am no longer in danger?"

"We're not quite ready to make an arrest, although we are very close. But as to your being in danger, I'm afraid you are in a great deal of danger. Let me explain."

As Holmes did, the ambassador's eyes narrowed to a fierce squint that never left Holmes' bright, untroubled face.

Watson told Miss Osterkos that he wished to see Mr. Coopersmith. There was no asking if he had an appointment, or call for an intermediary to escort him to Coopersmith's office. On learning of his arrival, Coopersmith, himself, came forward to greet Watson and lead him to his office.

"How can I help you, Dr. Watson? I should tell you I have asked Battel ... Mr. Battel, to take the remainder of the day to recuperate. He will, of course, receive full salary while he does so." A smile of recognition for his own largesse became a broad grin as an additional thought occurred to Coopersmith. "I believe Miss Kannapolis is helping him with his recovery."

"I suspect you may well be right, Mr. Coopersmith. I rather hope you are. And I'm sure your action was much appreciated. The young man appeared to have nothing seriously wrong with him, but was certainly badly used and in need of rest." Pleasantries exchanged, Watson set his face to reflect the seriousness of the issue he was about to raise.

"I have a small request to make, Mr. Coopersmith, and there is also something important I need to share with you. First, as to the request, Mr. Holmes would like you to schedule a small breakfast tomorrow to celebrate our athletes. Nothing elaborate, just yourself and your people in a modest tribute to the young men who've come so far on behalf of Queen and country."

Watson was afraid he might have laid it on a little thick. But he needn't have worried. Coopersmith's only comment was a surprising concern about the second member of the embassy's kitchen staff. "You are aware that Keeping will be engaged in his own bicycle race tomorrow. It starts in the early morning as I understand it, and goes on for a total of twelve hours. To tell you the truth, I tried to argue the young man out of it, not because of the work that needs doing at the embassy, but because I was afraid for the young man's health — I mean, seeing the condition Battel was in after four hours. But Keeping means to give it a go anyway." Coopersmith sighed his disappointment before continuing. "In any event, I'll schedule a breakfast reception if that is Mr. Holmes' wish. It's an easy matter. The athletes are to come by late this afternoon to retrieve travel documents we're holding for them. I'll issue the invitations then. In return, let me ask you and Mr. Holmes to join me, and as many of the embassy staff as I can encourage to be at the Velodrome at the end of the twelve hours."

"We will be there, of course. There is, as I say, something else I need to share with you. But first, I must ask you to keep what I am about to tell you to yourself. I would remind you there is still a killer at large, and it is not too much to say that if what I am about to share with you were to be divulged, one life and maybe several more would be at risk." Watson allowed a small pause, not to build tension, he had done that, but to gather himself to provide the news he suspected Coopersmith might find more troubling than the mere threat to life. "I think it only right to alert you that Lord Sterling will be joining us in the morning, and will be taking up his duties immediately after the reception you will be hosting. I tell you this because it would be unfair for you not to be prepared for Lord Sterling's appearance. You've done an admirable job in his absence that I'm certain will be recognized." In fact, Watson had no idea if the job Coopersmith had done was admirable, and from his days in government service was reasonably certain it would not be recognized, but he felt it the proper thing to say in the circumstances.

There was again a pause as Coopersmith digested the unsurprising, but unwelcome news. The smile that he'd worn since the discussion of Battel's recovery was gone, and would not return for the duration of their conversation.

"Thank you, Doctor. It's kind of you to say. May I know where Lord Sterling has been, or whether there is any special reason for his appearing tomorrow?"

"I can only tell you Lord Sterling was profoundly affected by his wife's death, as I'm sure you can understand, and so elected to withdraw from the world for a while. He feels himself sufficiently recovered to return to the embassy and his residence, and is anxious to do so while there is opportunity to pay tribute to the Olympic team."

"I suppose Lord Sterling plans to be present for the awards ceremony."

"I'm certain of it."

There was yet another pause, and then as a seeming afterthought, Watson expressed a wish to visit briefly with Lestrade. Coopersmith offered to guide him to the Inspector's office, but Watson told him it wouldn't be necessary. Watson gave Coopersmith a final warning of the danger that was certain if the secret was not kept, and the deputy ambassador swore his declaration to reveal their conversation to no one. The two parted from each other with the correctness of strangers. Watson then went to repeat to Lestrade the plan he had heard described by Mrs. Hudson, a plan the Inspector would assume had come from Holmes.

At the ambassador's residence, Mrs. Hudson was greeted by Mrs. Kasiris with a warmth rooted in the conspiracy they had forged over an afternoon of food and drink — with a particular emphasis on drink.

Now meeting in the front parlor, Mrs. Kasiris no longer chose the least comfortable chair available, selecting instead the easy chair although again sitting stiffly near its edge. With a new found coyness, she extended an invitation to Mrs. Hudson.

"I have half bottle of ouzo left. Would you like?"

Mrs. Hudson laughed, remembering her experience with the other half of the bottle. "Perhaps some tea if it's not too much trouble."

Her laughter was joined by Mrs. Kasiris. "I will put up water," she said by way of excusing herself. When she returned, Mrs. Hudson remarked on the attractiveness of the small statues and bowls in the room, and Mrs. Kasiris observed she had recently gotten several compliments on items in the parlor and dining room. Their banter led to a second round of laughter and the further strengthening of the bond between them.

"Mrs. Kasiris, apart from once again 'avin' a look at your collection, I wanted to let you know that things will be gettin' back to normal as of tomorrow. Lord Sterling will be returnin' to work in the mornin' and will be comin' 'ome in the evenin'."

Mrs. Kasiris took in the information with a sudden sobriety. She was, for the moment, the dutiful housekeeper. But only for the moment. Her curiosity overwhelmed the reserve appropriate to her station, and the relationship forged over ouzo and mezedes made possible her making direct question. "Does your Mr. Holmes know the man who did the terrible things?"

"I think I can safely say Mr. 'Olmes is on the edge of findin' everythin' out, and wants you to know you 'ave an important part to play in makin' that 'appen."

Mrs. Kasiris looked warily to Mrs. Hudson. "What do I have to do?"

"Nothin' that will cause you trouble. You will 'ave to let three men into the 'ouse before Lord Sterling gets home. You know all three; there's Mr. Sherlock 'Olmes, Dr. John Watson and Inspector Lestrade. They will arrive a little after 'alf six, and Lord Sterling will be 'ome a little after seven. There is no need for you to stay that late 'owever."

The housekeeper nodded understanding. "Is there any more I must do?"

"You might give them a little something to eat."

Mrs. Kasiris grinned her understanding, and the two women spent the next half hour drinking tea, and sharing stories about the men with whom they worked, and then about the men they'd known. Mrs. Hudson found it easy to be her usual circumspect self when she talked about Holmes and Watson, less so when she spoke of Tobias. Mrs. Kasiris, too, took care in discussing Lord Sterling, but became far more open in telling of her feelings for Mr. Seropopoulos, taking full advantage of having available a confidant who would be leaving Athens in a few days. The information did not surprise Mrs. Hudson, but left her wishing for a way to somehow influence that situation. For the moment, she couldn't think of any.

By the time the athletes gathered for breakfast at half eight the next morning, Frederick Keeping had been on his bicycle for three and a half hours, and had circled the Velodrome more times than he knew. Already four of the seven entrants had dropped out of the race. Like his colleague, Keeping had no intention of doing anything less than finishing his race, no matter the pain, no matter the fatigue, no matter the struggle that lay ahead.

At the embassy, the achievement of the man Coopersmith was now calling Battling Battel was being shared with the few who had not heard about it, and nearly every athlete and embassy employee found opportunity to shake his hand, or pat him on the back. At Battel's and Coopersmith's urgings, all pledged to be at the Velodrome at five that evening to cheer for Keeping at the conclusion of his twelve hour race.

Lord Sterling made entrance to the reception after everyone had had a chance to fill their plates from the hastily

210

organized buffet, and seat themselves at the half dozen tables set around the reception area. His appearance led to a silence that was punctuated only by audible gasps from several of his staff, indicating that Coopersmith had kept his promise to Watson. Silence was followed by a sprinkling of applause, and two or three staff members standing to register their respect, but only Coopersmith approached the ambassador, vigorously shaking his hand and smiling, while making clear to everyone assembled how much Coopersmith believed he had been missed, and how pleased he was to have him back. When he was done speaking, Coopersmith stepped back to wait with others Lord Sterling's explanation.

The ambassador had come prepared. He stood before the long table that held the buffet, looking to familiar and barely known faces before speaking. Later, staff members would tell each other how his clothes seemed to hang from him, how he was no longer the bear of a man they had known. The black armband he wore over the sleeve of his gray frock coat doubtless explained that. Some would swear there was more gray in his beard, some that there was white as well. All took note of his voice — still with the air of command, but now mixed with just the smallest bit of restraint. Indeed, his whole manner seemed to suggest a restraint none of them had seen before.

"I am pleased to be back with all of you, especially on such a pleasant occasion. There have been all too few such occasions in recent days. As all of you know, I have suffered a terrible personal loss, for which reason I have been away from my post. Let me say to my staff in that regard that I thank all of you for carrying on with the work of the embassy under difficult circumstances with your usual high level of efficiency, and let me thank, in particular, Mr. Coopersmith, who I know provided outstanding leadership during that trying period." Lord Sterling paused to allow applause to build for his deputy. When none materialized, he began the applause himself, and the room soon rang with a somewhat desultory display of regard for the small man who nonetheless beamed his appreciation to the crowd and the ambassador.

Lord Sterling smiled benignly to Coopersmith, then turned back to the crowd. "I don't want to keep people from their breakfasts, but I do want to give proper respect to our great athletes gathered here. I have learned of your exploits, and I know many of you will be receiving medals from King George tomorrow. More than that even, I know that all of you have conducted yourselves with a skill and sportsmanship that brings honor to the Empire and our Queen. I only hope you take as much pride in your accomplishments as I do." The ambassador again began a round of applause, this one was joined with vigor by both those described and those celebrating them.

"Now, enjoy your breakfasts, and I urge you to follow the suggestion I heard Mr. Coopersmith give you as I entered, and please make yourselves available at the Velodrome at five o'clock for what we hope will be Fred Keeping's victory ride. I'm afraid I've been away so long, and have so much to catch up on that I won't be able to get away from here myself until late, not before seven I fear. But I won't ask anyone to stay with me." What was meant as humor was welcomed with relief. "Should I be needed for anything, I will be returning home tonight after leaving the embassy."

With that, Lord Sterling left his position at the buffet table, allowing a second assault on the table's contents by those whose initial foray had been merely exploratory. The ambassador went from table to table accepting condolences, thanking staff members, and greeting the athletes as each stated his name to Lord Sterling. Having learned the results of events, he congratulated Flack on winning two races, and Elliot on his weight lifting accomplishment, diplomatically ignoring the events each had entered and lost. He pretended meeting Holmes for just a second time, praising him for what he understood to be a heroic Olympic performance. He clasped Benton's hand in his two, expressing astonishment for his tennis victories. He patted Ramsay's shoulder and commiserated with him about his loss at the pistol range. He managed a smile for Albert Needham, and hoped he could stay until the Archaeological Museum opened.

A short time later, guests at the embassy began the somewhat lengthy process of taking their leave from Coopersmith and Lord Sterling. An unexpected melancholy settled on the Empire's teammates as each man recognized this might well be the last time he would come together with his fellow athletes, and that, in participating in the first modern Olympics, every one of them had played a part in something important, something remarkable, something that would come only once in their lifetimes.

The remainder of the day at the embassy was spent with Lord Sterling attending once more to the duties associated with being head of the British legation in Greece. Topping the list, and occupying a good part of the day, was a task Coopersmith had happily visited on him — planning for the visit of Princess Beatrice. His Deputy had informed him of the delicacy of the situation, given this would be the Princess' first international travel since the death of her husband, the Prince. The celebration would need to be muted, but not so muted as to appear somber. Then, there were the problems with the guest list. The Prince was German. That meant members of the German delegation would be honored guests, but not too honored. Great Britain and Germany were still at odds over the Jameson Raid and the German telegram to Kruger in the Transvaal. The orchestra might play some German airs. Mendelssohn and Schumann would be acceptable. Of course, the Germans would expect Wagner. Lord Sterling detested Wagner. Then, there was the food to be served at the banquet. Was there anything to be borrowed from German cuisine that might have a hint of subtlety, and not leave everyone feeling bloated? He knew of nothing. Fortunately, he still had more than two weeks to plan for the Princess' visit.

While Lord Sterling busied himself with affairs of state, the athletes, he had lately celebrated, spent the rest of the morning and the afternoon purchasing souvenirs and gifts for themselves, and for those at home they wished to remember, or they knew would expect to be remembered. Shortly after four-thirty, the first of the athletes and embassy staff, together with Lestrade, began finding seats in the nearly deserted Velodrome. A short time later they were joined by Holmes and Watson. By four forty-five a small section of the stadium had been taken over by an enclave from the British Empire.

What they saw astounded all and repelled many. Only two riders remained of the seven who had begun the twelve hour race. One was their colleague, Keeping, the other an Austrian named Schmall. The legs of both men were swollen well beyond normal size, their uniforms were filthy with excreta, and their bicycles weaved side to side, the riders too fatigued to maintain effective control. What couldn't be seen was that the riders hadn't eaten, had not been allowed a bathroom break, and had been given only sips of water. Keeping was sometimes in front, sometimes behind, but it was impossible to know who was truly ahead since the race's ultimate winner would be determined not by crossing the line first, but by the distance covered at the end of the twelve hours. Tears mixed with perspiration as the two men neared the five o'clock goal. So painful was the race for both competitors and spectators that, after the Olympics of 1896, the twelve hour bicycle race would never be held again.

At the race's end, the Austrian was declared the winner, having pedaled a single lap more than Keeping over the half day event. Relief rather than celebration was felt by the two cyclists and those few who were there to cheer them. Battel ran to the side of his teammate and co-worker, followed closely by Watson, who was concerned with examining Keeping to assess his need for medical care. They were joined by Holmes, Lestrade and those members of the Empire's Olympic family in attendance. All stood by silently, frowning their undivided attention on Keeping and Watson. Finally, Watson spoke to the anxiety the men felt.

"His vital signs are fine. He is simply exhausted, but there's nothing that food, drink and especially rest won't cure."

His audience breathed a nearly audible sigh of relief and, once assured of the man's safety, several backed away from the painful sight. Battel volunteered to stay and help care for Keeping, but Watson urged him to go on, knowing he would be anxious to see Miss Kannapolis. He advised Battel that he would monitor Keeping's medical condition, and together with Holmes and Lestrade, would get Keeping cleaned up and see to it he got home alright. Calling best wishes to the still groggy Keeping, and offering profuse thanks to the three men remaining with him, the athletes melted away to enjoy what for several would be their last night in Athens.

Thirty minutes later, a partly cleaned and now coherent Keeping was put into a carriage over the protest of its driver, who demonstrated with fingers to his nose and arms waving, that he could happily forego Keeping's business. Holmes' display of a fistful of drachmas was able to persuade him otherwise. With Keeping safely on his way, attention turned to the evening's work that lay ahead of them. The three men summoned a second carriage, directing this one to the ambassador's residence.

They would be more than a half hour earlier than Mrs. Kasiris expected, and fully an hour earlier than the ambassador had announced he would be leaving work. They had mutually agreed the additional time would allow them to prepare for the unexpected, and perhaps more importantly, to coax Mrs. Kasiris into providing them some dinner.

Once arrived, Holmes was again struck by the barren expanse leading up to the ambassador's residence. The absence of trees, bushes, or anything that might block one's view had dictated the strategy Mrs. Hudson had devised. The three men followed the gravel path to the front door where Holmes knocked loudly, but to no effect. As seconds threatened to become minutes, Holmes knocked still more loudly, now using a staccato beat. The Mrs. Kasiris who finally answered the door was not the Mrs. Kasiris any of them expected. The usually impeccably turned out housekeeper showed surprising disarray. Her face was flushed, locks of hair had escaped the hasty efforts of a brush or comb and fell unchecked behind an ear. Her blouse spilled part way over her waistband where it had been hastily tucked into her skirt. Holmes guessed preparation for the evening that lay ahead had exhausted the woman. He suspected the bed in an upstairs bedroom would be unmade and rumpled. He looked to the landing above and the railing that ran the length of its corridor, but there was nothing to see.

"Mrs. Kasiris," Holmes began, "I believe you'll remember Dr. Watson and myself from our earlier visit at the time of Lady Sterling's death, and you'll recall Inspector Lestrade was here just the other day with two gentlemen."

"I remember. And your Mrs. Hudson told me you come."

"Good. I don't want to alarm you, but what may not have been made clear to you is that Lord Sterling could be in serious danger, and we are here to make certain he is well guarded."

Sharply raised eyebrows were Mrs. Kasiris' only response to Holmes' statement. He was prepared for alarm or questions, or both, and took advantage of their absence to outline the events planned for the evening.

"We will need to examine the rooms on the ground floor to determine where we will station ourselves to best protect Lord Sterling. You should not plan to stay until Lord Sterling's arrival however. You could find yourself in the way, and you might even place yourself at risk."

Mrs. Kasiris pursed her lips tightly and set her jaw before speaking. "I stay and welcome the master. I not get in your way. You not even know I'm here." The housekeeper drew herself to her full height, and with a determined stare, gave her final words on the subject. "I stay."

Before Holmes could respond, she turned from him with a flourish. "You look at rooms. I make tea, and maybe find some biscuits."

Watson, who had remained behind talking with Lestrade while Holmes spoke to the housekeeper, heard only Mrs. Kasiris' last comment, and called after her, "Perhaps sandwiches, Mrs. Kasiris, I'm afraid we've had no dinner."

As Mrs. Kasiris proceeded to the kitchen at the end of the corridor, the men began study of the rooms to determine how they would deploy themselves for Lord Sterling's arrival.

"I take it you have good reason for believing our murderer will come tonight, Mr. Holmes?"

"I'm certain of it, Lestrade. I assure you our time will not be wasted."

"Then I take it you believe you know who the murderer is."

"I do. We need to wait for Lord Sterling's arrival, and very shortly thereafter all will be revealed."

"I must admit, Mr. Holmes, I find some aspects of our plan confusing. If the murderer will be coming to the house later, why not engage the police to station their people outside before he arrives."

"Because, Lestrade, there's just the bare lawn and no place to station anyone where they couldn't be seen. The murderer would see the place is guarded, turn away and leave. Even if the person were to be intercepted, he could claim to be simply paying his respects to the ambassador or manufacture some other reason for calling on him, and we would have no reason to hold that person, much less charge him with a crime. No, we've no choice other than to catch our murderer in the act, attempting to finish the job he started, which is why we must take every precaution to prevent his success. I have informed Lord Sterling of the danger, and he understands the necessity of this action."

Lestrade shrugged acceptance of Holmes' reasoning, and joined with him and Watson as they methodically inspected the rooms on either side of the corridor extending the length of the ground floor. To their left, after entering the house, was the front parlor with which they were already familiar. Across from the parlor was Lord Sterling's study, and beyond it a library accessible to the study through pocket doors, as well as having a door to the corridor. Beyond the parlor was the formal dining room where the body of Lady Sterling had been found, and beyond that the breakfast room, and then the kitchen and pantry, with the kitchen having a door to the outside for deliveries. Beyond Lord Sterling's study was a music room, a grand piano prominently capturing one corner, a violin lying on its top and a cello beside it; the room providing space for a party or an entertainment. The second landing corridor overlooking the ground floor was briefly considered. A row of rounded columns beneath an oak railing provided a tempting cover, but was determined to be unnecessary, although they agreed one of the upstairs bedrooms would be a fit location for Lord Sterling to wait until the downstairs action was completed. The three of them had no doubt they could overwhelm the intruder, and almost certainly capture the killer alive.

They made their way to the parlor where Mrs. Kasiris, now properly coiffed and neatly garbed, was again the dutiful housekeeper. She had set out a pot of tea and three cups, lemon slices, a small pitcher of milk, and a tempting assortment of biscuits. She smiled her way from the room, announcing she would bring some sandwiches as well. Over tea and biscuits, they worked out where they would wait for their quarry. Holmes would station himself in the library, Watson the breakfast room, and Lestrade would remain in the study. When the killer entered, Lestrade would move to his back while Holmes and Watson faced the killer head on. Satisfied with their strategy, each man checked his revolver, making certain yet again his weapon was ready.

Lord Sterling, too, had a revolver in readiness. Watson had taken him aside at the breakfast reception to advise him there was no need to arm himself for the evening, he would have three well-armed protectors poised to act on his behalf. Lord Sterling had smiled, nodded, thanked Watson, and afterward had removed the revolver he had put back in his desk, and slipped it into the pocket of his frock coat. He appreciated Watson's words, and was genuinely grateful for the bodyguards, but he had no intention of having others fight his battles for him. If, as Holmes believed, Pamela's murderer would appear at his home some time after his arrival, he would be the one to avenge his wife's death. He was confident no court on earth would convict him for killing his wife's assassin — certainly no British court.

Prepared for his own homecoming, he turned back to the small stack of papers that had been gathered for his attention. Having set aside the information about Princess Beatrice's visit, he began leafing through the several pages of a complaint lodged by the owner of a Greek taverna against two British visitors, who, having witnessed a friend's Olympic discus throw fall well short of the winning heave, sought comfort through the consumption of liberal quantities of claret — which was, by coincidence, the same strategy they would have employed to celebrate their friend's win. Unfortunately for the peace of the taverna and the surrounding community, the second red brought them was a German pinot noir, and an inferior one at that. They discovered the insult after reducing the bottle by half, at which time they expressed their disappointment by hurling several chairs — one of them occupied at the time — through what was once the taverna's front window. No one was hurt and the situation had only come to the embassy's attention when the young men claimed that, in as much as they had come to Greece accompanying the Olympic team, they were entitled to diplomatic immunity. At the moment, the two wine connoisseurs were spending a quiet evening sobering up in a Greek jail. The ambassador was certain a fine and payment for the damages would resolve a not unfamiliar set of circumstances.

Lord Sterling slowly worked his way through four more issues of comparable gravity, making notes on each regarding the steps to be taken to effect their resolution. Two he would entrust to Coopersmith; two required contact with Greek officials, and protocol demanded he address those personally.

He turned back, not for the first time, to the telegram he had placed beside the stack. It expressed condolences on the death of Lady Sterling from the Secretary of the Foreign Office on behalf of the Prime Minister and the Crown. Underneath that was the document officially closing the investigation of the purchases of antiquities through the ambassador's household funds, having found no evidence of wrong-doing.

Turning back to the stack, and at its bottom, there were the usual communications regarding government actions, and reports of events in trouble spots throughout the Empire. These were typically no more informative than articles on the same issues in the *Times* and the *Standard*. However, since the *Times* and *Standard* were unavailable to him, the telegrams served as his only source of information. He skimmed a recent report from the Office of the Colonial Secretary concerning the state of affairs in the Sudan as revealed in a recent visit by a man named Lockhart with that Office. He remembered the man, a red-headed colleague he had met at one posting. Lockhart gave an optimistic account of the Sudan Campaign, seeing success in the fifteen-year war as having become imminent in consequence of Lord Kitchener's arrival with a flotilla of gunboats. It was a message Whitehall would want to hear, and its author just might benefit from the good will it generated, as Lord Sterling was certain would be well known to Lockhart.

He paid greater attention to a report of activities in South Africa. The Jameson Raid and the Kruger telegram that followed were seen as responsible for a tribal uprising in South Africa, and for Transvaal having put itself on a war footing. Separately, it was reported that Germany and Great Britain were engaged in a naval armaments race. Lord Sterling would have agreed with Mrs. Hudson that it was a situation that would not end well. It had already ended badly for Cecil Rhodes, who had been forced to resign from his position as Prime Minister of the Cape Colony.

When the reports before him could no longer engage his attention, he looked to his pocket watch and found he still had thirty minutes before he was scheduled to start for home. Unable any longer to remain confined in his office, he hurried past empty offices and the Greek policemen stationed outside the embassy at Lestrade's insistence. He strode to where Nikolos waited atop his coach.

"Drive. I don't care where, just drive until I tell you to stop."

Nikolos shrugged compliance. It was all the same to him whether he was taking the ambassador someplace or no place at all. Maybe even better to be going no place. He could make up whatever fare he believed he could get away with when they got there.

Chapter 11.
A Killer Calls

"The sandwiches are excellent. Thank you, Mrs. Kasiris." Watson's compliment was followed by a chorus of supportive grunts from Holmes and Lestrade, whose mouths were filled with the excellent sandwiches. Mrs. Kasiris acknowledged their praise with a polite smile. Holmes thought she still appeared distracted, glancing toward the upstairs as if anxious to straighten the room where she had been napping. Holmes suggested if she had unfinished business elsewhere, she might want to attend to it while there was a moment. Mrs. Kasiris fairly leaped at the opportunity and, as Holmes expected, went immediately upstairs, although he noted she appeared no less troubled on her return.

Watson also saw the concern on the housekeeper's face, and made his own assumption about its cause. "There's really no need for you to stay, Mrs. Kasiris," Watson said. "You've been very helpful — which we all appreciate — and there's no reason you should be exposed to whatever danger awaits us."

Lestrade mumbled his support for Watson's statement while Holmes simply nodded.

"I thank you for nice words," she said, looking from one man to another, 'but I mean to stay. I not get in the way, and I get Lord Sterling his dinner. It's what I should do."

All three men made brief argument, but found the housekeeper adamant about the need to fulfill her duties. In the end they only won her assurance she would retire to the kitchen shortly before Lord Sterling was due home to make certain she would be far from the front door, and the possibility of gunfire.

While they waited Lord Sterling's arrival, the three men followed their different interests to fill the time. Watson went to the ambassador's library, lit a pipe, and settled in to one of the several easy chairs with Baedecker's *Greece: Handbook for Travelers*, to discover what he hadn't seen in Athens. Remembering the violin, Holmes went to the music room and soon Tchaikovsky was filling the house for his own pleasure and others' tolerance. Lestrade's taste ran to the music hall and magazines featuring adventure stories, and he began a search through the periodicals that Mrs. Kasiris had neatly stacked on the table in Lord Sterling's study. He considered and rejected *The Ludgate Monthly*, finding none of the stories sufficiently diverting. He cast aside *The Union Jack* for the same reason, but eagerly picked up the third magazine in the stack, *The Strand*, seeing it contained the fourth installment of *Rodney Stone* by a Scottish writer, Arthur Conan Doyle, whom Lestrade rather admired. The story was just getting into descriptions of the bare-knuckles boxers of the day, and Lestrade was soon lost in their exploits.

Mrs. Kasiris, meanwhile, cleared the dishes from the parlor, and went upstairs again "to make certain the ambassador's bedroom would be ready for him" as she called to the three men, receiving an acknowledgment of "very good, Mrs. Kasiris" from Watson alone. After coming back down, Mrs. Kasiris did not again emerge from the kitchen, and the men assumed she was busy with dinner and remaining out of their way as she had been asked. As the time approached for Lord Sterling's arrival, Holmes put aside the violin and called to Watson and Lestrade that the time for action was at hand. They drew their revolvers preparatory to going to their stations when a man's voice sounded loudly from the kitchen.

"Each one of you come out from where you are and step into the corridor. Now! As you do so, place your guns on the floor in front of you. I know there are three of you so don't try any tricks. The housekeeper will be standing in front of me. I warn you, if you choose to fire at me, you will certainly hit her. If you do not do as I say within the next five seconds,

I'll see to it she loses the use of her left arm, if you do not do as I say within ten seconds, she'll lose the use of both arms. I suggest you move quickly if you have any concern about the woman's well-being."

The voice was known to all three men. It betrayed an accent with which they had become familiar. They filed into the corridor, guns at their sides. They faced a terrified Mrs. Kasiris, her mouth covered by a ribbon of white, her hands bound behind, and a revolver pressed to her right temple by Durand Ramsay.

"Guns on the ground if you value this woman's life."

Holmes acted first, placing his weapon at his feet. Watson and Lestrade grudgingly followed his example.

"You're early, Mr. Ramsay, or should I say, Mr. Ralston," Holmes said, "Mr. Denis Ralston."

A wry smile covered the face of the man newly identified by Holmes. "Kick the guns toward me just to be sure you won't be tempted to do anything foolish." He waited for them to do as he said before continuing. "We have a few minutes, Mr. Holmes, would you be so good as to tell me what it is you think you know about me."

"First, what about Mrs. Kasiris. You have our weapons. There's no need to hold her hostage. Won't you let her go free?"

"Later. After I have killed Lord Sterling. I may even let all of you go free. But that's still to be decided, and will depend on how much difficulty you create. For now, I repeat, please tell me what it is you think you know about me?"

"I know you are not who you pretend to be. That was clear from the time we met. You pretended to be from Australia, but Mr. Flack, who is from Australia, noted your accent was unfamiliar to him. You deferred to Flack to explain about a major transportation link — the Great Northern Railway — although it would connect the town you claimed as your own with the southern part of Australia. And

225

you described the indigenous people with whom settlers in Australia find themselves in frequent battle as 'the natives' when every Australian I've known refers to them rather disparagingly as 'aborigines,' as Flack did in correcting you." Watson looked to Holmes quizzically when he spoke of every Australian he'd ever known. As far as Watson knew, Flack was every Australian he'd ever known. Holmes got past that small difficulty by not looking in Watson's direction as he continued.

"All of which made questionable your claim to citizenship in a part of the world you thought sufficiently remote that you wouldn't be caught in your lie. It was your bad fortune that Flack was in London and decided to enter the Games."

"You intrigue me, Mr. Holmes, please continue with your tale in the brief time you have left."

"I must admit, at first nothing about what happened seemed to make sense. If it was a robbery of the letter the courier was carrying, why would the robber go in search of Lady Sterling to kill her when he could escape with the letter without being seen. And, while Lord Sterling's flight seemed to suggest his having committed the two murders in a fit of jealous rage, that theory was dashed when it became known that Lord Sterling's flight had taken him to the home of Lady Sterling's parents. Hardly the refuge of their daughter's killer."

"The only thing that made sense was that the murderer intended from the outset to kill two people. But not the two people you killed, Mr. Ralston. Your targets were the ambassador and his wife, whom you very naturally concluded would be the couple at home at the hour of your arrival. You killed Lady Sterling, but confused her visitor with Lord Sterling, and now you've come to rectify that error."

"But I don't understand, Mr. Holmes," Lestrade protested. "How could this Ramsay, or Ralston, or whatever, not know the ambassador? My understanding is that all of you met him at the reception he gave on the day of your arrival."

"Not all of us, isn't that right, Mr. Ralston?"

Ralston took the revolver from Mrs. Kasiris' temple, waved it in the direction of Holmes signaling him to continue, then set the weapon again at the head of his captive. The housekeeper seemed near collapse with the renewed threat.

Holmes winced at the sight. "Again, I ask you, Mr. Ralston, to free Mrs. Kasiris. She is an innocent bystander, and unnecessary to this action."

"Enough, keep talking. I'll decide what is necessary. Answer your friend. Tell him why I didn't recognize Lord Sterling."

Holmes' speech held none of the exhilaration of discovery it would have under differing circumstances. "Three people weren't present at the embassy, Lestrade. Oswald Benton claimed to have a prior engagement, Albert Needham pleaded exhaustion, and the man we now know to be Denis Ralston was so ill with motion sickness — or claimed to be — that he was unable to attend the reception. But he did get a card from Mr. Fitzhugh at the train station — as we all did — providing the address of the embassy, and of the ambassador's residence should an emergency arise. Ralston never met the ambassador that day. When he went to the house that night, likely claiming a need or wish to meet with the ambassador, he was admitted by Lady Sterling's visitor whom he assumed to be Lord Sterling."

Lestrade was so caught up in Holmes' revelations, he ignored for the moment the danger all of them faced. "Mr. Holmes, how do you explain the shooter's terrible inaccuracy in the murders? He took several shots to kill his victims, firing at relatively close range. Yet, Mr. Ralston is an Olympics marksman."

"Precisely. And because he's an expert marksman he could miss his victims' vital organs, forcing them to slowly bleed to death — exactly as he planned."

"Planned?" Lestrade queried.

"He wanted to be certain his victims would experience the pain he thought they deserved. You see, Lestrade, Mr. Ralston has a history with the Sterlings. I contacted my brother, Mycroft, and asked him to look into the ambassador's early career — in particular, his experiences in New Zealand, where he served with the Colonial Office. The telegram I received from my brother confirmed my suspicions. During their time in New Zealand, Lord and Lady Sterling were involved in a dreadful accident when a little girl chased her dog in front of the wheels of their carriage. The little girl was badly injured. The family's name was Ralston. They had a son, who would have been about 15 at the time. His name was Denis."

Mrs. Kasiris' body jerked back as Ralston tightened his grip on her bound hands. His voice was suddenly raspy as he struggled to control his emotions. "The girl's name was Helen. She was confined to a chair until she died of a blood clot last year. The doctor said it stemmed from the accident. Except it wasn't an accident. The Sterlings were drunk, coming back from one of their society parties. They made my sister a cripple, and the British Government did nothing to punish them. Well, I'm doing something." Ralston was breathing heavily now. He stopped to collect himself, then sneered an additional comment.

"There is one place you slipped up, Mr. Holmes. I told you I was in building trades and home construction. Not in Australia, as you've guessed. In Wellington, New Zealand. If you're in construction, you learn enough about locks to help people who lock themselves out, and to get past people who want to lock you out. It's not always quiet work, but thanks to someone's violin playing, any noise I made was easily drowned out. And when I got in at the back door, I found Mrs. Kasiris in the kitchen, where I understand you'd sent her, Mr. Holmes. So you see, it's thanks to you I had cover to get in and a hostage when I got there.

"But enough talk. It's nearly time. The three of you get up against that wall." Once again, he used the gun to give directions, waving his prisoners to the side of the corridor away from where the door would open. The three men moved slowly and reluctantly to where he gestured.

"Now we wait," he said. "I urge you to do nothing stupid. If you cooperate, you and this woman may survive."

They didn't have long to wait. Approaching hoofbeats sounded gradually louder, at the same time slowing and finally coming to a stop. They imagined the door to the carriage opening, Lord Sterling climbing down, and his starting up the walkway to the front door.

They considered the options available to them, and found none that offered even a remote chance of success. If they rushed the gunman it would lead to the certain death of Mrs. Kasiris, and the likely deaths of at least one, probably two, and possibly all three of them. Nor did they have any way to warn Lord Sterling. They faced the likelihood they were about to witness the murder of the man they had promised to protect, and could only then take some as yet undetermined and likely unsuccessful action.

The door opened slowly as if Lord Sterling, too, sensed the danger inside. Ralston waited until the ambassador's body was full in the doorway. Then, he threw Mrs. Kasiris to the floor in front of him, and trained his weapon a long moment on Lord Sterling, forcing the ambassador to become fully aware of the fate that awaited him. It was, Watson would tell Mrs. Hudson later, his fatal error. In the few seconds delay, a shot rang out from the floor above. Ralston crumpled, his own shot going harmlessly into the wall opposite where the detectives had been standing.

Now, all three rushed the wounded assailant. Lestrade kicked the gun from his hand. There was no need to subdue him further. The shot had struck him in the hip and left him writhing where he fell. Above them, standing at the second floor railing, still holding the gun with which he had saved at least one and possibly all of their lives, stood Mrs. Kasiris' friend, Mr. Seropopoulos, his eyes fixed on the person whose life most concerned him.

Seeing his intended assassin well in hand, Lord Sterling hurried to where his housekeeper had only been able to get to her knees. He took the gag from her mouth and untied her hands before being joined by a panting Seropopoulos who had raced down the stairs, and was now assisting him in getting Mrs. Kasiris to her feet. The appearance of Seropopoulos from a second floor bedroom, taken with the housekeeper's earlier flushed and somewhat disheveled appearance, explained Mrs. Kasiris' initial discomfort with their untimely entrance, and her insistence on staying at the residence even at the risk of confronting a killer bent on revenge.

With Seropopoulos now comforting his special friend, and Watson doing what he could to stanch the flow of blood from Ralston's wound, Lord Sterling went to the still open door to call for Nikolos. Together with Lestrade, the carriage driver would take Ralston to the hospital, where the Inspector would arrange for the Greek police to keep him in custody until he recovered sufficiently to be taken to England for adjudication. Holmes and Lord Sterling watched silently as Watson supervised Ralston's removal.

When that was done, all eyes and all attention turned to Mrs. Kasiris and her recovery. The ambassador invited everyone into the parlor and, while Seropopoulos cradled her in his arms on the sofa, he went to the dining room, returning a short time later with a tray holding five glasses and a bottle of ouzo. Gradually, words and liquor calmed the housekeeper and led to a more relaxed atmosphere. Lord Sterling raised his glass to Seropopoulos, and made an effusive declaration of his appreciation for saving his life and the lives of all the others. The ambassador's words were echoed by Watson and Holmes, and followed by Seropopoulos' claims that he had done nothing that any of them wouldn't have done under similar circumstances, a statement each man secretly believed, but proceeded to deny.

With tributes given and disavowed, a puzzled look came over Lord Sterling's face. "Mr. Seropopoulos, I am, of course, delighted you were here, but I can't help wondering how you knew to be here this evening?"

The response came from Holmes, as he smiled to Seropopoulos and Mrs. Kasiris, who now placed themselves at a decorous distance from each other. "I asked him to be here, Lord Sterling. I thought having a man on the second landing could be of value."

"You were certainly right, Mr. Holmes. I say again, I am in both your debts." He looked from Holmes to Seropopoulos, and then to his nearly empty glass of ouzo. He corrected the situation for himself and such others as shared his plight.

"One more thing, Mr. Seropopoulos, if I might," Lord Sterling began, "I couldn't help but notice your special concern about Mrs. Kasiris' well-being. Is it your intention to rob me of an excellent housekeeper?"

The ambassador chuckled appreciation for his effort to lighten the mood. Holmes and Watson gave tight-lipped smiles. Mrs. Kasiris blushed. Seropopoulos' expression never changed.

"I am afraid that may be the case, Lord Sterling. Mrs. Kasiris and I are engaged to be married."

His fiancée's eyelids flickered and her lips parted as she drew a quick breath. It was over in a moment, but all three men recognized that Mrs. Kasiris had learned of her engagement at the same time they had. An embarrassed smile replaced surprise as her face reddened, and its sharp features seemed to soften just a little.

"Is this true, Mrs. Kasiris?" Lord Sterling pressed the point.

"I've never known Mr. Seropopoulos to lie," was her soft reply.

"Then, we must drink to that as well." The ambassador raised high the bottle of ouzo, but found the glasses already full. He set the bottle down and raised his glass instead. "Syncharitiria! Congratulations!"

Holmes and Watson mumbled something approximating the Greek compliment, pointed their glasses to the couple and downed their drinks.

"You have all been most gracious, but I must take Mrs. Kasiris to home, and I must get to home myself," Seropopoulos raised himself and his fiancée from the sofa. Still in the role of housekeeper, Mrs. Kasiris advised Lord Sterling of the food set out for him in the kitchen.

There was a round of handshakes, and Seropopoulos had his back slapped several times. The headmaster lingered over shaking Holmes' hand, an act both Watson and Lord Sterling noted, but only Watson understood. After seeing the couple off, Holmes suggested that he and Watson should be going as well, remarking that the next day, the last day of the Olympics, would be an exciting one, unnecessarily reminding the ambassador that the King would be awarding medals and prizes to the winning competitors. They congratulated themselves a final time on an eventful and successful evening. Lord Sterling repeated his claim of being in their debt, and engaged in yet another round of handshakes before the two detectives left for their hotel and a description of the eventful evening to Mrs. Hudson, who was anxiously awaiting their return.

"It sounds a remarkable evenin', Dr. Watson," Mrs. Hudson said on hearing his account of activities at the ambassador's residence.

Holmes silently smoked a pipe throughout Watson's report, staring into the distance and affecting a splendid indifference, all the while paying close attention to every aspect of his colleague's description.

"I shudder to think what might have happened if Seropopoulos hadn't been there," Watson said. "You might well be getting an altogether different report from the embassy or the Greek police."

Mrs. Hudson grimaced and nodded, Holmes exhaled a stream of smoke.

"Mr. 'Olmes, do I understand that Lord Sterling told you 'e believed 'imself in your debt?"

"Indeed, he said it several times, Mrs. Hudson. Of course, that's not unusual. It's what people say in those circumstances."

"That's true, Mr. 'Olmes. But we will take 'im at 'is word. It will allow us to get one final stitch sewn. And it will again be up to you, Mr. 'Olmes to get it done."

Holmes removed the pipe from his mouth, and looked warily to Mrs. Hudson. "What exactly did you have in mind?"

"It's to do with the awards ceremony and the King of Greece."

Chapter 12.
Triumph and Tribute

The day of the awards ceremony was fairly bursting with sunshine as if determined to match the mood of the thousands of spectators who filed into the stadium and filled the hills beyond. A raised platform was set on the infield with six steps at either side. Atop the platform a long table was laden with the prizes King George would be awarding the athletes who were already seated with Olympics officials and foreign dignitaries in the infield area. The King had not yet made his appearance, and Holmes took the opportunity to engage Lord Sterling in a private conversation. In its course, the words "repaying a debt" were never spoken, but the thought was uppermost in both their minds. The ambassador spoke little. Instead, he seemed to concentrate hard on Holmes' every word. He nodded frequently, small head shakes that might have signaled understanding or agreement, and once he drew back appalled or amazed at Holmes' proposal. When Holmes had finished, the ambassador allowed himself a sly smile and a final emphatic nod, causing Holmes to adopt his own broad grin before turning to rejoin his fellow athletes.

Mrs. Hudson had meanwhile found Miss Kannapolis and her father in the area in which Mrs. Hudson had asked they meet, and now invited them to join her and Dr. Watson in the seats reserved for the ambassador's guests. Miss Kannapolis happily accepted, while Mr. Kannapolis agreed to the move, but looked furtively around as he advanced to the choice seats as if expecting to be accused of trespassing, and sent back to the less desirable seats where he belonged.

When King George entered the stadium, the crowd stood and loudly applauded. Princes Constantine and George accompanied him as he advanced to the elevated dais, stopping frequently to share brief pleasantries with the officials and ambassadors in attendance. When he came to Lord Sterling, he grasped both his arms to welcome him back and express his sympathies. Lord Sterling could be seen thanking him for his concern before drawing him close to whisper in his ear something that caused the Royal to adopt his own sly smile and nod his affirmation. A short time later a young man from the King's retinue came to sit with the ambassador, his face creased in concentration as he jotted down the ambassador's words. When he was done, he nodded correctly, never having said a word to Lord Sterling, and went to disappear into the small entourage that accompanied the King.

With the welcoming of officials complete, the King took a position behind the table and, after the reading of an ode to honor the occasion, he began the distribution of prizes. As a name was called by the King's herald, the athlete mounted the steps to cross before the King and receive an award commensurate with his achievement. Those who had won their competitions were presented with silver medals, certificates of merit, and olive wreathes taken from the trees of Olympia. Those who finished second in their competitions received copper medals, certificates, and laurel wreathes. Years later, third place finishers from the 1896 Olympics would also have their achievements recognized even as the medals awarded changed in color and content.

As Elliot crossed the platform to accept his silver medal for weight lifting, there was a hush followed by thunderous applause as the crowd seized on a last opportunity to celebrate the man who seemed to many to epitomize the Olympic ideal. Benton could not contain a small smile as he strode across the platform, amused at the irony of receiving two silver medals for athletic accomplishments that had been the cover for his investigative work. In recognition of his victories on the track, Flack also received two silver medals. The small bounce in his stride was in marked contrast to

Keeping's later acceptance of his award. The cyclist, still wobbly from his strenuous performance only one day before, moved slowly to stand with seeming effort before King George before accepting his copper medal with a small bow.

When all the medals, certificates and wreaths had been presented, the King announced there would be the awarding of additional prizes "for extraordinary achievement." To the crowd's delight, he called the names of two Greek marksmen, one of whom was awarded a hand-tooled rifle, the other an antique pistol. He presented a silver cup to another athlete, and a silver vase to yet another.

Holmes waited patiently for the King to fulfill the request Lord Sterling had made to him. He felt certain the King's smile and nod signaled his willingness to participate in the small scene they planned. He was wholly unprepared for the herald's call for "Mr. Sherlock Holmes."

Holmes made it to his feet, but was frozen in place by the unexpected tribute even as his fellow athletes applauded and urged him on. Finally, Elliot's large hand applied to the small of his back propelled him several steps in the direction of the platform. Regaining his customary composure, he bounded up the steps and walked with head high to a position facing the King.

"Mr. Holmes, I have, of course, heard of your accomplishments long before seeing you," the King said in English. "Now, I have witnessed for myself your acts of great courage, your selfless work for others, and, of course, your skills in fencing. I congratulate and honor you with this gift from myself and the people of Greece." He handed Holmes a silver bowl, the year "1896" and his name engraved on its outer part, and a pair of crossed swords etched on its inside bottom.

Holmes looked to his gift, then back to the King. "It is magnificent, Your Highness. It will remind me always of the great kindness and sportsmanship of yourself, and the Greek people."

As Holmes took his place again with the small crowd of athletes, he heard the name he had been expecting.

"Mr. Edward Battel."

Battel was as surprised to hear his name called as Holmes had been to hear his. Unlike Holmes, his confusion was never entirely replaced by composure. He crossed the platform to stand before the King, his expression making clear he still sought the reason for his being there.

King George glanced down to the notes his aide had placed before him, and did what he could to clarify things for the cyclist. "Mr. Battel, you rode a courageous race. I regret I was not there to see it, but I have heard about it from those who were. It is a feat worthy of recognition." At that moment, the King realized he was out of vases, bowls, statues or any other article suitable for presentation. He did not hesitate a moment. He unpinned from his chest one of his several medals, purposely choosing one that was large, and distinctive for being in the shape of a six-pointed star. "I want you to have this special medal as your reward, and to remember always the Olympic Games of 1896."

Battel stared at the medal he held, as if trying to fathom the honor he had been given. His mouth worked to frame words appropriate to the occasion, but never got past mumbling, "Thank you, Your Majesty," although he did so two additional times.

King George smiled with the gentle indulgence of one who has spent a lifetime relating to people reduced to near incoherence upon meeting him. He glanced to his notes a second time before speaking. "Mr. Battel, I am told your intended bride and her father are here. I should very much like to meet them. Perhaps Lord Sterling could escort them to the platform?"

Mrs. Hudson had been primed for the moment. Lord Sterling had never met Miss Kannapolis or her father, and Mrs. Hudson wasn't certain the ambassador would recognize her from their brief acquaintance. Accordingly, she had Dr. Watson stand, and urged Miss Kannapolis and her father to stand with him. Thus alerted, Lord Sterling took them in tow and shepherded them from their box to the platform. The young woman moved eagerly, if with undisguised bewilderment, across the infield to the King and Battel. Her father seemed to be pulled along, embarrassed at becoming the sudden focus of tens of thousands of his countrymen. He pushed back his thinning hair, smoothed his shirt-front, and resisted the temptation to wipe his shoes on his pants legs.

When he and his daughter were at last in front of the platform, he looked up from the ground for the first time, saw his King standing above and smiling to him, and again transferred his attention to the surface of the infield. Recognizing he was in danger of appearing disrespectful toward his King, Mr. Kannapolis summoned the courage to look again to King George, bowing deeply as he did so. When he was done, he nudged his daughter, who obliged him by making a small curtsy.

The King spoke to Battel in English, then in Greek to Mr. Kannapolis. "I am delighted to meet your fiancée and her father. I congratulate you, Mr. Kannapolis, on your fine family, and your daughter's upcoming marriage. You must send me an announcement when the happy event takes place."

Mr. Kannapolis stuttered a response that Miss Kannapolis later translated for Battel. "Thank ... thank you, Your Majesty. Thank you. Such an honor you do my family ... you do me. I ... bless you, sir. I will send an announcement, of course."

Lord Sterling reappeared at his elbow and led the awestruck couple back to their seats. Miss Kannapolis was too ecstatic to sit still through the remaining ceremony. Mr.

Kannapolis would be hours trying to fathom the event that had just befallen him, and years retelling it. Indeed, in fulfilling the King's request, the retelling of his narrative would span generations.

Beside them, though unacknowledged by them, Mrs. Hudson smiled her satisfaction. Everything was now complete. It was time to go home.

Within a day of their arrival, life at 221B Baker Street settled into a comfortable routine. Having assembled his papers, Holmes began writing his *Treatise on the Use of Bicycle Tires in Criminal Investigation*, later to be translated into six languages. Watson found two weeks of *Lancet* waiting his attention; and Mrs. Hudson had decided to experiment with the creation of raspberry infused scones. She made only a few, feeling there was no reason to waste the flour if they didn't turn out well. If they did turn out well — as she fully expected they would — she would bake enough to provide a proper welcome home for Inspector Lestrade when he returned from Athens to deliver Ralston to the Old Bailey.

Mycroft had scheduled his visit for two in the afternoon, an hour he regarded as far more civilized than the one imposed on him for his earlier visit. Mrs. Hudson was aware that Mycroft would want something stronger than tea and scones, and she had put aside a beverage she was certain would be suitable. On his arrival, he handed Mrs. Hudson his hat and cane, learned his brother and Watson waited him in the sitting room, and faced again the formidable task of mounting the seventeen steps to his destination. The journey was lightened somewhat by Mrs. Hudson's promise of liquid refreshment after he got settled.

The sitting room had been readied for Mycroft's arrival. One easy chair had been pulled from its position by the fireplace to face the sofa from the right, the basket chair had been moved to face the sofa from the left. Holmes and

Watson took the chairs, allowing Mycroft as much room on the couch as he found necessary to revive from his ordeal. He was finishing the last of a panting recovery when Mrs. Hudson arrived with the promised refreshments. She set on the breakfast table three glasses and one of the two bottles of ouzo she had brought back from Athens — and the only bottle her colleagues knew to have made the trip from Athens to London. Watson pulled a chair away from his roll-top desk and silently invited Mrs. Hudson to join them, at the same time taking a glass from the top of his desk to guarantee all could share in the bottle that was now in Holmes' hands. Holmes poured half glasses for himself and each of the men, and slightly less for Mrs. Hudson.

"Thank you, Mrs. Hudson, this is most welcome." Mycroft raised his glass to her, took a sip, then closed his eyes, tilted his head to the heavens and beamed. "Truly nectar of the gods." Mrs. Hudson took a sip, and returned his smile with eyes open. She ignored the heavens, aware that the liquor had come to her through the more worldly efforts of Mrs. Kasiris.

"Holmes, I can tell you that you are the subject of innumerable conversations at the very highest levels of government. I have been asked to communicate their appreciation for all that has been accomplished. I regret I was unable to make known the debt that is owed all of you without revealing more about your organization than I felt it wise or desirable to do." Once again, he tilted his glass toward Mrs. Hudson, and then to Watson in a broad sweep of his hand, before draining the glass it held. "I wouldn't be surprised to learn of some acknowledgement of your services, Sherlock, perhaps even an audience with Her Majesty. Of course, whatever is done will be kept quite secret. I'm afraid everything about the case is to remain quite secret. That means there cannot be another of your fancifully romanticized little stories, Dr. Watson."

Watson sniffed and found something of interest only he could see across the room. Holmes grunted acknowledgment of his brother's report without change of expression.

Their actions did nothing to dampen Mycroft's celebratory mood. He poured himself another glass of ouzo. "This drink is delightful. What is it exactly?"

"A Greek aperitif, I believe," Watson answered. "It was Mrs. Hudson's idea to bring a bottle back with us. It does have a rather nice flavor, wouldn't you say, Holmes?"

"Yes, it was really most thoughtful of you, Mrs. Hudson," Holmes replied, at the same time holding out his glass to have it refilled.

"Must you go, Mrs. Hudson?," Mycroft asked, as she rose to take her leave.

"I'm afraid I must. Thank you all the same, Mr. 'Olmes. There's orders to be placed with the butcher, and I've a list to make for a trip to the greengrocer, besides there bein' clothes to ready for the laundress."

"As you like, Mrs. Hudson." Mycroft turned back to his brother and Watson. He screwed his face in an effort at concentration. "I believe you were about to tell me about Athens. After all, I know you enjoyed considerable success, but I know nothing beyond what little was contained in your telegrams, and what I was told by Mr. Fitzhugh and Miss Pershing. A lovely young couple by the way. I wish them every happiness." Mycroft took another long sip of ouzo, and was joined in this latest tribute by Holmes and Watson.

As she closed the door behind her, Holmes had begun to respond to his brother's request. "I suppose we should start with the travel to Athens, and my suspicions of the man we came to know as Denis Ralston."

Once in her kitchen, Mrs. Hudson opened the second bottle of ouzo, and poured herself a part of a small glass, adding water to reduce its potency. She knew the men, naive to the drink's strength, would find themselves becoming increasingly self-congratulatory even as they became increasingly inarticulate. They had good reason to celebrate, and so did she. As she would later tell Tobias, they had concluded a major diplomatic initiative, saved the country from embarrassment if not scandal, brought to justice a double-murderer, and taken three romances from the dormant state in which they found them to set them on a sure path to the altar. All in all, it had been quite an Olympics. She raised her glass in silent tribute to herself, and emptied it in a single well-satisfied swallow.

Epilogue

When the Games were done:

Returning to England, Launceston Elliot became a fixture in British weight-lifting competitions, establishing four amateur records. He turned professional early in the 20th century (variously reported as 1903 and 1905), entering on a music hall career highlighted by his support of two bicycles and riders suspended from either side of a metal bar set across his shoulders. He later practiced farming for several years before retiring to Victoria in Australia where he spent his last years.

Edwin Flack returned to England briefly at the end of the Olympics before sailing to Victoria to work in the family accounting firm in Melbourne — aptly named Flack and Flack — and to breed championship cattle. Flack never again competed in track events, turning his attention to managing his firm's several branches in Australia and New Zealand. He did, however, represent Australia (after federation in 1901) on the International Olympic Committee. His statue in Berwick, Victoria was unveiled in 1998 by the legendary Australian track star and later governor of Victoria, John Landy.

Before participating in the hurdles event, Grantley Goulding paraded the streets of Athens sporting the medals he had won in earlier athletic competitions, leading his chief competitor in that event to remark, "I never met a more confident athlete." Nonetheless, Goulding lost his race, although by the narrowest of margins. After the event, he "stopped neither to linger nor say farewell, but went straight from the stadium to the station and took the first train out of Athens." There is nothing to indicate he laid claim to the copper medal he had won by finishing second. He later emigrated to South Africa, ending his days in the Natal, a former British colony; today Kwa-Zulu Natal, a province of South Africa.

No one by the name of Oswald Benton participated in the Olympic Games. However, a certain John Pius Boland of Dublin, who was visiting a friend in Athens at the time of the Games, was prevailed upon to enter the tennis competition, and proceeded to win both the singles and doubles events. At his request, an Irish flag was prepared to be run up the pole in addition to the Union Jack. Boland went on to become a Member of Parliament representing South Kerry from 1900 to 1908. He remained a strong advocate for the preservation of the Irish language until his death on St. Patrick's Day, 1958.

After participating in what remains the longest event in Olympic history, Frederick Keeping became the proprietor of a bicycle shop and garage in Hampshire, England. His son became a professional soccer player, and later coach of several soccer teams throughout Europe.

Nothing is known of Edward Battel. Even the spelling of his last name is uncertain.

The account of Sherlock Holmes' fencing competition is fictional. Holmes was not a competitor at the 1896 Olympic Games. Had he been, he would, of course, have proven victorious.

In the wake of the Kruger telegram following the failure of the Jameson Raid to overthrow the Boers in the Transvaal, Queen Vickie, the Dowager Empress of Germany, wrote to her mother, Queen Victoria, "William's [Kaiser Wilhelm] telegram to President Kruger [was] I think a deplorable mistake." She clarified further that the telegram was not an impulsive act, but represented deliberate German policy. Victoria responded that "the bad feeling" from that telegram would likely "last some time." The correspondence was part of the nearly 8,000 letters exchanged between the two royals from 1852 to 1900.

The bad feeling did last some time, contributing to a growing enmity between Germany and the United Kingdom, an enmity that found initial expression in the expansion of the German navy, and Germany's flirtation with Russia and France as potential allies against Great Britain. Of far less significance to the world, but of great significance to the Kaiser, it also found expression in Wilhelm's being denied an invitation, the following year, to the celebration of the diamond jubilee of the Queen of the British Empire, and his grandmother.

In Africa, the Jameson Raid destroyed any potential for rapprochement between the Boers and the British settlers. Ultimately, the distrust it fostered, in conjunction with the perceived maltreatment of British guest workers in the Transvaal — to say nothing of the gold and diamonds discovered there — led, in 1899, to the three year Boer War. At War's end, Cecil Rhodes' dream of a South Africa united under British rule had come to pass in spite of—or perhaps because of — his poorly planned and ineptly conducted attack six years earlier.

Also from Barry S Brown

Accompanied by Holmes and Watson, Mrs. Hudson crosses the ocean to attend the wedding of her cousin's daughter. They disembark to discover that the young lady's fiancé, a pitcher for the Brooklyn Bridegrooms, stands accused of an attempt on the life of JP Morgan and the death of his aide. A self-declared enemy of Morgan and the robber barons, the ballplayer ran from the scene of the crime and, when captured, was found in possession of a gun with two spent cartridges, the same number and caliber as that used in the attack. Before a wedding can be held, the unacknowledged sage of Baker Street will lead Holmes and Watson along a path of investigation taking them from JP Morgan's mansion to the gambling dens of New York's Tenderloin.

www.mxpublishing.com

Also from MX Publishing

MX Publishing is the world's largest specialist Sherlock Holmes publisher, with over a hundred titles and fifty authors creating the latest in Sherlock Holmes fiction and non-fiction.

From traditional short stories and novels to travel guides and quiz books, MX Publishing cater for all Holmes fans.

The collection includes leading titles such as *Benedict Cumberbatch In Transition* and *The Norwood Author* which won the 2011 Howlett Award (Sherlock Holmes Book of the Year).

MX Publishing also has one of the largest communities of Holmes fans on Facebook with regular contributions from dozens of authors.

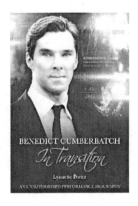

www.mxpublishing.com

Also from MX Publishing

Our bestselling books are our short story collections;

'Lost Stories of Sherlock Holmes' , 'The Outstanding Mysteries of Sherlock Holmes', The Papers of Sherlock Holmes Volume 1 and 2, 'Untold Adventures of Sherlock Holmes' (and the sequel 'Studies in Legacy) and 'Sherlock Holmes in Pursuit', 'The Cotswold Werewolf and Other Stories of Sherlock Holmes' – and many more......

www.mxpublishing.com

Also from MX Publishing

"Phil Growick's, 'The Secret Journal of Dr Watson', is an adventure which takes place in the latter part of Holmes and Watson's lives. They are entrusted by HM Government (although not officially) and the King no less to undertake a rescue mission to save the Romanovs, Russia's Royal family from a grisly end at the hand of the Bolsheviks. There is a wealth of detail in the story but not so much as would detract us from the enjoyment of the story. Espionage, counter-espionage, the ace of spies himself, double-agents, double-crossers...all these flit across the pages in a realistic and exciting way. All the characters are extremely well-drawn and Mr Growick, most importantly, does not falter with a very good ear for Holmesian dialogue indeed. Highly recommended. A five-star effort."
The Baker Street Society

www.mxpublishing.com

Also from MX Publishing

The Missing Authors Series

Sherlock Holmes and The Adventure of The Grinning Cat
Sherlock Holmes and The Nautilus Adventure
Sherlock Holmes and The Round Table Adventure

"Joseph Svec, III is brilliant in entwining two endearing and enduring classics of literature, blending the factual with the fantastical; the playful with the pensive; and the mischievous with the mysterious. We shall, all of us young and old, benefit with a cup of tea, a tranquil afternoon, and a copy of Sherlock Holmes, The Adventure of the Grinning Cat."
Amador County Holmes Hounds Sherlockian Society

www.mxpublishing.com

Also from MX Publishing

The American Literati Series

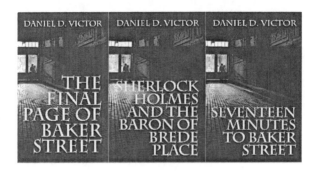

The Final Page of Baker Street
The Baron of Brede Place
Seventeen Minutes To Baker Street

"The really amazing thing about this book is the author's ability to call up the 'essence' of both the Baker Street 'digs' of Holmes and Watson as well as that of the 'mean streets' of Marlowe's Los Angeles. Although none of the action takes place in either place, Holmes and Watson share a sense of camaraderie and self-confidence in facing threats and problems that also pervades many of the later tales in the Canon. Following their conversations and banter is a return to Edwardian England and its certainties and hope for the future. This is definitely the world before The Great War."
Philip K Jones

www.mxpublishing.com

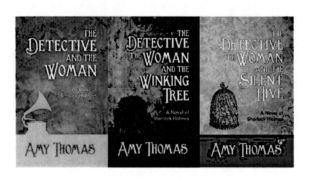

Also from MX Publishing

The Sherlock Holmes and Enoch Hale Series

The Amateur Executioner
The Poisoned Penman
The Egyptian Curse

"The Amateur Executioner: Enoch Hale Meets Sherlock Holmes", the first collaboration between Dan Andriacco and Kieran McMullen, concerns the possibility of a Fenian attack in London. Hale, a native Bostonian, is a reporter for London's Central News Syndicate - where, in 1920, Horace Harker is still a familiar figure, though far from revered. "The Amateur Executioner" takes us into an ambiguous and murky world where right and wrong aren't always distinguishable. I look forward to reading more about Enoch Hale."
Sherlock Holmes Society of London

www.mxpublishing.com

253

Also from MX Publishing

Sherlock Holmes novellas in verse

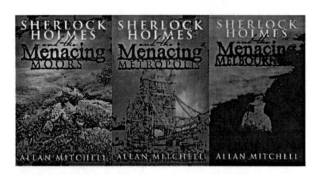

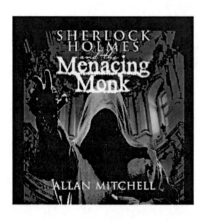

All four
novellas have
been released
also in audio
format with
narration by
Steve White

Sherlock Holmes and The Menacing Moors
Sherlock Holmes and The Menacing Metropolis
Sherlock Holmes and The Menacing Melbournian
Sherlock Holmes and The Menacing Monk

*"The story is really good and the Herculean effort it must
have been to write it all in verse—well, my hat is off to you,
Mr. Allan Mitchell! I wouldn't dream of seeing such work get
less than five plus stars from me…"***The Raven**

Also from MX Publishing

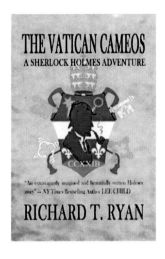

When the papal apartments are burgled in 1901, Sherlock Holmes is summoned to Rome by Pope Leo XII. After learning from the pontiff that several priceless cameos that could prove compromising to the church, and perhaps determine the future of the newly unified Italy, have been stolen, Holmes is asked to recover them. In a parallel story, Michelangelo, the toast of Rome in 1501 after the unveiling of his Pieta, is commissioned by Pope Alexander VI, the last of the Borgia pontiffs, with creating the cameos that will bedevil Holmes and the papacy four centuries later. For fans of Conan Doyle's immortal detective, the game is always afoot. However, the great detective has never encountered an adversary quite like the one with whom he crosses swords in "The Vatican Cameos.."

"An extravagantly imagined and beautifully written Holmes story"
(Lee Child, NY Times Bestselling author, Jack Reacher series)

CPSIA information can be obtained
at www.ICGtesting.com
Printed in the USA
LVOW10s1807091117
555649LV00012B/726/P